Jessica wasn't even aware that she was screaming

"Jess?"

Sam's voice broke through the demons. Jessica threw herself against his chest. "I was so scared," she breathed. Strong arms folded behind her back and pulled her close as she clamped her fists around the waistband of his jeans. She could feel him moving, retreating, pulling her along with him. Away from the unknown danger.

"Are you hurt?" Sam asked softly.

She was surrounded by strength and heat. Her cheek pressed against the warm skin beneath. Bare skin. She breathed in the clean, masculine smell of soap and the earthier scent of the man himself. She was hugging, grasping, clinging…. She waited for the shock of being clutched against a man's hard chest to undermine the comfort seeping into her. But she was okay. She was okay with this. She was okay with him. She nuzzled her cheek closer.

She needed him.

Dear Harlequin Intrigue Reader,

At Harlequin Intrigue we have much to look forward to as we ring in a brand-new year. Case in point—all of our romantic suspense selections this month are fraught with edge-of-your-seat danger, electrifying romance and thrilling excitement. So hang on!

Reader favorite Debra Webb spins the next installment in her popular series COLBY AGENCY. *Cries in the Night* spotlights a mother so desperate to track down her missing child that she joins forces with the unforgettable man from her past.

Unsanctioned Memories by Julie Miller—the next offering in THE TAYLOR CLAN—packs a powerful punch as a vengeance-seeking FBI agent opens his heart to the achingly vulnerable lone witness who can lead him to a cold-blooded killer.... Looking for a provocative mystery with a royal twist? Then expect to be seduced by Jacqueline Diamond in *Sheikh Surrender*.

We welcome two talented debut authors to Harlequin Intrigue this month. Tracy Montoya weaves a chilling mystery in *Maximum Security,* and the gripping *Concealed Weapon* by Susan Peterson is part of our BACHELORS AT LARGE promotion.

Finally this month, Kasi Blake returns to Harlequin Intrigue with *Borrowed Identity.* This gothic mystery will keep you guessing when a groggy bride stumbles upon a grisly murder on her wedding night. But are her eyes deceiving her when her "slain" groom appears alive and well in a flash of lightning?

It promises to be quite a year at Harlequin Intrigue....

Enjoy!

Denise O'Sullivan
Senior Editor
Harlequin Intrigue

UNSANCTIONED MEMORIES

JULIE MILLER

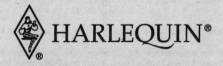

HARLEQUIN®

TORONTO • NEW YORK • LONDON
AMSTERDAM • PARIS • SYDNEY • HAMBURG
STOCKHOLM • ATHENS • TOKYO • MILAN • MADRID
PRAGUE • WARSAW • BUDAPEST • AUCKLAND

ISBN 0-373-22748-5

UNSANCTIONED MEMORIES

This edition published by arrangement with Harlequin Books S.A.

® and TM are trademarks of the publisher. Trademarks indicated with
® are registered in the United States Patent and Trademark Office, the
Canadian Trade Marks Office and in other countries.

Visit us at www.eHarlequin.com

Printed in U.S.A.

ABOUT THE AUTHOR

Julie Miller attributes her passion for writing romance to all those fairy tales she read growing up, and to shyness. Encouragement from her family to write down all those feelings she couldn't express became a love for the written word. She gets continued support from her fellow members of the Prairieland Romance Writers, where she serves as the resident "grammar goddess." This award-winning author and teacher has published several paranormal romances. Inspired by the likes of Agatha Christie and Encyclopedia Brown, Ms. Miller believes the only thing better than a good mystery is a good romance.

Born and raised in Missouri, she now lives in Nebraska with her husband, son and smiling guard dog, Maxie. Write to Julie at P.O. Box 5162, Grand Island, NE 68802-5162.

Books by Julie Miller

HARLEQUIN INTRIGUE
588—ONE GOOD MAN*
619—SUDDEN ENGAGEMENT*
642—SECRET AGENT HEIRESS
651—IN THE BLINK OF AN EYE*
666—THE DUKE'S COVERT MISSION
699—THE ROOKIE*
719—KANSAS CITY'S BRAVEST*
748—UNSANCTIONED MEMORIES*

HARLEQUIN BLAZE
45—INTIMATE KNOWLEDGE

*The Taylor Clan

THE TAYLOR CLAN

Sid and Martha Taylor:	butcher and homemaker ages 64 and 63 respectively
Brett Taylor:	contractor age 39 the protector
Mac Taylor:	forensic specialist age 37 the professor
Gideon Taylor:	firefighter/arson investigator age 36 the crusader
Cole Taylor:	the mysterious brother age 31 the lost soul
Jessica Taylor:	the lone daughter antiques dealer/buyer/restorer age 29 the survivor
Josh Taylor:	police officer age 28 at 6'3", he's still the baby of the family the charmer
Mitch Taylor:	Sid's nephew—raised like a son police captain age 40 the chief

CAST OF CHARACTERS

Jessica Taylor—Only one person knows what happened to her the night she wound up in an emergency room, brutally assaulted and half dead—and it isn't her. She needs a bodyguard and she needs the truth. Because her attacker wants to finish the job. And what she can't remember *could* get her killed.

Sam O'Rourke—FBI agent on an unsanctioned mission. He'll do anything—or use anyone—to find out who killed his sister and bring the man to justice. Will his quest for vengeance cost him the chance to redeem his frozen heart?

Alex Templeton—Jess's former lover in Chicago. Meeting the wife ended the affair. For Jess.

Derek Phillips—Jess's part-time help. He has a serious crush on his boss.

Boyce, Riegert and Winston—Jess's best customers. But are these mystery men who they claim to be?

Trudy Kent—She might come from old money, but there's nothing old-fashioned about the way this woman does business.

Charles Kent—The gentleman farmer is buying up parcels of land to keep out the undesirables.

Sheriff Curtis Hancock—Was he Jess's best line of defense? Or her worst nightmare?

Kerry O'Rourke—Inspiration or excuse?

Harry—The dog knew the truth. He just couldn't get his mistress to listen.

In memory of Lyn'da Simon Van Slyke.

A gentle soul with a brave heart.
A supportive fan and wonderful influence
on the youth of Nebraska.
I miss our long talks and shared hugs.
She loved her family best—
and I was lucky to have her as my friend.

Prologue

"Hell, O'Rourke. Don't you ever miss?"

With machinelike efficiency, FBI Special Agent Sam O'Rourke reloaded the spent magazine of his Bureau issue Sig Sauer pistol. He adjusted the protective goggles and insulated earphones to tune out the awed skepticism of his partner, Virgil Logan.

Lightly caressing the grip of the pistol between his hands, he took a bead on the image of John Dillinger at the end of the firing range and pictured a faceless man between the sights. *Head? Or heart?* Did it really matter? He emptied all fifteen rounds into the paper target before acknowledging his partner.

"It's just a matter of steady hands..." he dumped the spent magazine "...twenty-twenty vision..." he punched the button to pull the target forward "...and nerves like ice."

Virgil tried to laugh, but the worry lines in his coffee-dark skin had deepened with concern. "Usually a Feeb with sharpshooter status asks for a transfer to a TAC team. But you insisted on staying with drug enforcement."

"That's so I could be close to you, pal."

"Right." Virg was too smart to buy Sam's witty repartee, which lacked the heart that used to back it up. He ripped the target off its mounts and counted the holes inside each of the two circles that would constitute a fatal shot. "Fifteen for fifteen."

Sam released a slowly measured sigh. His grim expertise was about the only thing that gave him comfort and satisfaction anymore.

Each and every one of those bullets had been for Kerry.

His opportunity would come—one day—when he could put away his sister's murderer. One way or another. And he'd be ready.

"I have to practice to stay efficient with my weapon."

"Yeah, well, it's all that practice that has me worried." Virgil stood by as Sam stripped, cleaned and holstered his weapon. "Chief Dixon thinks the strain of your sister's rape and murder is proving too much for you."

A flare of Sam's Irish temper tried to show itself. "He's already stuck me on desk duty."

Virgil put up his hands in surrender, reminding Sam that he was just the messenger. And a concerned, loyal friend. "He wants you to take that bereavement leave. Get your head on straight before you shoot at something you shouldn't. Before you crack."

"Is that what you think, too? That I'm about to crack?"

Virgil shook his head. "I know you need the work to get your mind off things." His partner's mouth thinned into a grim line. When Virgil Logan got serious, Sam paid attention. "I just don't want to see you make a mistake that'll come back and kick you in the chops. I don't want to see you in a second career as a security guard somewhere because you lost your head."

Sam inhaled and exhaled deeply. He leaned forward and rested both fists atop the shooting deck. "I'm not trying to screw up anything, Virg. I only want justice done."

"You know I want that, too. But you gotta give yourself some time to heal. You haven't taken any time off since the funeral."

Sam pushed himself up straight and backed out of the booth. "Seeing that bastard lined up in the crosshairs of my gun is the only thing that'll help me heal."

Virgil followed him out. "That's the kind of talk that worries me. You're a damn good investigator when your head's on straight."

They turned and headed for the locker room. "You think the fact that I'm spending extra time on the shooting range means I can't run an investigation anymore?"

"No. I just don't want to have to break in a new partner. I had a hell of a time training you."

"Training me?" Sam twisted up a towel and flicked Virg in the backside before tossing it around his neck, catching the support beneath the gibe. "I love you, too, pal. I promise I won't be stupid. If I give you my word, will that do?"

They shook hands like men. Then they shook hands in a goofy secret code that only two people who had been friends through the best and worst times of their lives could share.

"That's all I needed to hear." Virgil stopped at his locker and opened it. He pulled out a folded slip of paper, rolling it back and forth between his fingers and frowning as if he wasn't quite sure what to do with it. "Because I got some information you'll be interested in."

Sam ran his tongue around the rim of his lips and tried not to betray the instant anticipation racing through his veins. "I'm the one who's supposed to be pushing the regs, not you."

"I know you've been accessing files you don't have clearance for. Reading hospital records and police reports on rapes that match the MO in Kerry's case."

Sam's jaw shook with the restraint it required to keep from snatching that paper from Virgil's hands. "So far I've matched up four rape-murders with the same binding and strangulation marks, and the souvenir lock of hair cut from the scalp. Kerry here in Boston. One each in Dallas, New York and Miami.'' He knew his sister's case backward and forward. ''The Bureau profiler and my gut tells me they were all victims of the same man. In each case the victim was dark-haired. She was single and successful, but she ended up in a bad part of town. She was kidnapped, tortured and ultimately raped. And then, as if that wasn't enough…''

Sam closed his eyes in a futile effort to block the image of Kerry's sweet round face bruised and frozen in death. He'd seen dead bodies before. But hers had unnerved him. She was his responsibility. Even as a full-grown woman she'd still been his baby sister. The sassy sweetheart he'd promised his father on his deathbed that he'd protect.

He'd failed.

Oh, God. Sam shook with the force of his emotions. Bile twisted in his gut and tried to poison the good memories he had left of his family. *He'd failed*. He tilted his head and swallowed hard, forcing down the gag reflex that convulsed throughout his body.

When he was in control of himself once more, he opened his eyes and looked deep into Virgil's cryptic expression. ''Did you locate another vic?'' he asked.

''It's not much. A rape in Chicago. Dark hair with a chunk of it cut off. That was enough to flag it for me. Listed as a Jane Doe.'' Virgil handed the paper to Sam. ''But there's one key difference between this case and Kerry's.''

''What's that?'' Sam unfolded the paper with impatient fingers and read the answer for himself. *No.* His heart thumped hard against the wall of his chest, trying to hope, trying to believe what his eyes were seeing. ''Jane Doe survived the attack.''

In a flurry of movement, Sam removed his holster, peeled off his shirt and hurried toward the showers. A biting sense of urgency nipped at his heels, making every moment too long, too precious to waste. This was the best lead—the only lead—he'd had since Kerry's murder nearly eight months ago.

An eyewitness.

If it was the same murderous son of a bitch who'd killed Kerry, this vic could ID him. Give him a name, a visual, a voice—anything that he could put in the profile and hunt down.

Virgil followed at a slower pace. "Should I tell the chief that you'll be taking that bereavement leave now?"

"Yeah." He didn't want his partner to get caught in a lie, so he played along. They both knew what he had to do. "Tell Dixon I'm leaving tomorrow. Tonight, if I can get a flight."

One way or another—sooner rather than later—he was going to track down this Miss Jane Doe.

Chapter One

One Month Later

Jessica first saw him from her porch, walking along the gravel country road, putting a determined distance between each step and the urban sprawl of Kansas City, Missouri. She watched him as he approached the crossroad that divided her property and the Kent estate.

The shaggy black German shepherd mix that lay at her feet shifted his big, rangy body to a sitting position beside her, eyeing the stranger. The dog's alert curiosity matched her own, and a ripple of uneasiness cascaded down her spine. Trouble was headed their way.

"What do you think, Harry?" she asked, trusting the dog's judgment and companionship more than she trusted most people's.

The front porch ran the full length of her one-and-a-half-story log cabin house, situated on the top of a hill. The high-school boy she'd hired for odd jobs around the shop and acreage had just driven home to his parents' farm for dinner, and the dust kicked up by his speeding truck never even slowed the man's stride. Rendered ghostlike until the curtain of dust settled, he just kept coming, moving toward

the iron gates of her property with a sense of purpose that
had her shifting back half a step.

Thrilling anticipation as much as cautious fear revved in
her veins and gathered speed as the blood raced from her
heart into her tingling extremities. Her lips parted to ac-
commodate the quicker pace of suddenly shallow breaths.

Was he the one? Was he finally coming for her?

Nothing about him seemed familiar. And yet, how could
she know?

The dog stood and circled her legs, antsy about her next
command. Would she order him to run down the stranger?
Stay and protect? Attack?

Jessica shook her head, answering the dog's unspoken
questions. "I don't like the looks of him, either."

She slipped back another step, into the shadow of a
wooden post. She needed more time to think, more time to
make a decision. She needed to remember.

But he just kept coming.

The sun hung low in the western sky, not yet at the point
on the horizon that would color the Indian-summer clouds
in a palette of orange, pink and gold. Silhouetted against
the sun, she could see he was a big man. The pack he
carried on his back seemed to hold a whole life's worth of
belongings, from the faded denim jacket tied at the top to
the sleeping bag that hit his hips. Yet he carried it all with
an easy posture and resolute stride that said he could carry
the weight of the world on those broad shoulders. And had.

Jessica reached down and scratched Harry behind the
ears, catching up a handful of his longish black coat, which
reflected more of his wolfhound heritage than his police
dog ancestry. She needed the comfort of contact with another living creature to forestall the sense of impending
doom that made her chest seize up. Had she felt this same
fear before? Reacted this same way? Had she gone numb
with shock like this? Choked on her helpless anger?

"Turn the corner," she coaxed the stranger beneath her breath. "Walk on by."

He could turn at the crossroads at the foot of the hill and head east. But long before he neared the brick posts and wood rail fence that surrounded her land, she knew he wasn't going to turn. He would come right through the gate, saunter up her long gravel driveway and invite himself up to the house.

And he didn't look like the type of man who'd hiked out into the countryside southeast of Kansas City just to buy antiques at her shop. He paused only to read the carved wooden sign, Log Cabin Antiques. He must have read the hours, knew she'd just closed at six.

Frozen in the shadows, Jessica curled her fingers around Harry's collar. "Walk on," she mouthed again.

The stranger's shoulders heaved in a controlled sigh beneath the taut fit of his faded black T-shirt. Then he lifted his eyes and looked straight at her. Sought her out in the shade of the porch. Made eye contact as if he'd known she'd been watching him all along.

Her breath stuttered out in a rush of panic. Harry growled and barked twice, sensing the exponential swell of his mistress's fear.

She grabbed the dog by the collar and pulled him inside with her, bolting the door behind them.

She hurried through the tiny living room, past the stairs to her bedroom loft, sidestepped a glass-front display case that housed doll dishes and campaign buttons and slipped into the private nook that doubled as office and dining room. She squatted down out of sight beside the rolltop desk that held her computer and hugged Harry close to her chest. She could scarcely think. Breathe. See.

She was flashing back.

Flashing back to what? she demanded of herself, trying to see through the blind haze of terror that filled her mind.

All she could remember was the fear, the sense of being trapped. A business trip and romantic evening gone horribly awry. She could recall that last dinner in Chicago with Alex almost word for word—how angry and heartbroken she'd been. She knew what the doctors and cops had told her when she came to in the hospital more than twenty-four hours later. But she couldn't remember anything in between.

Twenty-four hours of her life lost in the closed-off fog of a memory, purged by a mind that craved sanity in order to survive.

All she knew was that she should have been dead. That she'd been violated in a way beyond imagining and had lived to tell about it.

Only she couldn't tell about it.

She couldn't remember it.

"Damn," she muttered, as frustrated now as she'd been last March.

She came from a family of cops. Her brothers had taught her how to defend herself, had lectured her on how to be more observant than the average citizen. But it hadn't been enough. Somehow she'd let them down and *he'd* gotten to her.

The crunch of gravel beneath a heavy footstep reminded her of the danger at hand. Was *he* here? Was that *him* coming closer and closer?

Burying her nose in Harry's neck, Jessica could feel the dog's warmth and strength. She could sense his unwavering loyalty and devotion to keeping her safe. He licked her arm, his long, raspy tongue a gentle request for direction and understanding.

"I don't know, boy." She hugged him tighter, trading comforts. "I don't know what to do."

Hidden in the dining room behind a wall of shelves and an old walnut wardrobe filled with antique dresses and quilts, she could simply lock the doors and hide until the man went away.

But she had a feeling locked doors and windows wouldn't stop a man like him. She could hide inside the wardrobe itself or lose herself in the aisles of furniture and collectibles she had for sale—and he'd still find her.

Paralyzing fear warred with the less certain instinct to survive. Her brothers *had* taught her to protect herself. And although she had failed then, she was a different person now. One who was a lot smarter about the harsh realities of life. One who had a lot less to lose.

One who wasn't done living yet.

Besides, there was really only one way to know if the man who'd come to her remote cabin was *him*.

And more than anything—more than the fear itself—she wanted to know the truth.

Jessica leaned back and caught the dog's streamlined jowls between her hands. "You with me, Harry?"

Uncanny intelligence stared back at her from midnight-brown eyes. He'd had one hell of a past, too, before she'd found the giant mutt on death row at the pound. Maybe it took someone who'd survived the worst the world had to offer to understand what she'd been through, what she had to face every day of her life now. Maybe someone *could* understand—and love her anyway. The dog's unflinching support actually coaxed a smile out of Jessica.

And inspired a sense of calm that allowed her to think clearly once more. "Let's go."

Latching on to Harry's collar, Jessica pulled against the dog's weight and stood, quickly unlocking the gun cabinet beside her desk. She pulled out the Remington double-barrel shotgun she used for trap shooting and loaded two rounds. She stuffed two more shells into the front pocket of her jeans, whistled for Harry and headed out the double screened doors onto the back porch.

Matching the full-length porch on the front of the house, this one wasn't decorated to show off the cabin's rustic charms. This was a workspace full of rockers that needed recaning, wagons that needed new wheels, a 1910 buggy that needed one of its traces replaced. Wooden boxes, shutters, a washing machine, stools, barrels, trinkets, gadgets. It was a veritable fortress of camouflage, and Jessica used it to her advantage, keeping the faded green buggy between her and the stranger who approached.

"That's far enough," she ordered, hugging the rubber butt of the gun against her shoulder and leveling the business end at the center of his chest. It was a broad enough target. And she was a better shot than he could ever imagine. Harry bristled to attention at her side.

The man halted his steps, betraying more curiosity than alarm. "Not exactly the back-door hospitality I've heard tell about Missouri."

His voice was low pitched, smooth as whiskey and tinged with the barest hint of an accent.

And completely unfamiliar to her.

"This isn't a bed-and-breakfast," she warned. "It's private property."

He tilted the crown of his coal-black hair toward the front gate. "The sign says you sell antiques."

She held the gun steady, making her message clear. "We're closed."

He'd turned from the customer parking lot up the private driveway that bisected the grounds between the cabin and her storage barn. And though she stood three steps above him on the elevated porch, she was almost looking him straight in the eye. And they were the coldest eyes she'd ever seen. Icy gray. Almost colorless behind the squint of his expression. He was a man who didn't give a damn about anything. It was the best impression he could have made.

That meant he didn't care about her, either.

"Do you know how to use that thing?" he asked.

He might not be a voice from her past, but he was still trespassing. "Yes."

"And the dog?" His gaze never shifted off hers.

"I know how to use him, too."

"Look, lady, I don't—" He raised his hands in mock surrender and took half a step forward.

It was all the provocation she needed. "Harry, sic."

The snarling black powerhouse leaped from the porch and charged the man at a dead run. But despite the stranger's big size, his reflexes were quick. Before Harry lunged for his forearm, the man whipped the huge pack off his back and wielded it like a shield, absorbing the brunt of Harry's first blow. One hundred and twenty pounds of charging canine knocked the man back a couple of steps.

Harry bared his teeth and menaced in a horrible growl as he lunged again. The man used the pack to buffet the second attack. He twisted and blocked, countering Harry each time the dog tried to latch on to something with flesh.

The man was either trained in self-defense or damn lucky. But he would tire long before Harry ever surrendered. "Lady!"

Jessica almost smiled. *Good boy.* If Harry could best this man, she'd have a lot less reason to be afraid of him. "You lie down flat on the ground and I'll call him off."

Harry had a chunk of the backpack between his teeth now, and the attack had turned into a desperate tug-of-war. The man couldn't surrender his grasp or he'd be defenseless at the next charge. "Fine. Call him off."

"Harry, sit!" she commanded.

The dog obeyed, plopping down on his haunches beside the man's shoulder as he dropped his pack and threw himself prostrate onto the swath of fading grass at the center of her driveway. The man lay perfectly still beneath the dog's watchful eye.

Harry panted from the exertion, licking his muzzle, then letting his tongue loll out the side of his mouth. The man was catching his breath, too. But the instant he moved, a big black paw settled onto his shoulder and he went still.

"Is this how you greet all your customers?"

"You're no customer." Lowering the gun from her cheek and shoulder, she kept it trained in his general direction and left her finger near the trigger. "What do you want?"

SAM WASN'T READY to answer that question truthfully. He hadn't expected a warm, trusting welcome when he showed up with his vagrant cover story, but he was a little surprised to be greeted by a backwoods, Hatfield and McCoy, you's-trespassin'-on-my-land routine.

Where was the professional businesswoman with an eye for beauty and a penchant for history his contact in Chicago had told him about? Her face matched the newspaper photo of the elegant brunette at a museum exhibition opening he'd found in the *Chicago Tribune* archives—the same face the attending E.R. nurse had confirmed as his Jane Doe rape survivor.

He'd spent three weeks piecing together nebulous clues and putting a name to the face of the woman he was searching for. Then he'd run a background profile on her. And now he was here.

This was Jessica Taylor.

His Jane Doe had a name. And a definite attitude.

He suspected that earning her trust wouldn't be easy. Without the sanction of the Bureau, and with little more than a hunch to go on that she would be the break he needed in order to find Kerry's killer, Sam couldn't conduct a normal investigation. He needed to get to know Jessica Taylor better than he knew his own partner. He needed to become her very best friend and get her to start talking. About Chicago. Her attack. How she escaped.

Who did it.

Either she'd been too terrified to give a useful report to Chicago PD, or her attacker had been too crafty—too intimidating—for her to recall much. He might even have done a little brainwashing on her. Sam intended to find a way inside her head and learn the truth. Learn enough so he could match up her attacker to Kerry's and track him down.

But with that pump-action shotgun pointed his way and this hairy, black beast standing over him, his covert mission would be damn near impossible.

Kerry had always teased that it had skipped a generation, but Sam wondered if he could dredge up any of his father's Belfast charm. Lifting his cheek from the scraggly grass and dirt, he tried to restart the conversation. "What kind of dog is this?"

"The very protective kind."

Idly, Sam wondered if she'd always sounded this hard. Judging by the resonant tone and sultry pitch of her voice, Ms. Taylor could sound downright sexy if she softened up her articulation and dropped the sarcastic wit. It was probably an unfortunate byproduct of the attack. He'd be curious to know what other feminine attributes she was trying to hide.

Irrelevant, a stern inner voice warned him. Though curiosity was not the same as attraction, he wanted to argue, Sam wisely ignored the deviation from his quest. He turned his nose to the ground and inhaled the dank, musty smell of the dirt that reminded him of Kerry's funeral—reminded him of why he was here. "So I gathered. He looks like a black shepherd, but his muzzle is broader. And obviously he's bigger than any German shepherd I've seen."

"He's a German shepherd, Irish wolfhound mix." Irish,

huh? Maybe the hairy beast had some redeemable qualities, after all. "He was too big and too smart for his previous owners. But he suits me."

Sam tried to move his head so he could actually look at Jessica, but apparently the dog didn't feel the connection of their Irish roots. The growl in his throat became a deafening bark and a flash of sharp, white teeth. Sam forced his body to relax and resumed his prone position on the grass. "He seems well trained." He'd worked with K-9 units before, but had never been on the receiving end of such training. No wonder the perps usually surrendered without much of a fight.

"He is."

"I didn't show up by chance, Miss Taylor." He heard her feet shift their solid stance on the wooden floorboards, the first flinch in her protective armor. He'd called her by name. Better retreat a step. Even up the playing field. "I'm Sam O'Rourke. The clerk at the convenience store up on the Highway 50 intersection gave me your name and directions. If you let me have a chance, I can explain why I'm here." Silence. Damn, she was a hard nut to crack. "Do you need the dog and the gun both?"

"I don't know yet."

It was hard to be charming with his face pressed to the dirt and a wolfhound-shepherd beast sitting on his shoulder. Kerry had been right. He'd always done better with a more direct approach.

"Look, I can see this was a mistake. The guy at the store said your regular help wasn't able to put in enough hours and that you were desperate for an extra hand around the place." He looked around slyly and noted the overgrown patches of grass taking over the gravel parking lot and driveway, the dead branches of stately elms that needed trimming, the rust on the red-and-white metal storage barn, the tarp-shrouded load in the back of a pickup truck waiting to be unloaded. The man hadn't lied. "But he must have been mistaken. If you let me up, I'll go back into town and find work somewhere else."

"You're looking for a job?" She sounded skeptical. She might be stubborn, but she was smart. Deceiving her wasn't going to be easy. "Why didn't you call first? Where's your car?"

Technically his Kia was in a garage back in Boston. But the junker he'd picked up in Chicago had been easy enough to abandon at the side of the road outside Kansas City to establish his cover. "Until I earn enough money to fix it, it's sitting in the shop. I'm driving cross-country from Boston to San Diego. Sort of a sabbatical. It broke down on the highway."

"What kind of sabbatical?" she asked, her voice still filled with doubt. "You don't look like a professor."

"That's my business."

"Not if you want to work for me, it's not." Was she considering his proposition? "I'll let you sit up if you explain who you are and don't make any sudden moves."

It wasn't much of an offer, but he'd take it. "Deal."

She whistled—a bold, brassy tomboy whistle. Unexpected. Interesting. *Irrelevant.* "Harry, come."

A tremendous weight lifted as the dog immediately obeyed her command. The jet-black beast trotted up the steps onto the porch and cuddled at his mistress's side as if he thought he was a lap dog. Minding her warning, Sam slowly rolled over and sat up. He spun around on his bottom to face her, brushing bits of grass and gravel dust from his shirt and jeans. His arm had actually started to go to sleep beneath the dog's lucky guess at pressure points. Sam massaged at his shoulder and arm, easing the tingling rush of reawakening.

Using the massage as an excuse, he didn't say anything for several moments, giving himself his first opportunity to size up the woman who was going to make his mission a success. The stock of her Remington rested on the generous curve of one denim-clad hip. The woman up on the porch was a far cry from the sophisticate he'd seen in the newspaper's black-and-white photograph.

A hole in one knee broke the long line of leg that might be the most distinctive feature of her tall, subtly masked body. While the woman in the photo had worn a strapless evening gown that managed to look classy and seductive at the same time, this woman on the porch was a nature girl. No upsweep of long hair. No jewelry beyond a watch. And not much skin to catch the late September sun. Her modest blue Taylor Construction T-shirt looked as if it belonged to one of her brothers that had shown up in his research. The short sleeves hung past her elbows, and the collar rode high at the neck. The hem was loosely tucked into the waistband of relaxed jeans.

Body camouflage. She could be plump or thin or anywhere in between, but the outside world would never be able to tell. Sam wondered if Kerry would have hidden her fair-skinned attributes in the same way if she'd survived her rape. *Damn.* He didn't need to go off on a tangent like that.

Suddenly the enormity of all he had lost seized his throat. Sam squeezed his eyes shut and turned his head to choke the emotions back down. He couldn't let Jessica Taylor see how much he had at stake in this at-gunpoint job interview.

When he was in control of himself again, he turned back and lifted his gaze up to hers. He knew most of her stats by heart. Age: twenty-nine. Height: five-eight. Weight: 140. But the stats didn't do her bright-blue eyes justice. And to say her hair was brown was to miss the whole point of subtle auburn highlights and a loose, face-framing style.

Stats couldn't tell him word one about what was going

on inside that head of hers. And whether or not she could help him.

"Okay, Mr. O'Rourke." She nudged the air with the point of her gun. "Talk to me."

"I'm looking for some work to tide me over 'til the end of September, maybe mid-October. I like to get a feel for a place. And, hopefully, make enough money to fix the car and pay my way until the next stop." He braced his elbows on his bent knees and nodded back toward the road. "The clerk in Lone Jack said you were looking for some help. Seven miles straight down the road didn't seem like a terrible hike. So I took a chance."

"Ralphie, the clerk, likes to look out for me. My regular hand is one of the neighbor kids. Now that school's back in session, he can only work Saturdays and some nights after football practice." Was she opening up to him? She might be talking more, but the gun made it hard to tell whether or not he was making progress. "He's the one who almost ran you off the road on the way in. Derek Phillips. He's a sweet kid."

"He's a road hog."

"He's eighteen years old. What do you expect?" Okay, so clearly she was protective of her hired help. Or teenagers. Or this one in particular. Did that mean he could rule out a young man as her attacker? She did have a younger brother. Maybe the kid was just a reminder of him, and therefore she considered him safe.

She definitely didn't consider *him* safe.

Sam thought the conversation had died with his speculation. She stood in silence long enough for him to become annoyingly aware of the sharp gravel digging into his backside. "Can I get up now?"

"No, I—"

He got up anyway, slowly unwinding his legs and pushing to his feet.

"I said no!" She lifted the shotgun to her shoulder and had her finger on the trigger guard again.

Sam put up his hands in surrender and slouched his weight to the side. But he didn't retreat. He didn't want to scare her, but he wanted her to know he meant business. He had no intention of leaving Log Cabin Acres without this job. He had no intention of leaving, period. He'd let his hair grow out, and hadn't shaved for a couple of days, hoping his vagrant look would earn him an offer of room and board. Even if it meant bunking on a cot in the barn.

"I have a cramp in my leg," he said to explain his moderate show of defiance. "Believe me, you still have the advantage."

She had good form, he'd give her that. Steady, too. He could see one blue eye, clear and focused, as he looked into the over/under barrel of her gun and on up to the sight. She might have him lined up between the crosshairs, but the fact she didn't sic the dog on him again made him think she wouldn't actually shoot.

Progress.

"So what about that job?" he asked. "I don't know much about antiques, but I've worked with furniture—repairing and refinishing it. And I've done yard work and construction since I was a kid if you need help winterizing the place."

That blue eye squinted with doubt. "You're taking a sabbatical from yardwork and construction?"

"I have a reference. Virgil Logan." He'd tried to keep his partner as far removed from his off-the-clock investigation as possible. If anything about this quest for vengeance went south, Sam's career would be toast. But Virg would be free and clear of any wrongdoing. But surely his old buddy would be willing to say something nice about the cabinets he'd helped him install in his new kitchen last year. "I'll give you a number and you can call him."

Was that slight hitch in her shoulders a pensive sigh? Would a bit more gentle persistence wear her down?

"The clerk—Ralphie—said you lived alone out here." With his hands still in the air, he angled his head to the right and left. "It looks like you've got plenty of work. I think you need a few muscles to tackle some of these jobs. Unloading that furniture, regravelling the driveway. I tinker around with mechanics, too. I might be able to get that old steam engine tractor I saw out front running again. If you've got the parts."

She took her left hand off the gun and motioned him to be silent. "Fine. I have no doubt you can do the job. It's just…"

Sam lowered his hands to his sides. She was going to have to learn to trust him sometime. "It's just you're one woman, living out here on your own. And I'm a big, scary man. A stranger, to boot."

His understanding of her fears seemed to suck the argument right out of her. She was almost shaking as she lowered the gun once more and reached down to stroke the dog's head. "Yeah," she finally agreed on a soft, wistful sigh. "I have to stay safe."

He respected the admission of fear. Jessica Taylor's honesty would work in his favor. An admission of truth from him might be the first step toward earning her trust. He let just enough of the pain and guilt that riddled him seep into his expression. He kept the rest locked down tightly inside the prison of his heart.

"I, uh, lost someone very close to me earlier this year. My baby sister. We were all that was left of my family so we were pretty tight." He inhaled a steadying breath that wasn't all for show. "I took a leave of absence from my desk job, and I've been working on other things to try to get past it."

"I'm sorry." She sounded genuinely moved by his bare-boned version of the truth.

Sam looked up at her, and for a long, foolish moment out of time, lost himself in a sea of azure compassion. For that one brief instant, his world wasn't such a lonely place. He wasn't such a driven man. And his heart…

His heart almost felt something. Something hopeful.

Sam blinked and shook his head, looking away. Hell. What was that all about? The only thing that was going to make him feel better, the only thing that was going to make the pain go away, was to get the bastard who'd desecrated and snuffed the life out of the sweetest thing God had ever seen fit to put in his world. He'd swallow his pride, trade his life, whatever it took to put a bullet through that freak's head or watch him die by lethal injection.

"So, Miss Taylor…" There was more harsh than gentle in his voice now, and the light that he'd seen in her pretty blue eyes had vanished. "I need the job. I have no intention of harming you or putting the moves on you or any other damn thing that might get me into trouble." He curled his fingers into tight fists. "I just need to get my hands on something and work it out of my system."

"You need to forget."

"Yeah." But he never would.

To his surprise, she lowered the barrel of her shotgun and removed the ammunition. As she stuffed the unused slugs into her pocket, she looked toward the smaller log structure just east of the house. "There's an apartment over the garage you can use if you need a place to stay. Since you're on foot, I imagine it'd be more convenient."

Whoa. Sam shifted inside his dusty brown work boots. What just happened here? When had he missed the transition from Backwoods Annie to this efficient, articulate professional woman? "You're giving me the job?"

"I'll call your Virgil Logan in the morning to double-check you're who you say you are. If it pans out, you're hired for a month. But I have a few rules.'' She stepped back toward the double doors that led into the cabin. ''You're to come into the main house by invitation only. I'll fix or provide three meals a day. You can eat on the porch as long as the weather holds, or up in your room. That apartment is small, but the mattress is new. It'll hold a big guy like you. There's a coffeemaker and small fridge for snacks or cold drinks. I don't tolerate drunks, though.''

Sam reached down and slung his pack over his shoulder. Now that he'd broken the ice, he was getting somewhere. Had her attacker been drunk? Had Kerry's? He'd have Jessica Taylor sized up and spilling her secrets in half the time she'd offered him. ''I haven't been on a binge since college, and that's been a few years,'' he reassured her.

''No guests, no parties—''

''I don't know anyone here.''

''And no surprises. You give me one reason to doubt your story, and I'll call the sheriff and my brothers. Three of them are K.C.P.D. cops, and my cousin is captain of his precinct. You don't know overprotective until you've met them. Anything happens to me and they will track you down.''

So why hadn't they tracked down her rapist and put him behind bars yet? Maybe they weren't as good as she thought. Maybe he was better.

''Are we clear on the rules?'' she demanded, drawing his thoughts back to his first need—establishing his cover. He'd clue himself in to whatever the Taylors had found out about their sister's attack later.

''Crystal clear.''

She hesitated a moment longer, as if having doubts about her decision. ''Did your sister really die?''

Damn. Blindsided. He hadn't seen that one coming. He couldn't look at her. Not right away. Not until he got that instant image of Kerry's chopped black hair, and the bruises and cuts that mangled her porcelain skin out of his head. With a sharp curse on a sharper burst of pent-up air, he slammed that door shut in his mind. "Yeah."

That was all she needed to hear?

"I'll get the key." Before she opened the screened door and went inside, she paused. "Harry, stay."

After she disappeared inside, the hairy, black, monster mutt positioned himself squarely in front of the door, clearly reminding Sam of the stay-out-of-the-house rule.

Sam braced a hand on his hip and leaned in. "You and I are going to have to find a way to get along, big guy." If he wanted any chance to snoop through Jessica's things or get close to the woman herself, Sam would have to get the dog's permission. Or he'd have to find some way to get the furry guard beast out of the way. "Can I tempt you with a big, juicy steak?"

Jessica felt sorry for him. She thought she was helping him through the grieving process by giving him the job and a place to stay.

His lie must have been a tangible scent in the air. Because the damn dog glared at Sam, as if it knew he was going to take advantage of his mistress's foolish heart.

Chapter Two

"Die, bitch."

He pulled the belt tighter and tighter around her neck, loving the invigorating strain that burned through the muscles of his forearms and biceps and chest. Sweat beaded on his skin. He was the man. The world was his to control.

The voiceless words that formed at her cracked, swollen lips stopped as a dying sound gurgled up from her throat.

"What are you saying, honey? Is that too tight?" He loved the power. At the slightest nod of her head he loosened the tourniquet. "There. Is that better?"

Her breasts thrust up as she sucked in a deep gulp of air, but he was more intent on her face. Her lips sputtered one word. And he waited patiently for her to repeat herself. "Why?"

Not *please?* Not *sorry? Why?*

Damn her!

He jerked back on the belt, pinning his thighs around her hips as he sat on top of her. She thrashed beneath him, her struggles only adding to her pain and his delight as she tore her milky white skin against the bindings at her wrists and ankles.

He was almost giddy with the gluttonous rush of energy that pulsed through him. He was masterful. Thorough. He towered over her with his strength. "You don't have so much to say now, do you?"

He looked down on her as her eyes wept, beseeched, went blank, then closed.

"That's it?" he crooned in a soft voice, exhaling a dissatisfied breath of air. She should have protested more. At the very least, asked for his mercy. But this one had been too shocked, too damn full of herself to even scream properly. Disappointing. His entire body deflated as the energy that had jazzed him to yet another high dissipated.

He slipped off her quietly, not wanting to disturb her imitation of slumber. He rolled up the stocking mask that had covered his face and dropped it into his bag. He hadn't worried so much about hiding his identity as he'd enjoyed the symbolism of it all. He was man at his most base, his most powerful.

And he'd been triumphant.

A glance at his watch on the nightstand told him he had only a few hours before his flight. There wasn't much time to savor his victory. But he couldn't just leave.

He picked up his black jeans off the floor beside the bed where he'd stripped, and reached into the front pocket. He pulled out a pocketknife with a polished, inlaid ebony handle. It was a thing of beauty, a true find for his collection. He opened it up and tested its weight, appreciating the feel of it in his hand.

Padding across the threadbare carpet, he reached out and lifted a long, silky lock of her dark hair between his thumb and forefinger. Sawing delicately back and forth, he cut the lock from her scalp and lifted the fragrant strands to his nose. Beneath the odors of sweat and fear and that dusty mattress, he smelled the tangy scent of the woman herself.

It would be an appropriate souvenir of their night together.

"Unfortunately, I have to be leaving," he whispered to her. He didn't bother with meaningless platitudes. She'd served her purpose. There would be no next time for them. "Thank you."

He stuffed the hair and knife into his pocket and went into the tiny bathroom. He chased the roaches from the shower and quickly cleaned himself. In a matter of minutes he was dressed and packed and ready to depart.

But he wasn't done yet.

She'd learned her lesson. She didn't deserve to be found trussed up like a turkey.

Sparing her a few precious moments of his time, he went to the bed and untied her. He pulled her legs together and crossed them at the ankles. Then he freed her bruised wrists and laid them neatly atop her naked belly. He pulled the blanket from the foot of the bed and covered her up, tucking the cover around her, tenderly putting her to bed.

This one wouldn't cause him any more trouble. But that other one…that other one…

A fistful of that familiar rage tightened in his chest and made him forget for a moment his triumph here tonight. "I was in control tonight," he reminded himself. Not this dead bitch. "*I* was in control."

The anger left him almost as quickly as it had come. He pressed a hand to his chest and expelled a weary sigh. *Her* time would come. The one who got away—the one who could spoil it all—her time was coming. Sooner than she'd ever expect.

He smiled, feeling rational and benevolent and in control once more.

"Goodbye, love."

He leaned over the bed and kissed her gently on her cool cheek. Then he disappeared into the night.

"SHERIFF HANCOCK, this is a surprise." Jessica peeled off her gloves and dropped them onto the worktable beside the rusted toy wagon she'd been cleaning.

"Mornin', Jessie." Curtis Hancock slipped his broad-brimmed hat over his salt-and-pepper hair before climbing out of the white official county cruiser. "Fine September day, isn't it?"

Jessica didn't answer. She rarely judged her days by the quality of the weather anymore.

She wiped her sweaty palms on her jeans and whistled for Harry who was sunning himself at the far end of the porch. "Harry, come." Shaking off his snooze, the big dog stretched and trotted over as soon as she gave him a stern look. She rewarded his instant obedience with a "Good boy" and a vigorous scratching along his chest and muzzle. "Harry, heel."

Together, they walked down to the gravel parking lot while the sheriff adjusted his holster and utility belt around the waistband of his dark-brown uniform. Short and on the stocky side, thanks to his wife's Southern-style cooking, Curtis Hancock was every inch the proper, old-fashioned gentleman. Maybe that, and the fact he was closer to her father's age than her own, made her relax enough to smile. "Can I help you with something?"

The sheriff tipped his hat in a polite greeting. "Just making some rounds. I like to check on my favorite people in the county when I can." He leaned in with a conspiratorial whisper. "I let my deputies check on the ones I don't like."

He straightened with a wink and Jessica laughed on cue. "I'm flattered." She thumbed over her shoulder toward the cabin. "I still have some coffee in the pot. Would you like a cup?"

"No, thanks." He rested both hands near the buckle of his belt, assuming a casual stance. But his dark, darting eyes surveyed her place with a thorough curiosity. "I'm having lunch with Trudy Kent in half an hour. We're going over security for that big soirée she's throwing tomorrow night.''

"Security? For a dinner party?" Gertrude Wallace Kensington Kent was one of Missouri's wealthiest widows and liked to do things in a big way. But as the older woman's neighbor, she'd also learned that Trudy did them with grace and style. "That doesn't sound like her."

"Half the county's invited. It'll be more like a political rally, I imagine. She and her son, Charles, are determined that the city not buy up any more property to build a highway or new industrial complex. The Kents have lived in this part of the county since before the Civil War. They intend to keep a pristine countryside.''

She nodded. Trudy Kent had a standing offer to buy Jessica's adjoining property if she ever decided to sell. "And the business owners who are looking to expand or turn a tidy profit on land sales aren't thrilled with Trudy's plan. Are you really expecting trouble?"

"I just like to be prepared so I can control the situation should anything come up." His gaze lit and narrowed at a distant point beyond Jessica's shoulder. "Are you going to the party?"

His question was perfunctory and polite, but she could tell he was more interested in what he was watching than in her answer. She slowly turned to look over her shoulder, already guessing what had caught his eye.

Sam O'Rourke.

"I hired him yesterday." She answered his unspoken question first. "There's a lot I need to get done. Derek Phillips is busy after school with sports and farm responsibilities so he can't put in the hours he did over the summer.''

Sheriff Hancock nodded. "Looks like a good worker."

The big man with the shaggy black hair and granite eyes

was pushing a gravel-filled wheelbarrow from the barn to her driveway. Perspiration from honest work glistened on his golden skin, making dark patches on his black T-shirt at the center of his chest and the small of his back. His biceps and triceps corded with the effort as he negotiated the heavy load across the bumpy terrain. Though she knew he'd shaved this morning, the navy bandanna tied around his forehead gave him a dangerous, street-tough look.

It was all unnerving somehow, having Sam O'Rourke around the place. "He's doing fine so far." She tried to focus on conversing with the sheriff. "At the rate he's going, he'll have the driveway, the parking lot and the road up into the woods regravelled by the end of the week."

Though Sam hadn't spoken to her beyond proposing a list of tasks, asking about tools and thanking her for breakfast, she hadn't once forgotten he was there. She made a point of knowing where he was at all times.

But her vigilance wasn't solely due to commonsense safety and a lingering distrust of the man. With her eye for detail, she couldn't help noticing how his faded jeans hugged his lean hips and the solid trunks of his thighs. Sam O'Rourke was big. She was five-eight, and he towered over her by a good eight inches. He was in shape. His stomach was flat and his arms were corded like a man who worked out. And he was sexy. Not handsome. Not by any conventional definition of the word. Everything about his features was too strong, too angular—all set in stone without a smile or laugh line to soften them.

But he was undeniably compelling. A testament to honed strength and raw masculinity.

Jessica watched him fill three holes until he glanced her way and caught her staring. She quickly looked down, busying her attention with scratching Harry beneath his ears and praying the edginess that suddenly suffused her body didn't show.

But she doubted Sheriff Hancock was seeing the same details about Sam that she was. Her cheeks heated at the realization. She hadn't noticed a man's looks in months. Only to size up whether or not he was a threat to her, and to try to decide if he was *the one*. She couldn't remember the last time her body had buzzed with this long-forgotten awareness of a man.

Not since Alex. And her attraction for *him* had dimmed the moment he'd introduced his wife at that museum fundraiser. That had been during that same fateful trip to Chicago. Her sexual appetite had soured that night in the face of his arrogant deceit. Later, it had been destroyed by something much, much worse.

But she was noticing Sam O'Rourke.

And it scared her. Scared her enough to tighten her fingers around the cold steel of Harry's collar to steady herself. What was she thinking? Her therapist said when she started to heal, she'd begin to think of men in a sexual way again. That that was normal, and not to be afraid of the feelings.

But when she thought of how much she'd been hurt, how humiliated she'd been, how degraded and stupid she'd felt at letting a man…

No. You didn't let him do anything, she chided herself. *He attacked you. He used you.* The scars on her fingers and neck, her wrists and ankles reminded her of how valiantly she'd fought. The fact she'd been naked and battered beneath a threadbare blanket when she'd hailed that cab proved she'd been in fear for her life.

One man had done something unspeakable to her. One man.

Not the entire male population.

She loved her brothers and father. She could conduct business with men, carry on a conversation with them. She could look at—and even admire—them. That was all normal.

But she'd be a suicidal idiot if she allowed herself to get close to another man. If she allowed herself to feel anything—even empathy or attraction—for a man.

Not until she knew *which* man had stolen twenty-four hours from her memory and left her to die.

"Jessie?"

Jessica flinched, almost swinging out at the hand that grasped her shoulder. Harry growled in immediate response to her distress. Sheriff Hancock. Quickly orienting herself in the present and shutting off the vengeful commentary inside her head, she exhaled a calming breath.

"Easy, Harry." She smoothed the wiry hair atop his head, reassuring herself as much as the canine. Curtis Hancock didn't know what she'd gone through six months ago in Chicago. No one did. Secrecy was a necessary byproduct of her shame. Even if she never felt it again, she had to at least *act* as if she was normal. She even dredged up a shaky laugh. "I'm sorry."

The sheriff held up his hands and shook his head. "I'm the one who's sorry. Didn't mean to startle you."

Jessica shook aside his apology, moving on without offering any explanation. "I got my invitation to Trudy's, but I'll probably stay home. Since I've expanded my business onto the Internet, I'm having a hard time keeping up with orders."

"Is that why you hired the new man? What do you know about this new fella, anyway?"

Ah. The real reason for the unannounced visit. Curtis Hancock knew just about everyone in the county, from retirement-home residents to newborn babies. A stranger from the East Coast was definitely worth checking out.

Funny how a woman alone seemed to bring out the protective urges in every male. Except one. Sam O'Rourke seemed content to mind his own business and bury himself in his work. She could understand that need to lose himself in something long enough to forget the pain for a while. In the past months she'd treasured finding an escape like that—putting together her Web site to expand her five-year-old business, training Harry. Because the guilt and the pain never truly seemed to go away.

She'd better put Sheriff Hancock's concerns to rest before he took his questions any further and alerted her family. "Don't worry. I checked him out. This morning I called his supervisor back in Boston. He said that Sam had taken a leave of absence for personal reasons, but that he'd always been reliable and above reproach." She smiled and pretended complete confidence in her choice. "I wouldn't hire some bum with a criminal record."

"I know you Taylors are a big deal in the city. But out here in the county I'm your first line of defense." If Hancock could have puffed out his chest a little more when he said that, he'd have busted a button at the front of his shirt. "You won't mind if I do a little checking on this guy myself?"

"No." She didn't mind his interference as long as he didn't make a big deal out of it. "Just tell me if you find out something, before you let anyone else know."

"Absolutely."

"Thanks." She thumbed over her shoulder toward Sam. "Do you want to meet him?"

A soft, guttural woof from Harry alerted her to the gray-and-white tabby cat tiptoeing through the grass toward relative safety beneath the porch. Harry didn't much mind the cats who'd taken up residence in the barn and took care of the mice. He was more likely to go after the rodents and their larger cousins in the woods. But he was always careful to assert his dominance as chief pet.

"Hey, kitty." Sheriff Hancock's portly face creased with

a smile. "Here, baby." He circled around Jessica and Harry and scooped up the willing feline in his arms. "Aren't you a sweet thing," he cooed, stroking the cat's striped coat. "This one's not full-grown yet. How many of these you have?"

He turned and displayed the cat in his arms as if he'd just picked up a new grandbaby. Jessica drifted back a step, responding to an unfamiliar impulse. "I don't know. Ten? A dozen?"

"Would you consider parting with one or two of them?" He buzzed his lips, imitating the cat's purr. Jessica pressed her hand to her stomach, wondering at the sudden knot of nerves that clutched inside her. "I'd pay you a fair price," he offered.

Right now she was more creeped out by the cat he was petting than concerned about striking a business deal. Something toyed at the fringe of her subconscious mind. The cat. She was scarcely aware of the irregular pattern of her breathing now. "Take the cat."

"Are you sure?" the sheriff asked. "My wife's been bummed out ever since we had to put her yellow tabby, Peanut Butter, to sleep. Lord, how she loved that cat. Had her sixteen years."

Jessica didn't understand the panic that was sending intermittent shocks of terror through her system. She took a conscious step back, away from the cat. "Take however many cats you want. They're free. Just take them. With my compliments."

"Why that's right nice—"

"Is everything all right, Miss Taylor?" A giant shadow fell across her, temporarily blocking out the sun and breaking the inexplicable spell that had seized her. Sam O'Rourke pulled off his work gloves and stuffed them into his back pocket, circling around the sheriff and stopping at a respectful distance beside her. "I saw the sheriff's car parked—"

"Just paying a friendly visit." Sheriff Hancock angled his head to the side to mask how far he had to look up to see Sam's face. "It's my philosophy that the law needs to show up from time to time, even when there isn't any trouble." He shifted the cat to one arm and extended his free hand. "I'm Curtis Hancock, County Sheriff."

Sam's pale eyes narrowed as they studied the proffered hand and the man it belonged to. He paused long enough for the silent duel of wills between the two men to overshadow her own discomfort. Then he wrapped one big paw around the sheriff's and shook hands. "Sam O'Rourke. My car broke down outside of Lone Jack yesterday morning."

Sheriff Hancock pulled back, wise to Sam's subtle effort at intimidation. But he was the one with the badge, and Jessica watched him reassert his authority. "That's what Ralph Edmonds told me," he said, informing Sam he'd already been watching him. "So you're from Boston, huh?"

"Born and raised there. My parents were immigrants from Belfast, Northern Ireland." That explained to Jessica the hint of non-New England accent in his voice.

"Were they caught up in the conflict there?" asked Hancock.

"Yeah." He didn't elaborate.

Like a fool, Jessica hadn't even considered looking into Sam's personal background. She'd checked one work reference and trusted her gut that he was a loner without much of a stake in anything beyond his grief. Maybe she'd just invited some sort of Irish rebel to live in her garage apartment. Very foolish. Her hand automatically slid to Harry's collar.

"I see." Thankfully, Curtis's attention had shifted from her to Sam. Though she wondered at the unexpected relief she felt at having her hired hand join the conversation. "Where you headed?"

"San Diego," Sam answered. His voice was as clipped and unrevealing as his answer. "Is there a problem with me working here, Sheriff?"

The older man absorbed Sam's dare with a good-ol'-boy smile. "There's not a problem for me as long as there's not a problem for Jessie."

Jessica felt rather than saw the icy gray gaze sweep over her. But the deep voice was surprisingly warm. "I don't want to cause her any trouble."

Struck by the soothing tone of Sam's low-pitched promise, Jessica tilted her head and caught a glimpse of shadow darkening his pale eyes. A glimpse of what? Regret? The gray eyes shuttered and he looked away before she did. What a crazy notion. It was probably just the terminal sorrow he seemed steeped in that gave a false impression of caring.

As if she should trust her instincts about men, anyway.

Needing to end this torture of doubts and suspicions and constantly being on guard, she tapped on the crystal of her watch. "Oh, Sheriff, look at the time." She forced herself to smile. "You don't want to keep Trudy waiting."

He jumped in his shoes as if he'd just gotten goosed. "Oh, Lordy, no. Here." He thrust the gray tabby toward her. Jessica recoiled as if the furry creature had attacked. "Jessie?"

"I—" Oh, God. A giant door slammed shut inside her head, triggering an instant headache. Nothing rational could escape, only a tidal wave of instant, all-consuming fear. "Get away from me!"

She backed off, instinctively grabbing Harry and putting the big dog between her and the invisible threat that advanced on her.

"Jessie?"

"Miss Taylor?"

"No." She pummeled her way through the barriers inside her head. A flashback. Only she wasn't remembering any details about the attack or the attacker. She was only remembering the fear. "Stop it."

"Jess!"

Sam's sharp tone was punctuated by a bark from Harry. Like an electric shock stopping the defibrillation of a heart, hearing the personal abbreviation of her name snapped her out of that emotional hallucination. The darkness inside her mind vanished as if the combination of Sam and Harry calling out had switched on a light.

She was aware enough of her surroundings to see Sam's hand reaching toward her and to feel the bunching of muscles in Harry's shoulders as he prepared to defend her. "Down, boy. Harry, down." She waved aside Sam's attempt to help and commanded the dog to lie at her feet. "I'm all right."

"You don't look it." Sam dropped his hand to his side and retreated a step.

She felt faint and embarrassed and completely confused. But she flashed a fake smile and said, "I'm fine. I guess Harry's spoiled me. I've become such a dog person that I don't like cats anymore."

It was such a pitiful excuse for her behavior that it seemed neither man had the heart to question her.

Jessica studied the ground while both men studied her. Curtis Hancock was the first to break the awkward silence. "Well, I'd best not be late to Trudy's." He held out the cat, and she jerked away. Sensing the trigger of her discomfort this time, he set the cat down and shooed it back toward the barn. "I'll bring a carrier out Sunday afternoon, if that's all right? I'll bring Millie with me so she can choose her own cat."

"That's fine. Sunday's fine."

''I hope to see you at the Kents' tomorrow night. Jessie.''
He tipped his hat to her, then nodded to Sam. ''Mr.
O'Rourke.''

Jessica stared into the branches of the old elm tree that
grew near the corner of her cabin. She concentrated on
counting how many of its green leaves were turning gold
instead of dealing with the post-traumatic stress flashback
that had tried to take her back to that night she'd subcon-
sciously blocked from her memory.

Her therapist had told her that the memory would try to
assert itself. It might come in bits and pieces or all at once.
Something like the cat might trigger it, or it might come
back when her mind was relaxed and focused on something
else. Without any physical trauma to her brain, the only
explanation for her selective amnesia was that her mind was
trying to protect her from something.

Something she desperately needed to remember.

Something she was mortally afraid to.

She heard the sheriff's car door shut and the engine roar
to life. Without really seeing the white car, she turned and
waved as he drove off through her gate.

''Jess—''

''Miss Taylor.'' Jessica held up one pointed finger to halt
Sam O'Rourke's polite concern and remind him that he was
her employee, not a friend. She didn't think she could handle making nice and keeping her distance right now. ''It's
not your job to worry about me.''

He propped his hands on his hips, hesitating for a moment, standing far too close for her peace of mind. ''My
apologies. I'll get back to work.''

But when he relaxed his stance and headed toward his
wheelbarrow, her shoulders sagged. She felt inexplicably
abandoned. For a few horrible moments she'd been plunged
back into that horrible nightmare.

But a deep, Irish-laced voice had pulled her free.

She wouldn't explain what had happened. But he didn't deserve her censure. Jessica inhaled a cleansing breath and called after his wide, retreating back. "Find a stopping place and wash up. It won't take me long to throw together some sandwiches for lunch."

He stopped and turned. "Sounds good."

Then he strode away, his long legs eating up the ground while she watched the casual, controlled grace with which he carried himself.

Jessica shook her head and looked away. She had an eye for beauty, that was all. And the way Sam O'Rourke moved was a precise, powerful, beautiful thing.

She didn't need to be thinking of him as sexy. And she certainly didn't expect him to be her savior. Sam O'Rourke was just the hired hand. He had his own problems to deal with.

Harry whimpered, drawing her out of her depressing funk. She clicked her tongue and urged him to his feet, kneeling down and hugging him tight around his sturdy neck, finding strength in his unwavering loyalty. Finding comfort in the one male she'd let herself trust.

"I bet I can find a slice of turkey with your name on it in the fridge." She stood up and rubbed her nose against his damp one. "Shall we go inside?"

The dog's ears pricked up with excitement at the teasing tone in her voice. He ambled along beside her as she headed up the steps and into the house.

She tried to latch on to the dog's joy at a potential treat and ignore her lingering thoughts.

Sam O'Rourke wasn't looking for a relationship and neither was she. Besides, if he could dredge up one ounce of charm to go with that body of his, he could have any woman he wanted.

And he wouldn't give a skittish recluse of a woman like her a second glance.

Chapter Three

Jess. The name had slipped out as naturally and familiarly as if he'd known her for years instead of fewer than twenty-four hours. He'd shouted the word as if he had the right to personalize a nickname for her, a right to care about the deathly pallor and stark terror he'd seen etched across her face.

Sam breathed a sigh that did little to ease his frustration and guilt.

Jess Taylor was afraid of cats.

Interesting.

Not that she'd admit it, and it wasn't terribly helpful to his mission, but it was an interesting tidbit of information to add to her file.

Sam rolled the dusty, grit-filled wheelbarrow over to the hose and spigot at the west side of the cabin and turned on the water, letting it run until the sun-warmed water ran cold. He was starting to learn all kinds of interesting things about his eccentric employer, few of which were any help in tracking down Kerry's killer. But he took note of them, all the same.

Like the fact she cooked food as if she was feeding an army of gourmands. Her idea of throwing together sand-wiches for lunch had been a mouthwatering, deli-style feast, complete with homemade sourdough bread, deviled eggs and pecan pie.

He'd also learned that her legs were about a mile long, and she'd dangled them off the edge of the porch with an abandon that left him fantasizing about what they'd look like in something besides a ratty pair of work jeans. Something short. Covered in shimmery stockings. Or in nothing at all.

"Damn." Sam shook his head to dispel the image of long, shapely legs waltzing through his weary imagination. He squirted the hose into the air and let the cold water spritz across the sticky bare skin of his back and shoulders, easing the ill-advised heat that had been building inside him all afternoon. The unseasonable seventy-eight-degree weather and demanding physical labor weren't the only things that had him all fired up.

His fingers had itched inside his work gloves, longing to sift through the casual curls of Jess's hair to see if it was as light and silky as it looked. And her own hands were part earth mother, part artist. Long, strong fingers that moved with elegant ease through whatever task she undertook. The thought of her touching him with the same fine-tuned confidence with which she stroked her dog or curled them around the trigger of a shotgun had him breathing deeply and praying for a break in the muggy heat even now.

But despite his body's stirring interest in her long, leanly curved shape and soft blue eyes, Jessica Taylor was a woman who required a patience and expertise he didn't possess. Not in the relationship department, at any rate. He hadn't been with a woman since before Kerry's death. He hadn't even gone on a date. He'd lost his ability to connect with his heart that night he'd ID'ed his sister's body at the morgue.

The only emotions he'd been able to feel with any conviction were anger, sorrow and guilt.

Tenderness and compassion were foreign to him now.

The victim of a brutal rape would need both in abundant supply.

Sam sprayed the water across his shoulders again and tried to get a decent drink from the end of the nozzle. He had no business thinking personal thoughts about his new boss. She wouldn't be interested in any kind of intimacy with him—with any man—right now. And as much as he would love to hear that hot, steamy voice of hers couched in a seductive whisper, he wasn't the man with the skills to make it happen. He couldn't afford the distraction from his real purpose. His only purpose.

He had less than a month left on his leave. Less than a month to find out the truth. Less than a month to mete out the justice his baby sister deserved.

Thoughts of vengeance cleared his mind and tamped down his libido as nothing else could.

Sam turned the jet of water onto the wheelbarrow and rinsed it out. If only he could cleanse his soul of its guilt, his heart of its anger and sorrow so easily. He'd give Jess a couple of days to get used to having him around. And then he'd start a subtle push for information—and a not-so-subtle search of the place the minute she was gone. She must keep a journal or a planner or something that would give him a lead on the bastard who'd attacked her and killed Kerry.

Of course, there wasn't just Jess's distrust and stubbornness to get around. There was that damn mutt. Hopefully, Harry stayed by her side even when she traveled. He'd have a hard time explaining a drugged dog or a nasty bite if she left the Shepherd mix to patrol the premises while she was gone.

And he'd already learned that Jessica was protected by the watchful eye of the local sheriff. Curtis Hancock might be down-home-country personified, but Sam wouldn't underestimate the portly man's intelligence or skill as a law enforcement officer. This was his territory. He wasn't afraid to ask questions, and he picked up quickly on local gossip. Would he pick up on Sam's secret intentions as well?

Sam flattened his mouth into a determined line. The sheriff might be smart, but he was smarter. He wouldn't let Curtis Cow Pie or anyone else stand in the way of finding Kerry's killer.

He tipped the barrow over and attacked the wheel with the water, grasping the hose's gun-shaped nozzle between his steady hands and taking certain aim at each glob of dirt and grime. Yeah. *Poof.* Just like that. *Smack.* Right between the eyes. *Bang.* Dead center in the—

"You're pretty good with that thing. I don't suppose I should have you water the garden, though. The tomatoes would never survive."

Sam tensed at the sultry, smart-aleck voice behind him. He quashed the instinctive urge to spin around and point his facsimile weapon at the woman intruding on target practice. He wasn't sure how to respond to Jessica Taylor's ribbing sarcasm. He hadn't expected humor from her. He hadn't expected the urge to toss back a comment as if she'd made some type of flirty come-on instead of an astute observation.

Not that it mattered. How the hell had she gotten the drop on him? He couldn't blame it on the force of the water pinging against the wheelbarrow's metal frame. He'd been off his game. He'd been so focused on not noticing her that he hadn't…well…noticed her.

So much for not being distracted from his purpose.

"Hey. Is it quittin' time?" he asked.

"It's past time. I should have had you knock off half an hour ago."

Without betraying his surprise, Sam eased his grip on the nozzle and shut off the hose before he turned and looked at Jess. He was noticing all kinds of things now. The setting sun cast a rosy glow across her cheeks and ignited the deep red tints in her tousled hair. Despite his best intentions, a very basic awareness simmered along his nerve endings. Even without a speck of makeup, there was no hiding her classic beauty.

There was no hiding the determined way she held out the frosted glass of lemonade like a peace offering, either. "Here. I imagine you worked up a pretty good thirst this afternoon."

Her blue gaze boldly met his, but he suspected her directness had less to do with confidence than with keeping a careful eye on him.

"Thanks." Sam dropped the hose, wiped his palms across the hips of his jeans and extended his hand, taking careful note of the big furry beast standing guard between them, watching his movements with something like a dare in his brown-black eyes. With a cautious bit of challenge himself, Sam reached out. "He doesn't mind sharing, does he?"

She pushed the drink into his hand and smiled. "Lemonade isn't Harry's thing. Try it. It's my mother's recipe."

The glass felt icy cold in Sam's grip, and the condensation on the outside dribbled through his fingers. "Nice. I feel cooler already." He raised his glass in a toast of thanks, then tipped his head back and emptied half the delicious concoction in three long, throat-soothing swallows.

"Now, if I'd offered you a cheeseburger..." Sam glanced down as her voice abruptly stopped. The dog tilted his nose up and looked at her as if he understood the word. Or maybe he'd picked up on the sudden tension radiating from his mistress. Sam didn't need the dog's intuitive senses to see the way her smile flatlined and the color blanched from her cheeks.

"Jess?" Sam shook his head, quickly correcting himself

before she had any reason to walk away from him. Or, more likely, run. "Miss Taylor? Are you all right?"

Her gaze stuttered down his torso, then darted from pec to pec, shoulder to shoulder. She looked back and stared a hole dead center of his chest. "Where's your shirt?" She squeezed her eyes shut and turned her whole body away. "Don't you have a shirt you can put on?"

Sam splayed his fingers across the mat of black hair at the center of his chest, subconsiously shielding her from whatever had offended her prudish sensibilities. "I didn't know there was a dress code. Sorry, I…" He set his icy glass on the end of the porch and circled around Jess, the dog and a rainwater barrel that was being used for trash, striding toward the railing that led up the back porch steps. "I'll put it back on."

He snatched his damp, dusty black T-shirt from the wooden post at the end of the railing, and fumbled to get it turned right side out. He kept his irritation and concern to himself. Half a step forward and three steps back seemed to chart his progress with her. She'd seen his naked back when she'd walked up, hadn't she? Why hadn't she said anything then? He supposed *he'd* been the only one to feel an instantaneous attraction.

Still, the prick on his ego meant nothing. The last thing he wanted was to make Jess nervous in any way. She'd clam up, or fire him, making his quest for information practically impossible. He pulled the sleeves of his shirt free and scrunched up the material. He had one arm jammed into its sleeve when he felt five long, strong fingers latch on to his wrist.

"Wait. *I'm* the one who's sorry." Sam froze at the unexpected touch. He forced the tension from his body and looked down at Jess as she pulled his arm to his side. She came up to his shoulder, standing tall. But her deep-blue eyes were marred by a frown as they locked on to his. Her fingertips kneaded against his racing pulse. Although he suspected the gesture was meant to soothe, to silently apologize—if she even knew she still held him—Sam found the tender touch oddly seductive. He *was* reassured by her gentle show of bravery. "You must think I'm a total flake."

"No." Any irritation fled in the face of her courage to make things right between them. "I made myself at home, and you weren't comfortable with that."

He was beginning to get an idea of why his bare torso bothered her. She wasn't at fault. Her attacker had probably been shirtless, and just as close—even closer—to her than he'd been a moment ago. And he was a big man, strong enough to overpower her if he was that kind of male. But Sam wasn't supposed to know about the rape. He couldn't respond with sympathy or understanding of a victim's fears. He couldn't apologize for scaring her without giving himself away. So he shrugged his shoulders and opted for a humourous out instead.

"I just figured you didn't like the looks of me."

"No. It's a nice chest."

Sam grinned at her vehement argument. "Thanks."

Her cheeks flooded with color, flustering herself and flattering him all at the same time. "I mean, of course, it's a nice chest. You probably work out. And…" There had been nothing shy about her firm touch. But suddenly she snatched her hand away in a rapid release and retreat. She retreated all the way to the end of the porch. "This is silly. You'd think I was a gawky teenager again."

"Miss Taylor—"

"No." She spun around and faced him. Her fingers opened and closed in angry bursts of anger and self-recrimination. The dog danced around her feet. "It's almost eighty degrees out here, and the humidity's higher than that. Every one of my brothers would have had their shirts off if they'd been working the way you have. I apologize for the double standard.''

''Don't.'' He followed her, pulling on his shirt despite her protests. ''Something made you uncomfortable.''

Was it *him?* Did he look like her rapist? A tall Caucasian with dark hair? Great. Getting close to her would be damn near impossible if he reminded her of her attacker. On the other hand, it gave him a physical description he hadn't had before. Maybe if he could pinpoint exactly what it was about him that frightened her so he'd have a definite clue.

Now, to keep her talking. Sam picked up his glass, then leaned his hips against the edge of the wooden porch. It was a relaxed, nonthreatening pose, cutting a few inches off his height and keeping his distance. He took another drink of the sweet-tart lemonade and switched to a safer topic. ''Compliments to your mom. You say she taught you how to make this?''

Jess had shoved her fingers beneath the dog's collar, petting him and holding him close at the same time. ''Yes. Things weren't always easy for us growing up—I come from a big family. But always on our birthdays she'd fix us whatever we wanted. For me it was always a big fresh pitcher of lemonade.''

It wasn't so irresistible that she wouldn't come over to pick up her glass where it sat on the porch beside him. But he didn't point out the obvious. The goal was to keep her talking, after all. ''You have a summer birthday, then?''

Her wide, unadorned mouth blossomed into a smile. She shook her head, almost laughing. ''December, actually.''

Her amusement triggered his own urge to smile. ''Where'd she get the fresh lemons that time of year?''

''My mother's pretty resourceful.''

Must run in the family. It couldn't be just dumb luck that enabled Jess to survive her attack.

''Here.'' He picked up her glass and held it out. She kept

one hand on the dog but accepted the offer, not even flinching the way he almost did when their fingertips accidentally brushed against each other. Sam cooled his jets with another sip of the cold liquid and silently cursed the untimely awakening of his hormones. "I don't suppose you or your mom would share the recipe?" he asked, putting the conversation back on track.

"The secret is to add a few squirts of lime juice. And to cook the sugar down into a syrup before adding it. I keep some on hand." She took a long drink and savored it. "It tastes more like a fountain drink this way."

Sam drained the last of his. "That's it. It does taste like it was made in an old-fashioned soda fountain." Which brought them full circle back to his initial impression that she'd brought him the lemonade as a peace offering. "So what did I do to deserve the special treatment?"

His question hung in the muggy air, and after a moment Sam assumed Jess wasn't going to answer him. But he needed to learn to stop underestimating this woman's backbone. She hugged her glass to her chest, unmindful of the beads of condensation soaking into her baggy shirt. She looked him straight in the eye when she decided to speak. "I wanted to tell you a couple of things about me. Why I got weirded out by the sheriff and the cat. And, I guess, explain why your...bare chest...set me off."

Sam held himself perfectly still, masking the sudden flood of anticipation that tensed his entire body. This was it. He counted off each breath, tamping down the need to shake the answers he needed out of her even faster. He drew on the blarney of his Irish ancestors to keep his tone mildly curious. "I'm listening."

She looked down and stroked the dog, as if that constant contact gave her strength.

"I was...mugged...a few months back." It was only half a truth. Not even that. He'd learned that much just reading the sketchy report she'd given the Chicago police. "Sometimes…" She determinedly raised her gaze to his. "Things remind me of that night. I think the sheriff, holding the cat out—reaching for me like that—is what set me off."

Sam squeezed his fingers around his glass. He had the forethought to set it down before his frustration shattered it. A damn lie was less help than knowing nothing. Yet he couldn't call her on it. He couldn't demand the truth. But he did ask, "Your mugger wasn't wearing a shirt?"

"I…he…" Her expression clouded over. She closed up and turned away. She was done sharing info.

But he wasn't done needing answers.

"He didn't look like me, did he? Tall? Black hair?" *Gray eyes? Midthirties? Irish? Dressed in a sweat-stained black T-shirt and blue jeans?*

But Sam couldn't ask those questions. He couldn't follow up, he couldn't push, the way he'd been trained to run an investigation. But he needed something. He slowly rose to his feet. "I'd hate to think I remind you of him. That I scare you."

"You don't."

Liar. She'd backed off a step the instant he stood. What wasn't she telling him? "Did the police catch him?"

"No." At least that much was true. "I guess I'm afraid he might…"

"Might what? Come here looking for you?" Not likely for a mugger. A serial rapist, on the other hand…He had no doubt her fear was genuine. "I suppose he took your wallet and can find your address. Why don't you tell me what he looks like, so I can help keep an eye out for him. The dog's great protection, but—"

"I just wanted to tell you that so you wouldn't think I was crazy." Now she was mad, as if she resented him pushing for even that much information. Her voice caught on a husky croak of temper and fear. "I don't want to share the details.'' She picked up his glass, slipping beside him with a visible effort to avoid touching him. ''And I definitely don't want to share them with someone like you.''

''Someone like me?'' A sharp bark from the dog glued his hand to his side when he reached for her. Sam glared at the guard beast but wisely stood still while Jess stalked away. ''So I *do* remind you of your attacker.''

''Attacker?'' She spun around. ''I never said he…''

Jess's temper and posture sagged as if the switch that kept her running had been suddenly turned off. Sam heard the crunch of gravel the same time her eyes fixed on a point in the distance. Harry barked. He, too, had noticed the teal-green van cresting the hill and slowing as it neared the entrance to Log Cabin Acres.

''Expecting someone?'' Sam angled himself toward the approaching vehicle and made some quick mental notes. Two people—the driver and a passenger—inside. Missouri plates. His protective hackles rose, his senses fine-tuned with a hyperawareness of the intruders as they drove between the brick pillars at Jess's front gate. ''It's after six.'' He glanced back over his shoulder to remind her of the excuse she'd tried to use to dismiss him last night. ''You want me to tell them you're closed?''

''We can't turn them away. They're my parents.'' As the van came up the main drive toward the parking lot, Jess released the dog who was pacing back and forth at her feet. ''Go, boy.''

Harry took off at a lope to greet what must be a familiar vehicle. His bark and gait were considerably more joyful than the protective charge with which he'd greeted Sam's arrival.

But releasing the dogs, so to speak, was a stalling tactic, Sam realized. While Harry ran ahead to meet their visitors, Jess was smoothing out the wrinkles in her shirt, pinching her cheeks, finger combing her hair. More than that, she was breathing deeply, preparing herself. For what? Sam watched her transformation from defensive and upset to welcoming and wondered what was going on. Was she hiding something from her parents, too?

As the van's doors opened, Jess pasted a serene smile on her face and turned to greet them. "Hey, Ma. Dad."

Sam hung back and watched the scene unfold. A stocky man, six feet in height, with silver at the temples of his tobacco-colored hair climbed out from the driver's side and clapped his hands. Harry instantly propped his front paws on the man's shoulders and proceeded to lick his face. "That's my boy." The man grunted a sound that seemed to excite the dog even more.

Where were the bared teeth the dog had shown Sam?

"Good grief, Sid, you haven't even kissed your daughter yet." A tall, slender woman with soft, silvery curls framing her face climbed out the passenger side. She carried a covered dish.

The stocky man answered back with a laugh. "It's all right, Martha. Jessie and I like our dogs." He winked. "Don't we, sweetie?"

Sam's gaze immediately caught the elegant sway of Jess's backside as she strolled up to her father and greeted him with a hug and a kiss. "That's right, Dad. How are you feeling?"

"I'm feeling fine, thank you very much." He patted his hand against his chest. "Healthy as a ham."

"Hambone, you mean," chided Jess's mother.

Not to be outdone on the welcoming committee, Harry bounded around the van and met Martha Taylor halfway. He obeyed her "Down" command and was rewarded with a thorough scratch around his ears, some blown kisses and an indulgent, "How's my great big grand-doggie today?"

Harry ate up the attention.

"Hey, Ma."

''Hey, sweetie.'' The dog returned to his good buddy, Grandpa, while the women hugged.

Sam noted that genetics ran strong in the Taylor family. Jess was a younger version of her mother, matching her classic lines and height inch for inch. Yet she'd inherited her father's rich dark hair.

Jess's smile never wavered as they traded information about their drive from the city. And she still wore that mask of not a care in the world when she stretched out her arm and invited him over to join them. ''Ma, Dad, I want you to meet my new hired hand, Sam O'Rourke. These are my parents, Sid and Martha Taylor. They live in the city. Just north of downtown.''

Sid Taylor immediately stepped forward and gripped Sam in a firm handshake. ''O'Rourke.''

Sam understood that he was being checked out for his suitability to spend time in his daughter's company, even as an employee. Sam had done the same thing himself with his sister's dates and co-workers.

It was the one man he hadn't met who'd torn his life apart.

''Mr. Taylor.'' He could appreciate Sid Taylor's protective instincts and respected the way he sized him up.

Martha Taylor wasn't shy, either. She handed the dish she carried to her daughter and insisted on shaking hands. ''I'm Martha,'' she smiled. ''So tell us about yourself, Mr. O'Rourke. Where are you from? What kind of work are you doing for Jessie? Do you like antiques?''

''Ma.''

''Martha.''

Reprimanded on both fronts, she shrugged off her family's warnings and smiled. ''Pay no attention to them. You look like a healthy eater. I've brought some of my home-made lasagne. It's a low-cholesterol recipe for Sid's heart, but the whole family eats it up.''

Sam slowly withdrew his hand. "I'm sure it's wonderful."

"Does your wife cook for you?"

"Ma!"

"Martha."

This time she answered their warnings. "I can't help it."

Jess's cheeks bloomed with color, but Sam could only laugh. So Martha had been checking him out, too. But for entirely different reasons. "I'm not married, Mrs. Taylor."

"But you do like antiques?"

"I'm no expert at finding them. But I like working with my hands, rebuilding and refinishing old furniture. That kind of thing."

Sid Taylor wasn't so easily charmed. "That's not your regular job." He inclined his head toward the bridge of Sam's nose. "Your sunburn's fresh."

"Dad, he's the hired help. Nothing more. I checked his references." Jess intervened before the inquisition got fully underway. She slid in between Sam and her parents, bringing her close enough to breathe in the herbal scent of her shampoo on her hair. Sam retreated a step before his libido could get in the way of his duty again. "Sam's just working here for a month. He's passing through on his way to San Diego."

Sam? What happened to Mr. O'Rourke and keeping a polite distance? Why was she defending him?

"Is that so?" Sid challenged, glancing above his daughter's head. His brown eyes looked as doubtful as Martha's were intrigued. "You're a drifter?"

"Only part-time," he joked. Sid didn't laugh. "I'm on a leave of absence from my regular job. In Boston. I'm traveling the country, working my way when the money runs short. I ran short when my car broke down yesterday."

"I see."

Before Sid could follow up with any more questions, Jess

turned and lifted an imploring gaze. It was a silent plea for help. "Don't you need to finish cleaning up?" She strongly hinted that he make a hasty exit. "I already have dinner in the oven. It'll be ready in twenty minutes, tops." She refocused her smile and turned back to her parents. "Can you guys stay? We'll eat the lasagne tomorrow."

In the midst of excuses about having already eaten and being en route to baby-sit four grandsons, Sam took his leave, feeling three sets of eyes on him.

He rolled the wheelbarrow back to the garage and out of sight before he stopped to consider his immediate, heart-slamming response to the panic he'd read in Jess's unspoken appeal. The instant she'd turned those true blues and honest despair on him, something inside him had shifted into gear. The need to help her. To protect her. To keep her secret. The desire to grant even the simple request that he leave and take a good deal of her tension with him.

Ah, hell. He was falling under her spell. One she wasn't even trying to cast. He was getting personal, when this job should be nothing but professional. After just twenty-four hours he was thinking of Jess as a woman. A desirable woman. Jess. Not a victim. Not the answer to the mystery surrounding Kerry's death. Certainly not as a pawn he intended to use to uncover the truth.

"Ah, hell." He repeated the damnation out loud and tried to concentrate on the details of what he'd just witnessed.

Sid and Martha Taylor didn't seem overly concerned that their daughter lived alone out in the country. Or that she had a man they didn't know living on the property. Martha had even hinted at some unsubtle matchmaking. Sid had done his best to try to figure him out, yet he hadn't sicced the dog on him or ordered him to leave or offered to stay and chaperone.

And that didn't even begin to address Jess's effort to give

the appearance that everything was hunky-dory and under control in her life.

Sam closed the garage door and climbed the outside stairs to his apartment, letting the possibilities simmer in his mind as he headed for a quick shower. Either Sid and Martha were the most open, trusting parents he'd ever met—which, after that fatherly grilling, Sam suspected wasn't the case.

Or her parents didn't know she'd been raped.

Chapter Four

Jessica had assumed that sending Sam away would make it easier to face her parents and deal with their caring, curious chitchat. Instead she felt exposed, as if she'd lost some kind of shield between her and the outside world.

She loved her parents dearly, but keeping a secret from them—when they had to suspect something was wrong—was slowly eating a hole of guilt deep in her gut. Why else would they be dropping in so often? It wasn't as if she was on the way to her brother Gideon's house, where they had promised to baby-sit tonight. And now Martha was bringing food? They definitely suspected something.

"Sam seems like a nice man," Martha observed, following Jessica behind the long, narrow counter that divided her kitchen from her dining room and office. "Did I detect a trace of an accent?"

Jessica opened the fridge and found a spot for the lasagne. "His parents were immigrants from Ireland. But he was born in the United States."

"You know that for a fact?" Sid was still on a toot about protecting his little girl from the new stranger in town. He'd brought a thick steak bone from his butcher shop for Harry, and the dog had sprawled out on his rug inside the screen door to tackle the tasty treat. "What happened to that high-school boy who was working for you?"

"Derek still works for me. But during football season he can only come on the weekends, and when harvesting starts I'll lose him completely." Jessica poured some fresh glasses of lemonade and handed them to her parents. "Sam worked his butt off today without a complaint or any hassle. You can call his reference yourself. The number's there by the phone."

Sid crossed the room to her workstation and picked up the slip of paper with Virgil Logan's number on it. "I just might do that."

When her parents both sat at the table, Jessica was certain they were here for more than an impromptu visit. She put herself on guard and tried to guess at their concern.

"Have you heard anything from your brother Cole lately?" Martha asked, unable to hide the wistful tone in her voice. "I haven't seen him since the reception after Gideon and Meghan's wedding. I do worry about that boy."

That *boy* was thirty years old. But even though he was twelve months older than she, Cole and Jessica were as close as twins. She, too, had worried when he abruptly left the police force and drifted from job to job. His only contact with the career he once loved was in his occasional brushes from the other side of the law. But deep in her soul, where that almost empathic connection with her closest brother existed, she knew he was still a good man at heart. That he was searching for something. That his conscience, and the values they'd all been raised with, wouldn't fail him.

"I think he's okay, Ma." Jessica squeezed her mother's shoulder before sitting beside her and joining the mini family meeting. "I get an e-mail from him once a week or so, sometimes a phone call. He always asks about you and Dad."

"But if he's in trouble…" Sid reached across the table

and took his wife's hand. They traded a look that only two people who had lived and loved a whole life together could understand. "We just want him to be safe. And happy."

"He's safe," Jessica assured her. She didn't know it for a fact, but she felt it. She'd know if Cole was in real trouble. "I can't vouch for happy. But I think he'd come to us if he needed to."

Sid and Martha exchanged a look in a beat of silence, and Jessica realized discussing Cole had been a setup. Martha turned to face her. "Would *you* come to us if you needed to?"

As the only daughter in a family that included five close-knit brothers and a male cousin, to say she received some extra attention would be an understatement. She had to be the best-loved, best-protected female in the city. There wasn't one of her big, bad, loyal brothers who wouldn't come to her rescue in a heartbeat. Who wouldn't see that justice was done on her behalf. In their minds there were consequences for hurting her.

But she didn't want her family to face any consequences of their own making. She didn't want them to risk a career or put themselves in danger in their gung-ho effort to make the man who'd hurt her pay. Especially when she could do so little to help them—when she'd been able to do so little to help herself.

"Jessie?" Her father had moved to the chair on the opposite side of her.

Trapped. Could they have found out the truth? Jessica tried to brace herself without giving anything away.

"I know you had a gentleman friend in Chicago." Martha'a tone was kind, compassionate.

"Gentleman friend?" Relief rushed out on a noisy sigh. Of course. Alex. Old news. Not the rape. She tried not to be too eager to respond. "Alex Templeton is just a business partner. And he won't even be that as soon as I set aside enough money to buy him out."

"Then you're not still seeing him?" asked Martha.

"No." Jessica turned to include both her parents. "He wasn't the man I thought he was. It didn't work out between us."

"Did he hurt you?" Sid's question was more direct.

Had Alex broken her heart? Not really. Had he humiliated her? Yes. Would she tell them what had happened to her the night she'd broken it off with Alex? Never. She was more cautious with her response this time. "Why do you ask?"

"You haven't been the same since your March trip to Chicago." Martha's hand squeezed tight around her daughter's. "That's when you came home with the bruises on your arms. You said you'd been mugged, and that the Chicago police would take care of it."

"They did. They are. There's not much they can do."

Sid took her other hand. Jessica closed her fist to hide the scar that bisected all four fingers, a tangible reminder of that fateful night. Her father traced a circle around her wrist where the worst of the welts and bruises she'd borne had long since disappeared. "Did Alex put those bruises on your arm?"

"What? No." She could hear the pain in her father's voice. A helpless fear that his little girl had been hurt. He'd survived one massive heart attack already. He didn't need the added stress of worrying about her safety. "Alex didn't hurt me. I wouldn't stay in an abusive relationship. The bruises were from the…mugging."

There. She hadn't stumbled over the word too much.

"But you've been keeping to yourself," Martha reasoned. "You haven't come home for a Sunday dinner in months. I know you work more in the summer with the tourists, but it's a family tradition. It feels like you're avoiding us."

Avoiding a roomful of sharp-eyed detectives and scientific minds with fiercely protective instincts? Precisely. Jessica had to tell her parents something, or this discussion would wind up in the one place where she couldn't give them answers. She pushed her chair away from the table and circled to the opposite side. She crossed her arms in front of her and absently massaged her elbow. "Alex and I did have a thing going. I even thought he might be the one. He was handsome and exciting. Attentive. He wasn't showing up at the same sales I was going to out of coincidence." She forced a laugh.

"He worked in marketing, knew a lot about art. Our business skills complemented each other. It made sense for him to invest in my company. Eventually, working together led to something more." Her naive joy at his declaration of love seemed a distant memory. "I spent almost all my time with him when I was in Chicago. He traveled with me to the coast a couple of times. I thought I loved him. On some level, I did."

Sid and Martha seemed to relax, now that they were getting some kind of explanation. "Well, clearly he's not the one, or we would have met him by now."

Alex's betrayal still stung. "I found out he's married."

"What?" Sid's hand curled into a fist.

"Oh, sweetie." Martha got up and came around the table to hug her. "I'm so sorry."

Now her father was up and hugging her, too. "Is there something we should do?"

"No. I just need time. And space." She'd lie about the cause, but she couldn't lie about her feelings. "I should have known he wasn't being honest with me. I feel stupid. Like I was used."

"You were," Martha defended. "It's his fault, though,

lying about his marital status. You shouldn't feel embarrassed. Not with us.''

Jessica smiled. There was so much support, so much love in her family. She wished she could tell them everything. ''I just need some time to rebuild my confidence and believe in my instincts about men again.''

Sid patted her arm and pointed a stern finger at her. ''Maybe you shouldn't trust your instincts about Sam O'Rourke, then.''

''Dad.''

Sam wasn't her rapist. She'd know that, wouldn't she? Even if her mind was a blank, she was counting on recognizing her attacker if she saw him again.

Attacker. Sam had used that word earlier when she'd confessed to being mugged. Maybe in his mind, mugger and attacker were synonyms. Or maybe there was something more there that she *should* question.

Harry's deep, resonant growl ended her speculation.

''Knock, knock?'' Sam. Calling to her from the back porch through the screen door. ''Am I interrupting anything? You said dinner was at seven.''

The dog's early-warning system gave her only a split second to prepare for the sound of that Irish-tinged voice. How long had Sam been standing there? Had he overheard any of her private conversation? She hadn't heard his boots on the wooden floorboards. Had Harry?

Jessica blew out a silent breath and crossed to the side of the armoire that separated her living space from the sales area inside her cabin. ''It'll be ready in a few…minutes.''

She stopped moving when she saw his outline through the screen. He'd showered and changed. He'd tucked a white button-down shirt into fresh jeans and rolled up the sleeves to his elbows. His black hair was still damp against his collar, and it glistened in a lingering sunbeam. He was tall and broad and beautifully proportioned, and her heart skipped a beat with an emotion that had nothing to do with fear.

Suddenly self-conscious of her own sloppy appearance and the fact she'd been staring, Jessica tucked her hair behind her ears and whistled. "Harry, heel."

The black dog reluctantly left his post at the door and sat at her side, his head tucked beneath the stroke of her fingertips.

"Is it safe to come in?" Sam asked. "I thought I'd get the dishes and set the table out here like I did last night. Not that I'm hungry or anything."

Jessica smiled at the outright fib. "You put in a full day's work and then some. It's safe." She put her hand out by her side. "Harry, stay. Come on in while I say goodbye to my folks."

Sam opened the door, and Jessica squelched the urge to retreat a step. Harry and her parents were here. It was safe for him to come into the cabin. Safe, though not necessarily self-preserving. He was even more devastating without the screen to mask his rugged features. He walked around her and Harry, giving them a wide berth, his cool gray eyes and softly accented voice acknowledging her parents on his way to the kitchen.

Her dad mouthed the words, "I'll call this guy," and pointed to the reference number he'd copied down.

Martha hugged her tight and whispered in her ear. "*He* can help you forget about Alex."

"Ma!" Matchmaking was in her mother's blood. But Jessica couldn't be interested in a man in that way. Could she? She escorted her parents to their van, refusing to dwell on her unexpected fascination with her hired hand. "You'd better go or you'll be late to Gideon's."

"Oh, I forgot." Martha paused on the porch. "Tomorrow night Gideon and Meghan are throwing a birthday party for Matthew. He'll be five. That's why we're going tonight, so they can finish their shopping. The whole family's invited. Can you come?''

Jessica sighed. Her four newly adopted nephews had quickly worked their way into the hearts of all the Taylors, but one family inquisition per weekend was plenty. "I can't, Ma." She saw the protest rising to her mother's lips and added the first excuse that popped to mind. "I've already been invited to a reception at my neighbor's tomorrow night. You remember Trudy Kent? We'll be discussing some area land business, so I really need to be there."

"Are you sure?" her mother prodded.

"I'm sure." Of course, now she'd have to put in an appearance at the Kent soirée. She was already living a big enough lie without compounding it. But a houseful of neighbors making polite conversation about business and the weather might be easier to face than a houseful of nosy, well-meaning family. At least she wouldn't feel as guilty when she excused herself early from the festivities. "I'll take something over for Matthew later this weekend or Monday. Okay? Give him my love and tell him happy birthday."

Then it was a matter of trading kisses and hugs and good-byes before her parents were driving away and she returned to the cabin to put the finishing touches on dinner.

"Smells good in there," Sam praised her as she met him on the porch. "The table's ready. I just need to get the drinks. Lemonade? Water? Milk?" he asked.

"Water's fine."

Jessica carefully avoided being in the kitchen at the same time as Sam. Despite his apparent efficiency as a scullery maid, the space was too small and the man too big for her to think straight, even with Harry tagging along at her heels to guard her. It wasn't the fear so much she was worried about anymore, it was the other stuff her own mother had noticed before she even had. The attraction. The things she was feeling that she was fairly sure she wasn't ready to feel.

He can help you forget about Alex.

If getting over a busted love affair was all she needed, she might consider her mother's advice. Sam O'Rourke was more man than Alex Templeton could ever hope to be. Maybe he wasn't as conventionally handsome, maybe he wasn't as wealthy or urbane as Alex, the hotshot PR man, had been. But Alex had never worked up a sweat doing anything besides making love. He'd never shaken her father's hand and opened himself to her parents' scrutiny.

Alex had been offended, not hurt, when she'd told him to shove off. Losing his secret mistress had been a blow to his pride and his prowess, not his heart.

Sam was a man steeped in terminal grief, needing time and space and hard work to move past his sister's death. He was a man who could tease, a man content with silence. He had a depth to him she now realized Alex had never really possessed.

There was a lot about Sam O'Rourke she wanted to understand. But she lacked the courage to learn more. The quiche and salad she'd served for dinner had tasted like putty in her mouth. Every time Sam had asked a personal question, she'd turned the conversation back to work. Every time she'd wanted to ask him a personal question, she swallowed her food and her words and silently wondered if she'd ever be able to relate to a man in a normal way again.

She'd turned down Sam's offer to help with the dishes and waited until he'd climbed the stairs to his garage apartment before going inside and locking up all the cabin doors. She locked out the uncertain world that terrified her and locked herself in with only fear and loneliness and a loyal dog to keep her company.

THE LIGHT from the small television in Sam's two-room apartment created a strobe effect in his peripheral vision while he concentrated on reassembling the Sig Sauer pistol he'd taken apart and cleaned. He found solace in the familiar, mechanized precision of his reliable weapon. Keeping it in top working order was as much a part of his personality as it was of his training.

He was the job, after all. He was an FBI agent on a mission, albeit a very personal, unsanctioned mission. On some nights, like this one, the job was the only comfort he had, the only knowledge that made the gruesome memory of his sister's battered body and his broken promise to his family bearable.

Sam wasn't really interested in hearing that the Kansas City area's September heat wave might be broken by a chain of thunderstorms Sunday night. The nightly news was mere background noise to fill the sloped-ceiling cage he was calling home for the next couple of weeks.

There was no headboard on his bed, but he'd piled the pillows against the wall and propped himself against them. He should be sound asleep. His muscles ached from the day's hard labor. Despite the stilted conversation and health-food-central menu, he'd eaten a surprisingly filling dinner. The night was dark outside his window, with a haze of humidity that masked the stars and sliver of moon.

But the closest he'd gotten to hitting the sack was to untuck and unbutton his shirt, sit on the bed and pretend he was relaxing.

He slid the barrel of the gun into place with a satisfying click and cradled the empty grip in his palm, teasing the guard around the trigger with his index finger. He felt too edgy and restless to sleep. He needed to be doing something constructive. He needed to be moving forward in his investigation. He'd been stonewalled or distracted at every turn. Something had to give soon. He could feel it in his bones.

Sighting down the barrel, warming the cold steel in his hands, gave him a sense of purpose. It played into the sense of destiny that had brought him to Jessica Taylor in the first place. She was the key.

His backpack came into focus at the end of the gun. He held it steady. He breathed in and held himself perfectly still. He curled his finger around the trigger. "Bang."

The single, low-pitched syllable echoed in the room, reminding him of the emptiness in his soul. He'd lost everyone who mattered in his life—a mother to cancer, a father to the line of duty. A sister to some sick bastard who didn't know he had Sam O'Rourke coming after him. But he'd know soon enough. And then he would wish that he'd never—

The cell phone on the nightstand buzzed as it vibrated against the wood. Sam watched the silent ring summon him a second time before he reloaded the clip of bullets into his gun. He snapped the Sig Sauer into its holster and laid it next to the polished Bureau badge on the bed beside him.

Finally he picked up the phone and read the number of the incoming call. Something *was* about to break. He punched the talk button. "O'Rourke."

His partner, Virgil Logan, didn't bother with hellos, either. "How's life in the boondocks treating you?"

"Kansas City's a decent-size town."

"But you're not in town, my man. I'll bet there's not a coffee shop or gym for miles."

Sam shook his head and grinned. Like he needed to go anywhere else to get good food and a workout. "I'm managing."

He could hear the amusement in Virgil's city-born-and-bred voice. "You make a connection with your Jane Doe yet?"

Sam's gaze strayed to the window. Earlier he'd watched the cabin, trying to learn everything he could about the woman and her habits. The lone light she'd turned on was near the front window beside her desk where her computer was located. She planned a nightly check of her e-mail and Web-site orders, she'd said. He couldn't see the window from this angle, but the light was still shining onto the porch. Seemed like the only connections they shared were a willingness to work and insomnia. "I got a job with her. She's not much for talking, but I'm working on it."

"Work faster." Virgil wasn't laughing now. His articulated reminder was as ominous as a whispered warning.

Sam sat up straight. He swung his feet off the side of the bed and planted them firmly on the floor, literally and figuratively bracing himself for the reason behind Virgil's call. "You found out something," he challenged.

"Nothing good. There's been another rape-murder that matches the same MO as Kerry. In Las Vegas, sometime last night. Successful woman in for a convention wound up in the wrong part of town. Strangulation. Marks at ankles and wrists. Dark hair. A lock of it sawed off with a knife."

For an instant Sam couldn't breathe. The room swirled into blackness. Just like Kerry. He forced himself to inhale, forced himself to think instead of feel. As his head cleared, he spoke again. "You're sure it's the same guy?"

"Everything matches, right down to him using a condom and not leaving any DNA. I've got the forensic report right in front of me." Virgil hesitated, giving Sam the impression he was shifting uncomfortably in his chair. "This guy's sick. He's got a grudge against something or someone that just won't quit." He paused again. "Maybe you'd better tell your new boss who you really are and get her to a safe house. This guy doesn't strike me as the kind who'd let anyone get away. He's all about punishment and retribution. He might track her down."

The bastard coming here? Right into the sights of Sam's waiting gun?

The idea didn't give Sam the pleasure it would have two days ago. Jessica Taylor had been a statistic in a computer then. Now she was a living, breathing, vulnerable woman. She didn't deserve to be hurt again. Not by her rapist. And not by him.

The idea of her getting hurt didn't sit well at all.

"I'll think about it," Sam conceded. Confessing his true agenda might seal any chance of getting Jess to talk about her attacker. But if he was coming for her... "It's a catch-22, Virgil. If I show her my badge, I think she'll kick me out of here. But she's covering up for something. Or someone. And if I leave, she'll be alone out here."

"A sitting duck for our perp." Virgil's grim sigh matched Sam's mood. "You don't think she's holed up out there on purpose, do you? I've read that women who've been raped deal with a lot of shame. Depression sometimes. She's not suicidal or anything, is she? Hoping he'll come back and finish the job?"

Sam shot to his feet, defending Jess. "This lady? No way. She's smart and successful. She's got a dog who can take your head off, and she knows her way around a gun. She's a survivor—a fighter, not a victim."

Virgil laughed, deep in his throat. "We-ell. Looks like somebody's gotten under your skin, Irish. Let me guess, she's pretty, too."

He'd have knocked his partner flat if he wasn't half a country away right now. "*Pretty* doesn't have anything to do with it." Sam completely ignored the fact that he'd just confirmed Virgil's guess. "If this guy shows up, I don't think she'd hesitate to blow his head off."

"Then you make sure you get to him first," Virgil warned, ever the voice of patient wisdom. "Vigilante justice will put *her* in jail, not him. She doesn't need to be victimized twice."

Sam thought he detected a personal warning in there, as

well. "I'll do it by the book if the guy gives me a chance. But if he makes trouble…" Virgil knew all too well that Sam was more than prepared to snuff out the life that had taken his sister's.

"I know, buddy." What more was there to say? "I'll keep you posted if I learn anything more. In the meantime be careful. And I don't just mean watching your back for the bad guys."

"I will. Talk to you soon."

There were no goodbyes between them, either. Virgil hung up and would go home to his wife. Sam tossed the phone onto the bed, crossed to the window and stared into the night.

A yard light on the telephone pole between the garage and cabin cast a halo of illumination on the raised, wood-planked walkway that connected the two buildings. All was quiet, all was still outside.

He could see onto the end of her back porch and make out one of the spoked wheels on the old horse buggy she'd parked there for decoration and repairs. She'd asked him to help move it out to the repair shed on the other side of the trees that lined her property. But that was on tomorrow's agenda. Tonight she was working late on something else.

He looked at the lone rectangular window on the second floor of the cabin. When he'd been filling water glasses for dinner, he'd seen the stairs that led up to a loft where Jess's bedroom must be.

But he hadn't seen any lights go on upstairs. Either she was as incapable of sleep as he, or she made her way around in the darkness.

Though he didn't believe she was that eccentric, Virgil's idea made some sense. What if she was lying in wait for her attacker to come for her? But that was dangerous. Way too dangerous for a woman alone. The darkness was a perfect place to keep such secrets. And Sam wondered why Jess Taylor kept so many.

Sliding the curtain across the window for her privacy as much as his own, Sam turned and faced the empty room. Like it or not, he needed to get some rest. At the very least his body needed to recover so he could tackle the next big project at Log Cabin Acres. After he got her parking lot done and had moved the buggy, Jess wanted him to take a look at some oak furniture in her repair shed, to see if he could fix it up for resale.

But, most important, he needed to stay sharp. Catching a killer—and protecting Jess—depended on it.

He packed away his gun and badge and sprawled out on the bed, not bothering to change. If he did get sleepy, he'd just strip down to his boxer briefs. He picked up the TV remote and flipped through channel after channel of nothing that caught his eye.

Surfing through the dozens of stations from Jess's satellite dish had a hypnotizing effect on Sam. He was actually starting to succumb to long, heavy blinks when he heard a sound that jerked him upright on the bed.

Jess's scream.

JESSICA WASN'T EVEN AWARE that she was screaming.

She could only hear the words. Those two words on the screen.

He'd said them.

Die, bitch.

A voice tried to break free from the black void of her memory. A voice she should remember. A voice from above her, standing over her. No, kneeling over her. On her. Strangling the life out of her.

And the cat. Something about the cat.

"No!" She pounded her fists against the desktop and cried out as a blurry image began to form, then went blank, leaving her with fear but no knowledge, no power to sustain her.

Die, bitch.

The words were still there, typed in a generic e-mail along with the orders from her Web site. She clutched her hands over her ears. The voice still taunted her.

"Stop it!" She couldn't hear the intonation of the voice, but she was trapped in its spell, reliving every breath of its deadly intent.

But she did hear the footsteps pounding across the boardwalk and onto her porch. She did feel the cold, wet nose nudging her thigh beneath the hem of the oversize T-shirt she wore for a nightgown. She heard another man's voice shouting her name.

"Jess!"

Now she knew she was screaming. "Stay away from me!"

Panicked by the approaching footsteps and the vile message, waves upon waves of chill bumps cascaded over her skin. She leaped to her bare feet, sending her chair crashing back into the dining room table.

"Jess!" Terrible, thundering fists pounded at her door. Harry barked a deep, emphatic warning that vibrated along her nerves.

She scrambled over the tilted chair and knocked the next one with her shin, sending it flying into her path. Pain shot up her leg, but it didn't stop her from making a beeline for the gun cabinet.

"Jess, it's Sam O'Rourke." The floor shook as he pounded again. "Are you all right? Talk to me!"

She halted in her tracks as the deep-pitched lilt registered. Not *his* voice. Sam. Tall, annoying Irishman with the shoulders and the grace. Her mother thought he was hot.

"Jess?"

"Sam?" Her whisper didn't carry beyond her own ears.

Suddenly she was back in the present again. But the words were still there behind her. The blank memories, the fears, they still pursued her. "Sam!"

The pounding stopped. "Jess? What's going on?"

Demons nipped at her heels. She rounded the corner of the armoire and banged into a display case. Dishes toppled. Something broke. Jessica ran. The hardwood floor gave way to Harry's soft woven rug beneath her feet. She fumbled with the dead bolt, cursed the hardware before she slid it free of its catch. Then she was twisting the knob. Throwing open the door. Unlatching the screen.

The screen door jerked out of her grasp and Sam was there. A solid, unwavering savior in the shadows.

"Sam." Jessica threw herself against his chest. The door slammed shut behind her. "I was so scared." Strong arms folded around her and pulled her close as she clamped her fists to the waistband of his jeans.

"Scared of what? Are you alone in there?" One palm cradled the back of her head, the other skimmed the small of her back. She could feel him moving, retreating, pulling her along with him. Away from the unknown danger. "Are you hurt?"

For an instant she was surrounded by strength and heat. Sam's husky voice skittered like an urgent caress across her eardrums. Her cheek pressed against a bed of crisp, ticklish chest hair and warm skin beneath. Bare skin. Jessica came to her senses with a startled gasp and breathed in the clean, masculine smell of soap, and the earthier scent of the man himself.

She waited for the shock of being clutched against a man's hard chest to undermine the comfort seeping into her. But she was okay. She was okay with this. She needed this. Alone in the middle of the night with that *voice*, those *words,* wasn't a place she wanted to be anymore. She wanted this instead. She nuzzled her cheek closer. "Sam, I—"

One vicious, booming bark was the only warning before the screen door swung open and smacked her in the back, shoving her weight against Sam. "Harry!"

Sam stumbled back, catching himself and her on the top step. Jessica pushed away from his protection and solace, spinning around as her canine guardian burst out the door and lunged toward Sam. She blocked the dog's path and shouted a stern, "Down!" She flattened her hand in a visual signal to reinforce the command for the dog to drop to the ground. "Harry, down! Stay!"

Obeying the instinct to please her rather than the instinct to attack, the dog hunched down on his belly. His bark settled into his throat, becoming a low, growly woof. Jess knelt beside him, curling her fingers beneath his collar, just in case he still considered Sam a threat.

"Good boy, Harry. Good boy." She scratched the dog's ears, then swept her palm across the dog's raised hackles, smoothing the thick fur atop his shoulder blades. She talked in her gentlest, most playful voice. "I'm okay, sweetie. Sam's not the bad man. You're taking care of Mommy, I know. Harry's my good boy."

The threatening sounds ceased at his mistress's reassurance that all was right with their world, at least for this moment in time. Jess released a pent-up breath as the dog's tail began to wag. She continued to stroke Harry's flanks, but risked glancing up with an apologetic smile. "I'm sorry. He was just protecting me."

"Obviously. I hope he goes after real intruders the way he comes after me." Sam hovered behind her on the steps, his Irish roots more pronounced in his agitated voice. But she didn't think it was just the dog's attack that had his nostrils flaring. He pointed toward the door. "What exactly is going on in there that you scream bloody murder in the middle of the night and the dog thinks I'm the reason why?"

Jessica rolled to her feet, suddenly conscious of how far up her thigh her brother Cole's old T-shirt rode when she squatted down like that. Not that she thought Sam was looking at anything he shouldn't, but she had dropped her guard so easily, so completely with this black-haired man she scarcely knew.

The aftershocks of her fear still jolted along her nerve endings, leaving her feeling raw and vulnerable. The security she'd felt in Sam's arms seemed little more than a figment of her imagination right now.

She stared at the wide expanse of chest revealed by the open front of his white shirt. That same chest had terrified her earlier today; now she foolishly wished she was cradled against it once more. Jessica shook her head, looked away. No wonder the dog thought she needed protection. She apparently lacked the sense to take care of herself.

Tugging on Harry's collar, she urged the dog to his feet, using his vigilance as an excuse to turn their conversation away from her paranoia. She stepped aside to let the dog take a long, curious look at Sam. "I'm sorry. He went after you because I was spooked. He just needs to get used to you, to learn to trust you. Let him sniff you."

"He doesn't want to sniff me, he wants to take off a chunk of my face. And you didn't answer my question."

She summoned a game smile, though her gaze never made it above the jut of his chin. "I'm sorry if I woke you. I didn't—"

"Jess." He softened his voice in a way that moved around her defenses. "Quit making excuses. I can see you shaking from here."

Her gaze drifted higher. Sam O'Rourke wasn't a man easily put off. She had a feeling he wouldn't return to his garage apartment until she offered a plausible explanation for her erratic behavior. With his hands propped against his hips and his moonlight-colored eyes studying her with an intensity that never even blinked, she sensed he wouldn't budge until he heard the truth.

"I appreciate your gallantry, but I'm not…" That was a lie. She clutched her free arm across her stomach and decided to trust her instincts about the man. Decided she had no other choice. She prayed it was a decision she wouldn't regret. "Do you know anything about computers?"

"I know enough." One dark eyebrow lifted in a skeptical frown. "You're screaming about your computer?"

Jessica shook her head. Guiding Harry along at her side, she opened the screen door and silently invited Sam to join her inside. It might very well be the bravest thing she'd done since that horrible night.

Or the most foolish. Sam stepped up onto the porch, looking as big and powerful and dangerous as the day he'd first walked up her drive. She hoped he had it in him to be understanding, as well.

"I could use your help," she said simply.

"With your computer?" he clarified before moving any closer.

Jessica nodded.

If Sam O'Rourke thought she was a lunatic, he never let it show. He fastened a couple of strategic buttons on his shirt and offered her a curt, businesslike nod, accepting this task as easily as any other chore she'd assigned him. When he paused to allow her to enter before him, she shook her head. "You first. I don't want to see it again."

His probing gaze evaluated the dog's docile acceptance of his company as Harry trotted in ahead of him. Then she could feel him watching her with equal scrutiny as he cautiously stepped past her into the cabin.

Jessica followed a safe distance behind. Sam's watchful eyes took in the darkened showroom and living room, swept up the stairs toward her loft, then turned toward the light coming from her office area. When he circled around the armoire, he paused, and she knew he was surveying the mess she'd made in her desperation to escape her terror.

Thankfully, he made no comment. He picked up the first overturned chair and set it beneath the table. He straightened the chair in front of the computer, but he read the words on the monitor before he ever sat.

Jessica swallowed hard at the stiffness that suddenly infused his graceful posture. When he turned to face her with an unspoken question, she was huddling against the opposite wall, hugging herself. She knew she was conveying every bit of her fear.

"I can't bring myself to touch it. I need you to make it go away. Please?"

Chapter Five

Sam read the vile e-mail on the computer screen and forced himself to remember he wasn't supposed to know anything about her past. Was this her rapist's sick idea of a calling card? Jess had apparently interpreted it that way. Had she been threatened that way during her attack? Were those the last words that Kerry had heard?

He swallowed hard, choking back the bile and curses that clogged his throat. "Is this what spooked you?" he asked. But he had the presence of mind to push for a little information. "Pretty damn crude what can get sent across the phone line these days. This isn't from someone you know, is it?"

"I don't..." Jessica kept the full width of the room between them. She hugged her arms around her chest and stomach like a suit of armor. And while her clear-blue eyes revealed her debate over answering him, he could see the fine tremor of nerves along her jaw and chin as she clenched her teeth too tightly. "Can you just delete it for me? I know it's simple to do, but I just can't—"

"I'll do it," he reassured her.

Her eyes flooded with such gratitude, such relief, that right now he wanted nothing more than to close the distance between them and take her in his arms again. In those few seconds before the dog had tried to turn him into a late-night snack, he'd been completely aware of her as a man—not an agent. Not a big brother intent on justice.

His body had awakened to the soft press of her breasts and the needy clutch of her hands. Her silky hair had caught beneath his chin and palm as he'd tried to drag her away from the unknown danger. The earthy femininity of her fresh ginger scent had sparked latent desires that had lain dormant inside him for months.

Something primal, territorial, had lit in his veins and coursed through him. She was afraid, in danger, and she'd turned to him. She was his to protect. And in those few charged moments in his arms, something had shifted inside him. The feeling was still there, simmering inside, making it tough to think with the objectivity he needed right now.

The objectivity *she* needed.

Sam inhaled deeply and calmed his fiercely protective reaction to Jess Taylor. She didn't need the man right now—to hold her and comfort her. Whether she knew it or not, she needed him to be that ice-in-his-veins agent. She needed a champion to slay her beast, even if it was only the computerized kind.

And in order to do that, he needed to start thinking like an agent—not a lonely, loveless man.

Sam stretched his shoulders and forced some positive energy into the room that was being sucked dry by fear and mistimed longing. "You wouldn't happen to have any decaf coffee, would you? Or maybe a pot of tea?" Staying busy would divert her attention from the sick message and give him an opportunity to do a bit of sleuthing. "I have a feeling neither one of us will be getting any sleep for a while."

She looked surprised that he could think beyond the moment. But she seemed to stand taller; the tension in her seemed to ease a bit. "Right. I'll go make us some coffee. I'd like it if you'd stay…for a little while."

"Sure."

With a brief nod and game smile, she headed into the kitchen, clicking her tongue for the dog to follow behind her. Sam sat and went to work quickly, ignoring the twinge of guilt that tried to distract him from his purpose. There were ways to trace the message to its source. But he couldn't do that here. Not in front of Jess, not with this equipment.

The subject line indicated the sender was looking for old watches, a misleading attention-getter that seemed as innocent as the preceding message from something that sounded like a law firm—Boyce, Riegert and Winston. Sam pursed his lips in a silent whistle. BRW had been so pleased with Jess's last order of Missouri historical items to decorate their offices, that they were willing to spend up to $5,000 on any holiday collectibles she could supply them with. "A five-thousand-dollar shopping spree," he whispered. "Not bad for a day's work."

There was another message from an Alex, complimenting her on the number of Web site hits she'd been receiving. If half of those hits were orders, he claimed, she'd be on the Forbes small business list in no time.

Jess Taylor's business was clearly thriving.

So why was such a successful professional woman afraid to tell her family and the police the true details behind her "mugging"? Was she hiding something? Protecting someone?

Sam listened for the sound of Jess grinding coffee beans to ensure she was busy while he scrolled through a half-dozen other e-mails that had come through her Log Cabin Antiques Web site. All were chatty and business themed and involved a tidy profit except for the one that had sent her flying out the door. He went back to the original, two-word message.

Coming4U was the return address listed at a free server

that could have been accessed from any point across the U.S. He recognized a server popular with students and public institutions that couldn't afford subscription rates to an ad-free provider. The colorful advertisement floating at the bottom of the screen was for a national online mortgage company, so he couldn't even narrow the source to a particular region of the country.

"You come for *me,* you bastard." He memorized the sender's address, knowing even that particular choice of words had been meant to intimidate Jess. He forwarded the message to Virgil and asked him to track it to its source. Then he deleted the message and address from both the inbox and the sent-mail files. He wasn't going to find any other leads on her computer tonight.

"You want me to shut this down?" he asked in a voice loud enough to carry into the kitchen.

"Please." Jess appeared around the corner of the counter that separated the kitchen from the dining room. "The coffee will be ready in a minute. Why don't you go ahead and have a seat in the living room. I'll bring it out."

Jess slipped into the bathroom, leaving Sam with only the hiss and bubble of the coffeemaker to keep him company. It was a prime opportunity to search through her desk to try to find a journal or planner, but the interior walls of the cabin were too thin to risk being overheard. Besides, Harry was lounging on the floor between the dining room and kitchen. And though the dog gave the relaxed impression of boredom and exhaustion, he was watching Sam's every movement.

"I know, I know," he muttered to the dog, "keep my hands and my hormones to myself, right?"

The dog snorted as if his claim to Jess was obvious. And when the big, hairy mutt followed him through the shop area into the living room, Sam knew he'd have to wait until the cabin was completely empty before conducting an in-depth search. Though he could tolerate Sam's company if ordered to do so, Harry just plain old wasn't going to allow anyone to hurt his mistress.

"I don't want to, big guy," Sam confessed. But finding out the truth had been the only thing to keep him going, after Kerry's death. If breaking Jess's fragile trust and condemning his own soul were the only way to get the job done… Sam nodded at the dog. "You can tell I'm as big and bad as I look, can't you?"

Sam turned on a lamp and settled into the leather recliner in front of the cold stone fireplace while the dog circled in place three times and finally plopped onto the rug between the coffee table and sofa. Harry rested his snout on his front paws, but his brown-black eyes watched Sam just as steadily as the glass eyes of the buffalo head mounted over the fireplace.

Sam leaned forward slightly, shaking his head. "You and I have to find a way to get along, big guy."

"Making friends?" Jessica walked around the screen that divided the public showroom from her personal living space. She'd stopped to put on a short, terry robe over her T-shirt, but with it cinched loosely at her waist, it accented rather than concealed all the alluring parts of her long-limbed figure.

Sam stood as she set a tray of cups, homemade cookies and the coffeepot on top of the table. "I wouldn't go that far. I think I'm still on his hit list."

He wasn't sure if it was the rich scent of freshly brewed coffee or Jess's soft, musical laugh that made the shadowy walls of rock and wood feel suddenly very cozy. She handed him a cup of the steaming drink and sat on the rustic-print sofa, curling her long legs beneath her and settling in to sip from her own cup. "Harry takes his job very seriously," Jess explained. "I think most dogs just want to know what their role in the pack is, and then please the pack leader by doing that job well. And I think rescue dogs are especially grateful to find that place where they're needed and fit in.''

Sam resumed his seat, silently wondering what *his* place in this odd pack might be. ''And you're the leader?''

Jess nodded. ''It's important when training a dog that he knows who's boss.'' She reached down to pet Harry. ''I'd hate to have this bruiser running around thinking he was in charge.''

''You mean he doesn't?''

Sam decided then and there that Jessica Taylor didn't laugh enough. When she did, she tilted her face back, exposing a swanlike arch of neck. Her eyes glittered and her lips blossomed from that composed Mona Lisa grin into something radiant and confident and full of life. His interest in her shifted well south of any kind of investigation and his nerve endings buzzed with the urgent desire to kiss her.

The single lamp beside the couch cast a soft halo of light around them, separating them from the darkness of the rest of the world. Under any other circumstances, with any other woman, Sam might have told her how beautiful she looked. He might have shared her laughter. He might have moved to the couch and tasted those smiling lips for himself.

But tight fists of guilt and determination kept him rooted to the spot, kept him wishing. Jessica Taylor wasn't any other woman. And he wasn't sharing coffee at midnight under anything close to normal circumstances.

So he let the laughter die. He let his body's needs go unappeased. He drank his decaf and searched for some smooth line to lead him in to the questions he needed to ask.

But Jess saved him the trouble.

She shifted into the far corner of the couch, giving him a glimpse of one long, creamy thigh. But the sensual mood caught in the circle of dim light dissipated as she tugged the robe down over her lap and curled herself into a tight, protective ball. She stared down into the flowered cup she cradled between her hands for a long moment before her chest expanded with a pensive sigh and she raised her clear-blue gaze to his.

"If you're not too tired, I think we should talk."

Sam's pores opened with the heat of anticipation. Was this it? Was this what he'd come to find out? But he sipped his coffee and kept his cool, not wanting to frighten her off the topic. "Talk about what?"

"I should probably tell you a little bit about me. So you don't think I'm a complete lunatic."

"I don't think that."

"I would." She smiled. She was back to that Mona Lisa look—friendly enough but holding something back. "You don't think I'm the least bit eccentric?" she challenged.

"I'm hardly one to talk."

She set her cup on the table and leaned back, picking up one of the dark-green pillows that decorated the couch and hugging it to her chest. "I haven't always walked around with a shotgun and a guard dog, you know. I haven't always screamed at my computer or been overly suspicious of strangers."

Sam polished off his drink but held on to the cup to keep himself from doing something unwise like reaching out to her. As flip as she sounded, her body posture told him how difficult this was for her to discuss. "Obviously, you know your way around a gun."

She nodded. "My dad taught me how to shoot when I was a teenager. Most of my brothers are cops, so there were always firearms in the house and it was important I knew about gun safety."

"Sounds smart."

"Several months ago when I was on a buying trip in Chicago...well, I told you I'd been mugged." She squeezed her eyes shut and jerked her head to one side, as if she was unable to avoid a painful image that popped to mind. Sam's grip tightened around the delicate porcelain in his hand. Maybe he didn't want to hear this, after all. She must have suffered. Kerry had suffered the same way. Jess's eyes opened. Such sad, haunting eyes. "Actually, I was—" she swallowed hard and said the vile word "—raped."

"Son of a bitch." The cup nearly cracked in his grip. Sam hadn't counted on the intensity of his reaction when he actually heard her admit it. He swiped his palm across his mouth and jaw. He needed to detach his emotions from this, and fast. "I'm sorry." He set down the cup before he broke it. "I know it's an old-fashioned notion, but I've always thought women should be protected. And that, no matter how strong or independent they are, it's a man's responsibility to care of them. Not to…" Oh, man, he was rambling now. He shut himself up. "I'm sorry."

Her shy smile softened the sharp scrutiny of her eyes. "You remind me of my big brother, Brett. Well, actually all six of them think they're big brothers." She felt a *sisterly* connection to him? His ego would deal with that one later. Though maybe it would be easier to keep from feeling anything for her if he only saw her as a sibling or employee. She seemed to read his mind. "I don't mean like that."

Sam wondered if his double take showed on his face. Oh? So she *had* noticed him as a man who might, in some very foolish way, be attracted to her? "How do you mean?"

"You seem very protective. Coplike. On guard. Observant. Quick to respond." Sam bit down on the inside of his lip, showing no reaction to her on-the-mark intuition. "I figured it was safe to tell you about Chicago since you've come to my rescue a couple of times now. I try to lead a normal life, but I can't. I'm always…watching for him.''

Those coplike instincts made him ask, "Your rapist wasn't caught? You did report it, didn't you?"

Jess studied the dregs of her coffee and didn't immediately answer. "The Chicago police know I was attacked."

But there was no physical description of her attacker on file. No details of the event on record. No damn way to track the man until she decided to identify him or, if that wasn't possible, share everything she did know and let a pro like him piece together the clues.

Sam watched her studiously withdraw back into herself. Patience didn't come naturally to his Irish temperament. But he was going to have to find it somewhere. Jess had been brave enough to open up about the attack. She hardly knew him well enough to risk sharing anything more. Tonight, at any rate. He'd bide his time. But he wasn't about to give up.

"So you believe that e-mail was from him?" he asked.

She nodded, slowly raising her gaze to his. "I just wanted you to understand. And I wanted to thank you for trying to protect me."

"My sister—" No, he couldn't admit to that, the similarity of the crimes would be a dead giveaway to a smart woman like Jess. He covered the glitch. "I wish I could have protected Kerry better. I wish I could have been there when she needed me."

"You weren't there when she died?" Her sympathetic tone eased his frustration and had him thinking about her as a woman instead of a witness again.

"No, I was on another—" *Case.* Dammit, he'd almost slipped up. Forget digging up facts. He needed to end this conversation before he really blew his cover. He pushed to his feet and crossed to the fringes of the light, standing half in and out of the shadows. He propped his fists against the mantel and tipped his head back to stare into the cold, life-less gaze of the buffalo trophy. "I was in another city. Working."

That sounded vague enough. It was the truth. If he'd been in Boston with her at the time, maybe he could have saved her. He should have nailed the guy before any other woman got hurt. His senses flooded with anger and grief. *Could have. Should have.*

A tall, lithe shadow materialized in his peripheral vision the instant before a strong, warm hand folded over his where it rested on the mantel. Sam dropped his gaze and stared in awe at Jess's long, artistic fingers twining with his. It was a tender, totally unexpected touch of comfort, of connection.

It pulled him from the past and centered him squarely in this moment with her. "Guilt's a terrible thing to live with, isn't it?"

The husky croon of her voice was a balm to his shattered heart and weary soul. "Yeah."

He turned his hand and caught hers up in his larger grasp, palm to palm, absorbing her peace and strength when he had no right to. It would be the most natural thing in the world to lean down and kiss her. To hold something good and strong and sweet in his arms and ease the aching emptiness inside him.

But Virgil had been right in his warning. There were limits to what Sam's conscience could withstand. He settled for the generous gift she'd offered and simply lifted her knuckles to his lips to press a grateful kiss there. Her skin was velvet to the touch, and the delicate spice of her soap or lotion teased his nose.

She'd watched the movement with curious, cautious eyes, so that clear-blue gaze was right there when he smiled at her.

"What do you have to be guilty about?"

A startled look washed the drowsy fascination from her expression and she pulled her hand away. She crossed to the coffee table and gathered their things onto the tray. Her long legs carried her swiftly and purposefully into the kitchen. "I should have been smarter. I've been trained in self-defense by some of Kansas City's finest. I should never have let that man hurt me."

"What?" He hurried after her. Now he had plenty of reason to get riled up. "You didn't *let* him do anything. Rape is a violent crime. I know damn well you fought back. No one ever asks for it or deserves it."

Good God, is that why she hadn't told her family? Because she thought she somehow deserved to be raped? He rounded the corner of the cabinet bar that blocked off her kitchen. Though she didn't yell, "Get out!", her frantic gasp and instant retreat warned him that he'd unintentionally trapped her in the tiny area.

Sam put up his hands to placate her, cursed his impulses and backed out far enough that that damn dog could squeeze in between them. The same hand that had reached out to him, automatically reached for the dog's fur. He shook his head in frustration. It was always a half step forward and three steps back with this woman. But she had to understand.

"You were the victim, not the instigator," he insisted, quoting the research he'd done after Kerry's death. "No matter how you were dressed. No matter where you were or what you were doing. If you said no, if you protested in any way, you have nothing to feel guilty about."

There was a long pause after his vehement spiel when he thought she'd either sic the dog on him or burst into tears. But Jessica Taylor had more backbone than he gave her credit for. Instead of lecturing him, she made a wry smile and teased, "So, how do you really feel about it?"

Sam lowered his hands. "I'm sorry. I didn't mean to get on my soapbox."

"It's okay. My head knows all that's true. But logic doesn't dictate our emotions. It's nice to hear it from somebody besides my therapist, though." Sam retreated as she stepped around the dog and gestured toward the dining room. "It's late. We'd better get some rest. There's an auction I want to get to early tomorrow morning. I need you to come along and be my muscle. Hopefully, I can find a cabinet or pie-safe to fill an order. Then we'll have to get back and open up for our own customers after lunch."

Sam stopped at the outside door and turned. After spooking her in the kitchen, he was compelled to ask. "Do I remind you of him in any way? Do I frighten you?"

Bold lady that she was, she tipped her chin to look him straight in the eye. "No. And yes. But not because you remind me of him." With that enigmatic statement she touched his arm and nudged him toward the door. "I'll try not to wake you again. See you in the morning."

He stepped out onto the porch. He wasn't ready to leave her, but she had already latched the screen and was closing the door. Smart woman. He turned to face her through the screen. "Good night, Jess."

She paused. "Good night, Sam."

He waited until he heard the dead bolt slip into place before he turned and headed back to his apartment. The garage wasn't that far, and yet he felt as if it were miles away.

Sam breathed a heavy sigh that blended with the still night air and admitted it wasn't just the answers she could provide that he was reluctant to leave behind.

BY 8:56 A.M. Saturday morning the weather was already unnaturally warm. A dewy layer of perspiration made the blue-striped material of Jessica's cotton blouse stick to the small of her back. But the autumn heat wave hadn't stopped an eager crowd from gathering at the Stuyvesant Farm, just off Highway 50, a few miles east of Lone Jack.

Rebecca Stuyvesant was a ninety-four-year-old widow who had moved into a nursing facility and put the family farm up for sale. At her request, her children had packed up the family heirlooms they wished to keep and were auctioning off the rest of her belongings to help with her expenses. Jessica had arrived early and quickly scanned the tables and displays set up in the front yard that held nearly a century's worth of true collectibles and accumulated junk.

She'd already made note of the items she wanted to bid on—for her own shop and for clients—and had picked up her buyer's card from the cashier. There was a palpable energy in the air as the auctioneer team tested the sound system. Anticipation thrummed along her nerve endings as she greeted a few acquaintances and other dealers. She enjoyed the competition of an auction almost as much as she loved finding a wonderful treasure a less-observant or less-experienced eye might overlook.

Of course, the nervous tension that made her heart skip a little faster might not have anything to do with the temperature *or* the auction. She suspected at least some part of her anxiety stemmed from the tall, raven-haired Irishman who followed her through the rows of tables, pointing out items of interest and asking questions about others.

Dressed in faded jeans and a black T-shirt that hugged the broad expanse of his shoulders and chest, Sam O'Rourke didn't look like any of the other attendees. Wearing dark glasses that shaded his watchful eyes, he looked dangerous. Sexy. Mysterious.

He was an anomaly who turned heads and set curious tongues wagging. In the time before her attack, a day like this would have been a perfect date. Chatting with an intelligent man, admiring the way he looked and smiled and carried himself. Sharing secrets.

The trouble was, the man who'd rescued her from her fears in the dark shadows of the night was the same man she hesitated to trust in the bright light of day. Last night she'd been drawn to his strength. She'd felt a soul mate, steeped in emotions that were sometimes too powerful to bear. This morning that virile strength and aching heart terrified her.

She wasn't in any emotional shape to trust her judgment, to handle a relationship, to love another man. But Sam O'Rourke seemed to find a way around all her barriers and common sense. He wasn't a part of her safe, secluded world, but he was bulldozing his way into it. And the more time she spent in his company, the more they talked, the more feminine and confident she felt. She felt stronger when she butted heads with him. She felt normal. He tempted her to think more like the woman she once was than the woman she'd become.

Terrifying, indeed.

"Did you see this?" he asked, stopping in front of a locked glass case full of small trinkets and jewelry.

Jessica moved beside him and peered through the glass. "There are some pretty pieces in there." Mrs. Stuyvesant must have been a fan of silver jewelry. All of the items had a dull, pewterlike finish from years of disuse, and a few rings and a pendant were missing some of the semiprecious stones and crystals that decorated them. "If they sell the lot together, you could probably recoup your investment by selling a couple of pieces. Everything else would be pure profit."

"I don't know about that part, but," Sam pulled off his black-framed sunglasses and leaned in closer, "there's a Celtic-designed ring and necklace that remind me of my mother."

The elegant symmetry of the cross and knot motif wasn't half as interesting as the faraway look that relaxed Sam's ever-alert features for a moment. Jessica tried not to stare. "She was born in Ireland, right?"

Putting his sunglasses back on, Sam straightened. His mouth creased into a wry grimace as if sharing something personal made him uncomfortable. Maybe the light of day made him feel more vulnerable, too. "Yes," he finally answered. "Born and raised in Belfast."

"Do you miss her?" He'd once mentioned that he and his sister had been the last of their family.

He nodded. "For a lot of years, it was just Da and Kerry and me. But Da talked about her almost every day. Ma sold all of the jewelry that had been handed down through her family for generations to pay their way to come over here. They were determined that their children be born and raised in a country in which they didn't have to fight a war every day."

"They sound like wonderful, caring parents."

"They were. Cancer took her. Da was a policeman. I think he always thought he'd be the one to die young. He never did understand why she had to go first."

Ah, the son of a cop. Maybe that's why she recognized such an air of duty and authority about Sam. His expression was hidden behind the mask of his glasses, but she could hear the wistful note in his voice. Jessica curled her fingers into a fist, resisting the urge to reach out to comfort him as she had last night. He seemed so alone. Bereft of family, crossing the country without a friend to share the road. Maybe that's why she felt so drawn to him. She and Sam both understood what it meant to be alone, to interact with people without letting any one of them close to their hearts.

She didn't dwell too much on the notion that while having Sam around was often a scary prospect, since he'd walked up her road to her cabin, she hadn't felt quite so alone.

Turning her focus back to the silver items in the case, she tried to think of something inconsequential to say that would turn the conversation away from such intense personal matters. "Maybe you should bid on this lot. The jewelry looks authentic, and I know Mrs. Stuyvesant traveled to Europe after her husband…" Her train of thought stuttered as her gaze focused on the multiple strands of a silver wire necklace inside the display case. She tried to continue, but her mind was already playing tricks on her. "It might remind you…"

Silver wire.

Thick, pliable strands.

An unwanted gift. Delicate. Twisting.

Jessica's blank mind tried to pull out a memory.

She inhaled deeply, then caught her breath as she traveled back to a bright, moonlit night. *Shining in through the window, the only light in the room.*

Her fingers flew to her neck, and she coughed.

Beautiful silver around her neck. So tight. Too tight.

She splayed her fingers across her throat. She could see it there. She could feel it. *Her body jerked as the decorative noose tightened.*

Her eyes squeezed shut and she could see it. Feel it. Remember it. *She curled her fingers into a knot, pulling with all her might as the wire sliced through her skin.*

She breathed in hard, but her lungs wouldn't expand. And there was pain, such pain. In her mind's eye she could see the gloved hands at her throat. *She forced herself to look. Along the corded muscles straining in his bare forearms. Up farther, over his taut shoulders, across his naked chest.*

She couldn't breathe. But she would fight. She would see. She would know. She looked up to see the face above her.

"Jess?" She jerked at the very real touch of Sam's hand on her arm. The air whooshed from her lungs.

The image vanished before it ever came into focus. "No," she protested, trying to snatch it back. She smoothed her fingers across her undamaged neck. "I was so close."

Sam shook her slightly and demanded her attention. "Are you all right?"

Jessica tipped her head back. He'd pulled off his glasses and his cool gray eyes blazed with concern. She reached up and touched her fingertips to the jut of his chin. His skin was warm, the bone solid, the muscle trembling underneath.

He was real.

It wasn't the face she'd expected to see; it wasn't the one she needed to recognize. But Sam's roughly chiseled features brought her firmly back to the here and now. She was safe. She could breathe. She wasn't dying in some dusty, moonlit room.

Heat that had nothing to do with the muggy temperature flooded her cheeks. Self-consciously she pulled her hand back to her chest. "Did I say anything?" she whispered. She glanced to either side to see if she had an audience. "I didn't cry out, did I?"

"No. But you went about a million miles away. You mumbled something and then you couldn't catch your breath."

Oh, God. She felt each one of his fingers and thumb wrapped in a velvety vise around her upper arm. Her knees felt weak, but his grip kept her standing. "Does this have something to do with what you talked about last night? You have flashbacks, don't you? Do you know what triggered it?"

Too many questions. "I was—" Her gaze dropped to the center of his chest. How could she explain what she couldn't remember? *I know I was hurt. But I can't tell you how. Or who. Or why.*

The auctioneer's speedy, articulate whine registered, giving Jessica the excuse she needed to file away those random images and pull free from Sam's grasp. She straightened the collar of her blouse and planted herself squarely over her own two feet, dismissing his concern. "The auction's starting. I want to bid on the third lot."

She turned to go. Anywhere away from that intense scrutiny that seemed to pry her secrets free, away from those strong arms that made her want to share. "Jess, don't—"

"Jessica? Is that you?"

Her attention tuned to a smoothly politic voice, the essence of genteel charm, calling from the opposite direction. She scanned the crowd until she spotted a familiar face. Now that they'd made eye contact, he separated himself from the gathering of bidders and was striding toward her. "Jessica Taylor. You're pretty as a picture. Where have you been keeping yourself?"

She smiled. "Charles."

Though only a few years older than she, Charles Kensington Kent had gone prematurely gray. But the silver crown added to his air of impeccable style and wealth. Even on a Saturday he wore a lightweight navy blazer and khaki dress slacks. The fact he'd skipped a tie with his button-down shirt was the only indication that this was his casual look.

"Jessica." He bent the few inches that separated them in height and kissed her cheek. It was a polite, comfortable gesture claiming more than mere acquaintance, though stopping shy of public affection. He cupped her elbows in his palms and leaned back, studying her with a close-lipped smile. "It's good to see you. You're looking well."

Jessica grinned, more grateful than she should be to deal with the familiarity of friendly chitchat rather than Sam's probing questions. Hopefully, he'd attribute her flushed skin and uneven breathing to the heat. "I can say the same for you. Looks as if the real estate business is thriving."

He nodded. "Between that and managing Mother's affairs, I'm staying busy." He thumbed over his shoulder toward the house. "I didn't realize you were a friend of the Stuyvesants."

"More of a business associate. I've sold some of her furniture on consignment. I'm looking for things to resell now. Hopefully, one of her Queen Anne or Chippendale pieces."

"It's a shame her children don't have the wherewithal to keep…" He paused, his blue eyes narrowing as he looked beyond her shoulder. That would be Sam who'd earned Charles's curious scowl. Did he think the man towering a little too closely behind her was eavesdropping? "Jessica?"

"Oh. Sorry." She stepped to one side, more to put some distance between her and Sam than to be polite. "Charles, this is Sam O'Rourke. He's working for me at the cabin now." She finished the introductions. "If you ignore the four miles of farmland between us, this is my neighbor, Charles Kent."

Even without his sunglasses, Sam's expression was a neutral mask as he extended his hand. "Mr. Kent."

Charles studied Sam for a moment before accepting the offer to shake hands. "O'Rourke. Nice to meet you."

Instead of striking up some sort of get-acquainted conversation, Charles angled his attention back to Jessica. "Will you be joining us this evening? I know Mother sent you an invitation—I saw the guest list."

Jessica nodded. "I'll stop in for a while. I'm curious to hear what your mother has to say about the new land developers moving in."

"Well, they won't get an inch of Jackson County if she

has her way.'' He pulled back the corner of his jacket and slipped his hand into his slacks pocket, assuming a model-like pose. ''I just made an offer on the Richter property this morning. When that goes through, we'll own land all the way to the Little Blue River.''

''Impressive.''

''Boring, actually. They were ready to surrender the farm and let it go cheap. I prefer the challenge of negotiating.'' The auctioneer droned on in the background as Charles looked around her, making no effort to hide his avoidance of Sam. ''Well, I won't keep you from making your grand purchase. I want to bid on her collection of Osage Indian baskets.''

He reached for her hand and raised it to his lips to graze a gallant kiss across the back of her knuckles. When he released her, Jessica quickly wrapped her fingers around the leather strap of her shoulder bag, confused by a sudden, self-conscious chill. Sam had kissed her in much the same way last night. The gentle rasp of his beard-roughened skin had sent tendrils of heat blooming along her arm, while Charles's touch inspired no reaction whatsoever.

She shouldn't be noticing things like that about a man. She shouldn't.

But before she would admit to any sort of chemical combustion with her hired hand, she realized that Charles was still talking. ''…tonight and see my arboretum. The gardeners and I have worked diligently to bring the lushness of the Amazon here to Kansas City. I'm sure we'll be asked to do the garden tour next summer. But I'll give you a sneak preview.''

Jessica nodded. Charles just wanted acknowledgment of what seemed to be a pet project. ''It sounds fascinating. I look forward to seeing it.''

''Until tonight, then.''

''Bye.''

A deep-pitched touch of Irish vibrated close to her ear. "He's a snob."

"He's an old friend." She defended Charles against the accurate assessment because she needed something to focus on besides her shivery response to Sam's husky whisper. "His mother is one of the richest women in the state. She inherited all kinds of land, and her grandfather owned one of the largest stockyards in Kansas City during the late 1800s. Charles is intent on preserving his family's contributions to westward expansion and community development. That's probably why he and I connected in the first place. We share an appreciation for history."

"He'd like to *connect* with you in a more personal way."

Jessica rolled her eyes up and glared at him. "First, what Charles may or may not feel is none of your business." She remembered her chilly, spark-free response to Charles's kiss. "Second, you're wrong. We're friends. Period." And if Sam meant to impugn Charles as some kind of suspect in her attack, she wasn't going to stay and hear it. She stiffened her shoulders and headed toward the auctioneer. "Now come on. Our chest of drawers just went on the block."

Three steps across the lawn and a firm hand on her arm stopped her. Her instinct to jerk away from the unexpected touch stilled when she spun around and saw the raw emotion that shaded his eyes. "What?"

Was he upset? Frustrasted? Concerned? What did Sam O'Rouke *need* from her?

He dipped his face close to hers, close enough to feel the caress of each soft breath across her cheek. "Where were you a few minutes ago? Before Charles of the Ritz showed up." His grip and his tone gentled. "You were scared to death. Something in that jewelry case set you off. What was it?"

Jessica shook her head, twisting her arm in his grasp.

She couldn't do this. She couldn't fall prey to Irish charm or her own confused heart. She had to keep herself—and her feelings—safe. "I'm not going to discuss it with you. Not now, not ever. Now let me go."

Sam stepped back, his hand raised in what she guessed was only a temporary resignation to her wishes. She turned and left him behind, excusing her way into the thick of the auction, raising her card when she spotted the Queen Anne breakfront she wanted already going for $185. "Two hundred," she bid.

But though she immersed herself in her quest to strike a few quality deals, Jessica never lost the sensation that a pair of intense, ice-gray eyes were watching her every step of the way.

Chapter Six

Sam had investigated numerous crime scenes, interviewed countless witnesses and interrogated dozens of suspects in his eleven-year tenure as an FBI agent. But nothing had ever plagued his conscience the way digging through Jessica Taylor's lingerie drawer did.

In the hour since she and the dog had left to attend Charles Kent's party, he'd picked the lock on her front door, rifled through her desk, scanned her computer and climbed the stairs to her bedroom loft. He didn't need a search warrant, he wasn't on an official mission. Nothing he found would ever stand up in court, but then, he wasn't sure he trusted justice for Kerry to the legal system, anyway. He was hoping for a showdown with the bastard, long before he ever got to court.

His coldhearted detachment had served him well. He'd been quick and neat, and had learned that his pretty boss was a unique dichotomy of creative chaos and businesslike efficiency. She kept meticulous financial records on her computer, yet marked client folders in some sort of code with colorful stickers or frowny faces drawn in black marker. Boyce, Riegert and Winston, a local PR firm for whom Jess had purchased some items at the auction and who had placed the big order yesterday, must be a partic-

ularly good customer, judging by the stars and teddy bears
pasted to their file.

But no clues. Nothing to piece together her fateful trip
to Chicago. No letter or journal where she'd written down
a name or detail he could use to track the man he hunted.

He should give it up, lock the cabin and go back to his
apartment to establish his alibi for the night. She'd said
she'd be gone a couple of hours. He figured he only had
about fifteen minutes more to find something and get out,
in case she left the party early. The clock was ticking.

On his entire investigation.

But as he stood in front of the open top drawer of Jessica's refinished oak dresser, Sam had the feeling that *he*
was the bad guy here. That he'd taken his quest for vengeance too far.

This was too personal. The delicate scents of rosemary
and ginger wafted up from the clothes before him. It was
her smell. The clean, natural delight of herbs and citrus
from her shampoo or perfume. Part of him wanted to
breathe in deeply, to cleanse his battered soul with her fresh
scent and shy touch.

But the saner, less selfish side of him ached at the transformation of personality he saw inside that drawer. Jess's
rapist had stolen much more than her sense of security.

He'd stolen her confidence.

Plain, functional bras and panties of white cotton were
piled in neat stacks at the front of the drawer. Though Jessica Taylor would be a beautiful woman in anything she
wore, he could tell she'd once been a more adventurous
woman. More daring. More fun.

Tucked into the back of the drawer were undergarments
that belonged to a woman who was proud of her attributes,
a woman who indulged herself in a ladylike way. Gathering
dust in the back were bras of black lace and red silk. A

sheer silver camisole. Panties and thongs cut high at the thigh and low at the waist. Sexy things.

He couldn't bring himself to touch them. As much as his fingertips had itched to wind themselves into the silky waves of her hair or stroke across her velvety skin, he couldn't disturb her most private things. It was too great a violation. If the answer to his quest was in her top drawer, Sam wouldn't find it.

Reverently he slid the drawer closed and moved on to the rest of her bedroom. He was ready to resign himself to the fact that she'd erased all trace of her attack from her life when he uncovered a thick manila envelope beneath the blankets in the antique trunk at the foot of her bed.

Sam sank back on his haunches and exhaled an anticipatory sigh of air. Chicago PD. The official label on the front of the envelope showed that these were the personal effects recovered from the scene of her "mugging." He cradled the package between his hands and searched for a calm, objective center before he looked at the contents inside. If the MO of Jess's attack was identical to Kerry's, then she'd been snatched on some seedy, remote street and taken to an apartment or motel room nearby. These items would have been found at the abduction site.

Swallowing his hopes and suspicions and fears, Sam opened the package and pulled out a copy of the same sketchy report he'd read in Chicago. "Items stolen: purse. Coat? Jewelry?" The reporting officer had speculated, but could only write down what the victim said. Apparently, Jess had been too distraught to even remember whether she'd worn a watch or earrings.

Or, since she hadn't wanted the rape on record, the omission of anything she'd lost during the attack might have been intentional. Had her rapist stolen a sick souvenir she never wanted to see again? A scarf? A necklace? Is that what had set her off this morning? Had Jess seen something in that jewelry case that reminded her of that struggle?

"Oh, crap." Sam swore as the memory of his sister's battered face caught him off guard. She'd struggled. Not every wound on her body had been inflicted as a means of torture. She'd fought hard. And lost.

A new image crept in to expand the nightmare. Jess. She would have struggled, too. He could picture cruel hands against her throat, and that sweet, sweet mouth shouting for help, begging for mercy.

"Damn!" Sam shot to his feet and paced to the top of the stairs and back. Maybe, for the first time, he truly understood that Jessica had suffered just as much as Kerry had. Maybe more so because she had to live with the memory of what had been done to her.

"Tell me the truth." He prodded the still air of the empty cabin for answers. "Give me a name, a face, and I will find him for you." His vow reverberated in a low-pitched whisper. "I won't let him hurt you or anyone else again."

But, of course, the cabin had no answers for him. And he'd lost too much in his life to believe that some kind of divine inspiration would gift him with the answer he needed.

That left the facts and Jessica herself.

And she wasn't willing to talk. Yet.

There was only one item besides the report in the envelope—Jessica's black leather day planner. Sam turned on his tiny flashlight and thumbed through the pages of the book. He found the addresses for her family, business cards from dealers and flea markets all across the country, and a flat, dead flower, pressed with loving regard between the last two pages of the book.

He flipped to the date he knew by heart. He found the record of her March trip to Chicago. A Thursday flight from KCI to O'Hare. Friday had "Alex" and a heart written across the top. The rest of the day had a line drawn through it. Saturday had two entries: "Eppley Estate Sale" and "Museum Fund-raiser—8 p.m." The photo he'd seen in the newspaper must have been taken that very night, hours before her attack. Had she been abducted on her way home? Had she taken a walk to get some fresh air? And how had she gotten all the way from the fine arts museum near Lake Michigan down to the low-rent, high-crime district more than seven miles away?

It wasn't much, but it was something. He could talk to the guests who'd attended the fund-raising event, see if any of them remembered anyone suspicious lurking around Jess. A waiter. A cabdriver.

Downplaying his disappointment that he hadn't uncovered anything more concrete, Sam carefully replaced the planner and report and knelt down in front of the trunk at the foot of Jess's bed. He was up to his elbows in blankets and quilts when the telephone rang.

Sam jumped inside his skin as if he'd been caught. But when he breathed out, he was calm and thinking clearly. The ringing phone served as an alarm, reminding him it was time to get out. With everything secured in its original place, he hurried down the stairs. He'd reached the armoire that divided her office space from the sales floor when the answering machine clicked on and Jess's professional voice invited the caller to leave a message.

"Where are you, kiddo? It's Cole." Sam paused to eavesdrop on the strong, yet weary man's voice. "I'm in town for the day and wanted to take my favorite sister to a late dinner. We haven't talked for a while. I could use someone to…" Her brother hesitated, then shifted gears. "Ah, hell. You're probably out on a date. Hopefully, with someone better than that Chicago jerk. I had a bad feeling about him the moment I laid eyes on him. But, hey, he's history, right? I love you. Tell Ma and Dad the same. I'll call you next time I'm around.''

The caller had disconnected and the machine was beeping by the time Sam was out on the porch, locking the door behind him.

That Chicago jerk? Interesting. What if Alex and the "jerk" were the same guy? He wondered if said jerk *had* hurt Jess. And Kerry. And four other innocent women.

Inside his apartment, he dug out the file photo of her from the newspaper. In the background of the picture, there was a tall man with dark hair. Sam read the caption. Alex Templeton.

He looked closer at the picture. Alex was standing in the same group with Jess, smiling for the same camera. But his arm was tucked behind the back of a cool, Nordic blonde, not Jess. The caption listed the blonde's name as Catherine Templeton.

This was the Alex with the heart in Jess's book?

"You son of a bitch."

Jerk was right. Templeton sure wasn't holding on to his sister. The creep might not be guilty of anything more than adultery, but if he had no compunction about leading a woman on, about using her...

Sam picked up his phone and put a call in to Virgil.

GERTRUDE WALLACE Kensington Kent should run for political office, thought Jessica, hiding a yawn behind her cider punch while admiring her hostess. The sixty-five-year-old woman was a force of nature. Standing tall and slender with a stunning upsweep of silver-blue hair, Trudy Kent worked the room like a pro, making her agenda clear. She wouldn't sacrifice the natural beauty or quiet pace of small-town, country living to economic development and the population explosion of Kansas City's suburbs.

She'd filled her Monticello-inspired home, with its

stately white columns and domed roofline, with guests from all walks of life. City politicians, local farmers, small business owners like Jessica, old-money landowners and capital investors. Though ostensibly gathered to celebrate the apple crop from the Kents' orchard, there was no mistaking the underlying message of this party.

The Kents liked things the way they were, and they were doing everything they could to keep it that way.

But Jessica had already heard the spiel and pledged her support. She, too, enjoyed country living. And she was close enough to the city to enjoy its activities and culture and opportunities, as well. Trudy had reiterated what Jessica had already promised Charles when he'd shown her the massive, colorful, indoor jungle he modestly called an arboretum. If she ever decided to sell Log Cabin Acres, she'd give the Kents the opportunity to buy it first.

There was no point in prolonging the evening. She had a long day ahead of her tomorrow since Sunday was generally her busiest time for customers. And two hours of putting on her just-like-old-times face for old friends and new acquaintances had stretched her nerves to the limit. She wouldn't feel guilty for lying to her parents and missing her nephew's birthday party now, but she was tired of making nice and pretending her life was normal. She wanted to go home, kick off her low-heeled sandals and relax.

The decision made, she set her cup on the tray of a tuxedo-clad waiter and caught Trudy's attention as she moved from one group to the next.

"You're not leaving us, are you?" Just as she had when she'd first greeted her, Trudy hugged Jessica and pressed her cheek to Jess's in a lipstick-saving version of a kiss. "The night is young."

Jessica shrugged as the older woman pulled away to adjust the sleeves of her bronze silk jacket. "I'm an old-fashioned working girl with a business to run. The customers will be there tomorrow whether I'm ready or not, and I prefer to be ready.''

"Absolutely." Trudy linked her arm through Jessica's and escorted her through a high, white archway into the marble-tiled foyer. "You Taylors have always had a wonderful work ethic. And you have some of the dearest, quaintest things at your shop. I still have those Polly's Pop soda bottles I bought there. Reminds me of my childhood.''

"I'm glad you're enjoying them.''

As they passed another archway leading to the west wing of the house where other guests had gathered in the conservatory, Trudy's friendly tenor changed. "Charles." It was the strict, no-arguments-allowed call of a mother to her recalcitrant child.

It made no matter that the child was thirty-six years old and engaged in a conversation with an attractive redhead. Jessica bristled right along with Charles and offered an apologetic smile as he turned to face them.

"Jessica is leaving." Trudy stated the obvious. "You need to thank her for coming and say good-night.''

"Of course." After the slightest of bows toward her and his mother, Charles dipped his mouth close to the ear of the auburn-haired woman and whispered. The woman laughed in response and Charles smiled. The smile stayed fixed in place as he adjusted his yellow silk tie and joined them in the foyer.

He walked right up to Jessica and kissed her on the cheek, just as he had that afternoon. "It's wonderful to see you again, Jessica. Don't be such a stranger.''

"I don't mean to be," she answered, appreciating his low-key counterpoint to his mother's imperiousness. "Work keeps me tied up so much, it's hard to get away from the cabin sometimes.''

But Trudy wasn't out of the conversation yet. She

brushed a microscopic crumb from the lapel of Charles's gray Armani suit. "If we could get you out of that garden of yours, maybe you could pay Jessica a visit sometime."

"Mother." He caught her hand and gave it a swift kiss. "It's an arboretum. The garden is outside." He released Trudy and grinned like a schoolboy. "You see what I put up with, Jessica? It's a work of art. I designed it from the ground up. Literally. And she doesn't even appreciate that I'm helping the economy by hiring a few of the locals to do the work."

"I thought it was gorgeous. Imagine, orchids blooming year-round here in the Midwest. I'm sure you'll appreciate all that greenery after our ninth or tenth snowfall."

"You'll have come see it then," Charles offered. "We'll have dinner."

Jessica's good humor vanished for an instant. She squeezed her eyes shut, fearing the onset of another flashback. Right here. In front of friends. In plain sight of a hundred guests.

The flashbacks were coming more frequently now. She needed to call her therapist. Maybe it was a sign that her memory was returning.

"Are you all right, dear?" Trudy Kent's face swam into focus as Jessica blinked open her eyes.

No image, no emotion flooded her senses. She forced herself to breathe. It wasn't a flashback, after all. More like a panic attack because it sounded for all the world as if Charles Kent had asked her out on a date. Was that all it was? A nervous, adolescent reaction to being asked out by an attractive man?

Would she ever feel self-assured again?

She pinched the bridge of her nose between her thumb and index finger. "I'm coming down with a nasty headache." It wasn't a lie. The stress of the evening had wound a taut twist of pain behind her left eye. "I'd better be getting home."

"Do you need me to drive you?" Charles's forehead creased with concern.

"I'll be fine. I have Harry in the truck, anyway." As dear as Charles and Trudy could be, she knew neither one had a love for any creature that shed. Especially in Trudy's Mercedes or Charles's Range Rover. She pulled her keys from the pocket of her cobalt linen slacks, buttoned the matching jacket and headed for the door. "Thanks for everything. Good night."

Jessica closed the door on their responding good-nights and inhaled a deep breath of the muggy night air. It wasn't all that refreshing, but it was quiet. And after waving off the valet's offer to fetch her truck and acknowledging the uniformed deputy watching the front door, she was alone.

She hoped.

There was no need for pretense now. Carefully sweeping her gaze from side to side, Jessica stepped off the well-lit porch and headed down the front walk, away from the people and lights and noise. She armed herself with the tiny canister of pepper spray on her key chain and wished like hell Harry was here beside her rather than snoozing in the cab of her truck at the end of the long, shadowed driveway.

"Go on, boy. Go get it." Jessica leaned back and hurled the tennis ball as if she was throwing out a runner from the wall in center field. She laughed as Harry leaped to try and catch it, tumbled over his feet with excitement, then took off at a dead run across the length of the yard to retrieve it.

She was always amazed at how entertaining a tiny tennis ball could be to a 120-pound dog. Harry had an uncanny ability to find his favorite toy, even during a nighttime romp like this. She cringed to think how well seasoned the ball must be in order for him to track its scent, its fluorescent-yellow cover having long since been chewed to a dingy beige.

When he came bounding back into the circle of light cast by the yard lamp near the porch, Jessica braced herself. He would never hurt her intentionally, but, in enthusiastic mode like this, he could knock her flat without meaning to. Harry skidded to a halt on the patchy grass between the cabin and barn and dropped the ball at her feet. His pink tongue lolled out the side of his mouth as he panted with exertion and excitement and eagerly waited for her to launch it again.

"Don't you ever get tired of this game?" she teased, feeling herself relax as she helped the dog unwind. He deserved a good run after being cooped up in the truck for a couple of hours at the Kents' estate. She'd briefly considered walking him up to her metal work shed in the woods and back, but it was pushing ten o'clock and the security lights attached to her buildings didn't light all of the gravel road in between. So she'd settled for a rousing game of fetch.

Harry looked down at the ball, then up at her, one black ear flopping over to the side as he cocked his head. His brown-black eyes and dancing version of a sit communicated as clearly as if he had spoken.

Jessica shook her head, unable to stop herself from smiling. "Okay. One more time." She picked up the ball and lobbed it into the woods at the far end of the barn. "Go get it."

Harry charged after it, disappearing into the brush and darkness at the edge of the trees.

"Have you ever thought about pitching for the Red Sox?" A dark voice, tinged with a little bit of Irish and a whole lot of humor startled her.

Surprised by the unexpected company, her breath initially caught in her throat. But Jessica quickly exhaled and settled into banter mode. "The Bosox? Are you kidding?"

"Hey, don't knock the Bosox." Sam sauntered down the stairs beside the garage, looking big and lean in a pewter-gray work shirt and smooth-fitting jeans. He rolled up his sleeves as he approached her, exposing the muscular strength of his forearms. His sunburn had cooled to a light golden tan which complemented the sprinkle of dark hair across his skin.

Jessica stood taller, feeling more aware of herself and her surroundings, as if each color, each sound, each scent intensified with every step he took toward her. It was a heady, scary, normal feeling.

"I'm a Royals fan from day one," she avowed. "It's an annual tradition for Dad and me to go to the season opener at Kauffman Field. I would never play for the competition."

"Loyal to the bone, eh?" He slipped his fingers into his pockets as he stopped beside her in the circle of light. "I noticed your team isn't headed for the World Series this year."

"Yours isn't, either," she glibly pointed out. The night air warmed and softened as she traded taunts with this stern-faced charmer.

Their camaraderie remained in place when Harry came loping back into the yard, the tennis ball proudly clenched between his jaws. The dog's long stride hitched a step when he noticed Sam standing beside his mistress, but then he ambled on up to Jessica's feet and dropped the ball. Maybe he could sense her comfort at the moment, or maybe the thrill of the game made Sam's presence only a minor distraction.

"That's Mama's good boy." She reached down and scratched the dog around the ears and muzzle, praising him and loving him and savoring this ordinary, peaceful moment.

"You think he'd let me throw one?" Sam asked.

Jessica straightened, surprised by the offer. "You want to be friends with Harry?" That was almost like being friends with her. But the idea of growing closer to Sam didn't alarm her as much as she'd thought it would. "We can try."

She scooped up the ball, conscious of the dog's attentive gaze as she held the ball above Sam's outstretched hand. "I warn you—slobber ball is not for the faint of heart."

Sam's stony expression lit with a cocky grin. "Well, that wouldn't describe me, now, would it."

He snatched the ball from her fingers, spun his arm back in a huge windup and sent the ball flying like a bullet deep into the trees. "Go get it!"

Jessica laughed as Harry vaulted into the woods and disappeared. She pursed her lips together and whistled in mock awe. "We won't see him for three days. Are you sure *you* don't want to pitch for the majors?"

Massaging his shoulder, Sam offered a wry smile. "I think my pitching days ended somewhere around the ninth grade. I developed other skills instead."

She'd be curious to know what special skills this tall, dark mystery man possessed. But right now she was more concerned about the wince of pain that tightened his lips. "Did you hurt yourself?"

He shook his head. "Just a little stiff. You've got me doing more physical labor than I've done in months." He stopped her protest before it started. "I'm not complaining. In fact, I'm enjoying the mental break. Besides, I saved the toughest part of the hauling and shoveling for tomorrow when your high-school friend can help. We'll use the mini-bulldozer to—"

Sam stopped abruptly at what sounded like a drawer full

of silverware being dumped on its side—out in the middle
of the woods. The distant shattering sound was punctuated
by a deep-pitched bark.

Jessica turned toward the trees where Harry had disappeared. Every muscle in her body clenched with a sudden,
expectant tension. "You hear that?"

"I heard it." Sam patted his side, then glanced up at his
apartment door before turning his head and peering deep
into the night. Whatever stiffness he'd felt a moment ago
had transformed into a fluid alertness. He was already moving—lightly, surely—on the balls of his feet. A second
crash, then a third, splintered the heavy air. "Sounds like
your storage shed. Wait here. I'll check it out."

"You'll check—" Harry barked in the distance, calling
out a terrible, ferocious alarm. "Harry?" Jessica's caution
became fear for her dearest friend. Adrenaline poured
through her veins, pushing her leaden feet into action.
"Harry!"

Sam had already rounded the end of the barn, and Jessica
ran to catch up. She pressed her tongue against her teeth
and whistled. If nothing else got Harry's attention...

She was halfway through the three-note call when a
large, hard hand slipped across her mouth, muffling the
whistle and a startled shriek of terror. "I love that you can
do that, lady, but you've gotta be quiet."

The rueful admiration in that hushed voice pressed
against her ear didn't immediately register. Instead, the
panicked instinct to fight for freedom had her kicking out
and swinging wide with her fist. Strong arms lifted her off
the ground and thrust her up against the side of the barn.
A tall, dark silhouette of controlled strength trapped her in
the shadows. But her heels hit dirt and her fist bounced off
an immovable shoulder.

"It's me." Sam quickly identified himself and pulled his
hand away.

She couldn't remember enough to say that a hand stifling her mouth or being grabbed from behind reminded her of her attack. But the feelings she remembered were crystal clear. Trapped. Foolish. Strong enough to want to fight, not nearly strong enough to win.

"Don't…" Jessica breathed hard, from short-circuiting emotions more than exertion. "Don't startle me like that."

"I didn't mean—"

"Ever."

She splayed one hand across her chest, as if that could somehow soothe the frenetic aftershocks of her pounding heart. The other hand clung to the cool ridges of steel that formed the wall behind her. Now that she knew where she was and whom she was with, she was torn by the need to wrap herself against Sam's warm, solid chest to find comfort the way she had all too briefly last night, and the self-preserving urge to run away and put as much distance between him and her needy desires as possible.

He propped one hand on the wall above her shoulder as if sensing her thoughts of escape. He wasn't touching her in any way, but he didn't back off an inch, keeping her pinned in place with nothing more than his proximity. Her body pulsed with an edgy alertness of every taut stretch of his soft cotton shirt, every nuance of expression that darkened his moonlit eyes with shots of gunmetal gray, every gram of heat that radiated between his body and hers.

"I'm sorry I frightened you." His stern mouth hovered close to her face. "But what the hell do you think you're doing?"

Boldly she tilted her gaze to meet his. "Saving my dog."

"By charging blindly into who knows what?" Sam's voice never rose above a whisper, but there was no mistaking the admonition there. "He's a guard dog. Let him guard."

"We don't know what's out there." Jessica flattened her

palms across the dangerous territory of his chest and shoved him back a step, slipping away the instant she was free. "I have to call him back. What if he's hurt?"

A snarling combination of barks and growls filled the night. Sam grabbed her arm and jerked her to a halt. "He doesn't sound hurt."

"He's not *your* dog." Jessica twisted free. "And I said not to touch me like that." She pushed aside a bramble of tall weeds and fading grass and plunged into the woods.

"Dammit, Jess."

Dead branches and scattered ground cover snapped beneath each step, poking and scratching her feet through the open sides of her sandals. Sam made no sound when he moved, but she knew he was coming after her. Just like that first day on the road. Always coming. Ever closer. For her.

"I'm going to take your hand."

"What?"

He declared his intention an instant before he folded his hand around hers, locking them together. Jessica stumbled and caught herself, more startled by the announcement than by the actual touch.

"I don't want you to be frightened of me," he explained, never breaking stride. He pulled her along with him, crouching behind the fat, gnarled trunk of an ancient oak. "There could be something worse out there to worry about. We'll go together."

That he would spare precious seconds to reassure her with his low-pitched promise was a consideration that warmed her from the inside out. The gentle pressure of his grip told her they were a team. She wasn't a victim or a crazy lady or anything except his equal.

"Remind me to thank you later." She squeezed his hand in gratitude. Harry was howling now. "But can we hurry?"

Jessica matched his hunched posture and held on as they

jogged through the trees. Sam kept them hidden in the shadows and avoided the road, somehow finding his way without compass or flashlight in the dark.

The dark? They should be approaching the work shed by now. "What happened to the light?" she whispered. "There should be—"

Sam suddenly ducked behind a stand of pin oaks and dragged Jessica in beside him. "Come here." He warned her of his intention an instant before releasing her hand and dropping his arm around her waist and tucking her to his side. He pressed his index finger against his lips in a request for silence. "Stay close."

Jessica complied. She wrapped her arm behind his back and clutched a handful of the front of his shirt, pulling herself closer to his protective strength. He anchored his hand at the curve of her hip and completed the embrace. She turned her cheek into the pillow of his shoulder and held her breath. There. Just on the other side of the trees. She could hear the voices over the barking now, too.

Along with the abrasive scratch of Harry's claws against the shed's steel door. Someone was holed up inside.

"...you idiot!" That voice came from outside. "C'mon. That dog'll wake everybody up." It was a man's voice she didn't recognize, hoarse and deep. The urgency of his command was emphasized by the rev and rattle of a big engine being coaxed into running smoothly. "If it hasn't already. Move it!"

Sam angled his back against the tree and pulled Jessica right up into the V of his legs, wrapping his arms around her back and holding her impossibly closer. Shielding her from view and danger with the bulk of his own body.

"He won't let me out!" A second voice, muffled by the walls of the shed, sounded frantic. "Damn dog."

Go, Harry. Jessica silently cheered. A couple of yahoos

had trespassed on her property and broken into her shed.
But the dog, apparently, had trapped one man inside.

The man who must be driving swore, a long and colorful
diatribe that made his impatience perfectly clear. The engine gunned and tires kicked up gravel that pinged against
the steel wall of the shed. The dog squealed in pain and
Jessica jerked in Sam's grasp. The barking ceased.

"Harry?" She breathed the name against the wall of
Sam's chest and wedged her arms between them to push
away and go to his aid. But Sam held her firmly in place.
He dipped his mouth beside her ear. "Easy, babe. He's
okay."

Harry snarled again, right on cue, turning his attention
to the pickup truck wheeling around the corner of the shed.
With its headlights off, it was just a big shadow careening
through the night. A deadly shadow that could be used as
a weapon to hurt her dog.

She didn't speak her fears out loud, but Sam could sense
them. The lips beside her ear became a gentle kiss at her
temple. "He'll be fine," he reassured her. "If he can handle me, he can handle these bozos."

Harry's renewed barking was drowned out beneath the
noise of the truck as it spun a U-turn and slammed to a
stop so close to the front of the building that Jessica cringed
at the screech of metal grating against metal.

"Use the window!" the voice from the truck yelled.
"Climb in."

There weren't many details she could make out around
the thrust of Sam's shoulder, but she caught a glimpse of
a figure crawling out through the front window of the shed.
He dove straight into the bed of the truck. It was too dark
to make out shapes and faces, or even be sure there were
only two intruders.

"I'll be ready for you next time, you damn dog." The
man in the bed shouted the threat and tumbled out of sight

as the truck peeled away from the shed and fishtailed onto the gravel road.

"Stay put." The instant the danger was moving away from them, Sam set her firmly aside. Her body flushed with chill bumps as she was suddenly denied his surrounding heat. He slapped his hand against his side, then gritted his teeth and swore. "Damn."

"Sam?"

Shaking off whatever inconvenience had frustrated him, he gave chase, making no pretense of stealth as he leaped into the clearing and ran after the speeding truck.

"Sam!" Jessica ignored his warning and followed. This was her place, her haven that had been violated. Her dog that had been in danger. *Next time* the man had vowed. They'd be coming back? *She* was the one who wanted to demand answers.

But though she'd run cross-country in high school, her sandaled feet were no match for the jagged gravel. She quickly realized she was too far behind to catch Sam or the truck. And when Harry dashed past her to join the pursuit, apparently neither injured nor in need of her attention, she turned around and jogged back to the shed. There'd be answers there, too.

The darkness and at least one of the crashing noises was easy to explain. Broken glass crunched beneath her feet as she neared the shed's front door. Jessica paused and looked up. The security light that hung over the entrance had been smashed, leaving only a few shards of the globe and light socket hanging from the metal frame.

She debated about five seconds whether or not she should go get her shotgun before opening the door. But she hadn't been able to help herself that night in Chicago. She wouldn't repeat that mistake. She wouldn't run and let Sam or anyone else take care of this problem *for* her when she had smarts and character of her own to draw from.

Though the lock had been broken, the door wouldn't budge. Studying her options, Jessica took a cue from the intruder and hoisted herself up and in through the broken window. Her burglar had either used a flashlight or disabled the lights inside, as well. In the pitch darkness inside, she stubbed her toe against a block-shaped object on the floor. She ignored the sharp jab of pain that radiated through her foot and made her way toward the doorway to find the light switch and circuit box.

When the light switch proved inoperable, she trailed her fingers along the connecting electrical conduit and reset the circuit breaker. She squinted her eyes shut as the one-room structure flooded with light.

As her eyes adjusted to the brightness, the sabotage became obvious. Shock slowed her reactions, forcing her to process the scene bit by painful bit. She slowly turned, her mouth agape as she inspected the damage of what would have been complete destruction if Harry hadn't intervened.

"Jess?" The crunch of gravel outside the shed told her Sam had returned. "Jess!"

Reacting to Sam's frantic call, she quickly pried loose the ax that had been wedged beneath the doorknob and swung the door open. "In here. I'm okay."

When he would have taken her in his arms, Jessica backed away. After clinging to him in the woods, she didn't think she could stand to be touched by him—by anyone— right now. Still clutching the ax in her grasp, she hugged her arms around her waist, afraid she'd break into tears if she surrendered what strength she had left to him.

Accepting her rejection with a stoic lack of argument, Sam paused in the doorway. His nostrils flared and his chest expanded and fell as he caught his breath. "They drove straight north toward Highway 50. There was too much dust to read a license. All I got was a beat-up truck. Two-tone stripe on the side. I couldn't see anything in the back," he reported. ''Harry must have interrupted them before they had a chance to steal whatever they came for.''

''I don't think anything's missing,'' she said, a dull, dead tone in her voice. Jessica knew with bone-chilling certainty that this break-in wasn't about theft. The old buggy had been turned over on its side in the corner. The chest of drawers she'd bought at the auction that morning had been chopped into irreparable pieces, probably using the ax she held in her hand. The drawers had been pulled out and crushed with equal ferocity.

But that wasn't how she knew.

''Son of a—'' Sam saw it now, too.

Scarlet spray paint, trickling down the walls like bloody tendrils. Six letters. Meant to be eight.

D-I-E B-I-T

She thought of the message on her computer the night before and wondered how an anonymous stalker from somewhere in Chicago had wound up in her own backyard.

Chapter Seven

"That's a pretty serious message for a couple of teenagers just out gettin' their kicks. Seems more like they want to throw a scare into you for some reason." Sheriff Hancock rolled the brim of his hat in his hands, leading this night-time summit of sorts on her front porch. "Of course, it could be they just singled you out because you're a woman alone out here. Easy prey and all."

"She's not alone."

Jessica slid her gaze to the black-haired Irishman leaning against the post at the far end of her porch. Sam's emphatic assertion thrummed through her body. His matter-of-fact defense of her was both enervating and a tad frightening. It wasn't right for him to intimate that he was willing to do more than haul her furniture and repair her driveway, was it?

She wasn't the only one who questioned his presence here.

"It doesn't have to be that way, kiddo." Mac Taylor was her second-eldest brother, a relatively quiet man on the Taylor scale. But there was no mistaking his strength and authority. "You know Ma and Dad have room in their condo over the shop with all of us moved out. And you're always welcome to stay with Jules and me."

To keep Sam from placing the call himself and putting

her name and address over the dispatch wire where someone in her family might hear it, she'd phoned the sheriff at home to report the "incident." Interesting how one of her brothers had managed to find out about it, anyway.

Jessica settled back on the bench beside the front door. "I appreciate the offer, Mac. But no one's scaring me off my place. That sounds so…Perils of Pauline-like. This isn't a melodrama. I'm a professional woman. I've been running a business here for five years."

He raked his fingers through the short spikes of his burnished hair. He looked tired. He should. He'd been working a crime scene when he'd somehow intercepted the information about the break-in and driven out to her cabin. "Then the family can take turns staying with you."

"No." She tempered her refusal with a smile. "I don't have that much space to put anybody up. The extra bed in the garage apartment is being used right now."

Sheriff Hancock leaned in and whispered in a voice that was still loud enough to carry to the end of the porch. "You sure your new guy's got nothing to do with it? Wouldn't be the first time organized groups have come from the coasts to steal antiques here in the Midwest to resell back in the big cities where the demand's so high."

"I'm sure Sam had nothing to do with it." She was pretty sure of a couple of other things about Sam O'Rourke, and was anxious for him to verify what she already suspected. Being a thief wasn't one of them.

Though the sheriff didn't seem satisfied with that particular answer, he continued to ask a few more routine questions. He paced off the length of the porch and stared out into the dark toward her driveway as if the trees and gravel could tell him something useful.

She certainly couldn't. Yes, she kept the shed padlocked. No, she didn't think anything was missing. Yes, her insurance would cover the damage to her property.

No, she didn't know any reason why someone would want to hurt her.

Jessica studiously ignored the pair of ice-gray eyes that drilled holes through her when she answered that question. It wasn't a complete lie. She understood the threat behind the words and vandalism, she just didn't know who was responsible, or why she was being targeted like this again.

But she didn't feel the need to justify her omission to Sam. She'd listened to his perfunctory report of the night's events to the sheriff—the details he'd picked up, the way he described them.

She wasn't the only person on her front porch keeping secrets tonight.

Jessica stole a look at Sam, hovering in the shadows at the far end of the porch, opposite from Sheriff Hancock. She should have recognized that miss-nothing intensity in his gaze from day one. Lord knew she saw that same look at every family get-together. There'd been other clues that should have given him away to her discerning eye. But she'd been too attuned to his alleged grief over his sister to pick up on them. She'd felt the pull of the charm he'd tried to hide. The kindred spirit her soul had longed to reach out to. She'd sought out his protection, even welcomed his touch when it hadn't startled her.

But Sam O'Rourke wasn't everything he appeared to be. She'd bet Harry on it.

Jessica turned away and petted the dog stretched out at her feet. Harry had suffered a few bruises from the flying gravel, but nothing serious enough to impede his mooch and cuddle drive. She was glad because right now Harry seemed like the only male she could trust.

When the sheriff turned to face her, she automatically buried her fingers in the fur beneath Harry's collar. "You sure this incident isn't something more personal?" he asked.

Mac certainly wasn't the most reactive member of her family, but he was definitely the most perceptive. He adjusted the gold-rimmed glasses that masked the scar tissue around his blind left eye and addressed the sheriff.

"Of course it's personal." He pushed away from the post he'd been leaning against, straightened his jacket and sat on the bench beside her. He placed his palm between her shoulder blades and began rubbing soothing circles across her back. "You should be looking into any employee she's had to fire who would know about that shed back in the woods. Old boyfriends. Disgruntled customers."

"It's okay, Mac." She reached out and squeezed his knee through the khaki work slacks he still wore. As a forensic pathologist, he was more scientist than cop. But he still wore a gun and a badge, and he was all big brother. She smiled, anxious to ease the lines of strain bracketing his mouth.

"Tell me what old boyfriend is going to cause trouble with the six of you watching over me. And I don't have any disgruntled customers. My prices are fair and I know how to make a deal." She purposely ignored the deceiver at the end of the porch she *should* fire. "And I've only had to discharge one employee. He's since gone back for his GED and, last I heard, has a job repairing telephones and making more money per hour than I ever paid him. What reason would he have to vandalize my property?"

"You should still—" Mac began.

"I'll get a name and look into it, just in case," said the sheriff. Jackson County was *his* jurisdiction, and while the sheriff's department got along well with KCPD, he wasn't about to turn over his authority to an outsider.

But Mac was thorough. If he had a point to make, he would make it. "If it is just a couple of teenagers out partying on a Saturday night, I'd like to know who they are and why they don't have anything better to do."

"Mac—"

"We're working on it." Curtis Hancock defended himself before Jessica could. He propped his hands on his belt and the butt of his gun as he crossed back toward them. "I've got a description of the truck from that handyman of hers, and what men I can spare are out looking for it now." Mac stood as the sheriff came closer to make *his* point. "I have other security priorities at the moment, Mr. Taylor. But Jessie here is a citizen of my county and a friend, to boot. I take the protection of her property and her person very seriously."

"Well, since you're booked up with other priorities right now, I don't suppose you'd mind letting me take that ax back to my lab to dust and run for fingerprints."

"I don't mind a bit. We run a lot of our evidence through KCPD's lab." Hancock's expression creased with a good-ol'-boy smile. "As long as you share the results with me."

"Absolutely. You do your job, I'll do mine." They exchanged a businesslike, if not exactly friendly, look before Mac pulled her to her feet. "Need anything else, kiddo? It's been a long day and I'd love to see my wife before she goes to bed."

"Go. Say hi to Julia for me." She stretched up on tiptoe and welcomed his familiar hug. "Don't say anything to Ma and Dad, okay? This may be nothing and I don't want to put any more stress on Dad's heart than necessary. You know how they worry."

Mac released her with a smile. "We all do." He thumbed over his shoulder toward Sam. The two men hadn't spoken directly beyond introductions, but she had a feeling Mac had been observing him the entire time. "You're sure you're okay alone here with this guy?"

"I'm fine." She was actually looking forward to a few minutes alone with Sam. Though not for reasons he might expect. "He's been very helpful."

Mac slid Sam a look to let him know he was being watched. "If you say so. I'll let you know what I find out." He brushed a kiss across her cheek. "Love ya."

"Love you."

Jessica stood in place, watching Mac and the sheriff walk down to the parking lot together and then drive away in their separate official vehicles.

"So am I suspect number one?" Sam didn't waste any time addressing the tension in the air. He left the relative exile he'd withdrawn to and strolled toward her with an easy, pantherlike grace. "Your brother doesn't like me."

"He doesn't trust you. There's a difference."

"Why didn't you tell him and Hancock that this wasn't the first threat you've received? That whoever sent it is a hell of a lot more dangerous than a couple of bored teenagers?"

Jessica shook her head. "Uh-uh. It's my turn to ask questions." With a snap of her fingers, Harry rolled to his feet and sat by her side, pressing his head up into her hand as his reward for obeying. She obliged him with a thorough scratch around his ears. "Let's go inside. I think we'll want full-strength coffee for this discussion."

Sam's eyes narrowed to slits of gray. But he said nothing more as he held open the door and waited while Harry pushed his way inside first. Before she could follow, Sam snatched her by the wrist and held her back while he pulled the door closed, trapping the dog on the other side.

Sam released her before she could protest his trickery or his touch, and held his hands up in front of him in peaceful surrender. "He'll be fine on his own for a few minutes and so will you."

Oddly enough, Harry gave one surprised bark, but then went on in to find his food or a place to sleep. Apparently, he wasn't alarmed by this separation. *Traitor.* "This isn't your—"

"Forget about the coffee." He lowered his hands and kept his distance, but there was no mistaking the challenge in his voice. "If there's something eating at you, let's hear it."

Fine. She could do this without Harry or the distraction of keeping her hands busy. She inhaled deeply, crossed her arms in front of her and tilted her chin. "Earlier tonight, when we were running through the woods, and then when you took off after that truck, you kept reaching for something at your side. You even cursed when it wasn't there." The images of Mac adjusting his jacket, the sheriff using his belt as an armrest, made what was missing so vividly clear now. "You were reaching for a gun."

There was a beat of dead silence. But he never blinked, his expression never changed. "No, I—"

"Dammit, Sam. Don't lie to me." Her temper overrode any misgivings she had about a confrontation. "I've been around men like you all my life. I said you reminded me of a cop. Are you?"

His pause was even longer this time. And the expression that darkened his features was resignation, maybe even regret. "No. I'm not a cop."

Jessica pivoted and stormed away, angry that he would lie to her face. The signs were all there. The awareness. The protective instincts. The readiness to take action. She knew.

"I'm a special agent with the FBI." The soft-spoken admission stopped her in her tracks. She hadn't really expected him to be honest with her. And when she slowly turned to face him, she hadn't expected to see the weary sag in his posture as he sank onto the bench and leaned back against the cabin's log frame. "My badge and gun are up in the apartment. In my backpack. I'll wait here if you want to check. Take the dog with you or leave him here to stand guard. I promise you're not in any danger from me.''

Oh, but he was the worst kind of danger. The kind that bulldozed around her defenses and got under her skin. He triggered her temper and taunted her hormones and tempted her heart. He made her feel needy, compassionate, womanly things. Things she hadn't felt for a very long time. Things she'd never felt this intensely.

''The FBI?'' She should be gloating that she was right, that she'd caught on to his deception. But all she could see was the bitter twist to his handsome mouth; all she could feel were the unanswered questions in her own heart. ''Your friend, Virgil, whom I called as a reference—''

''He's my partner. We work out of the Boston Bureau. Drug enforcement mostly.'' Sam looked at her then. But his attempt at sarcasm fell flat. ''I did do some carpentry work for him, and he will vouch for my character most days.''

Jessica sat on the opposite end of the bench, just out of arm's reach. She wasn't sure she'd believe what any man told her right now. But she wanted to understand. She wanted Agent Sam O'Rourke's reason for conning his way into her life to be valid. ''So what are you doing all the way out here in Missouri? You're not really on any kind of sabbatical, are you? Are you working a case?''

''I *am* on leave. Bereavement.'' He hesitated, and Jessica held her breath along with him. ''I told you my sister died. She was murdered.'' His mouth flattened into a hard, grim line as he controlled his emotions. ''She suffered.''

That he said so little so bluntly probably said a lot about how much he had suffered, as well. His fingers silently tapped the bench, one at a time, the only outward sign betraying his tension. His expression eased when he looked at her, but the fingers kept tapping. His eyes were dark, empty shadows. ''I'm looking for the man who killed her.''

Jessica scooted an inch closer. But she wasn't sure if comfort was what he needed, or would accept, from her. He'd lied to her, but with that bleak edge drawing all the color from his voice, how could she not feel his pain? "Sam. I'm so sorry. You don't blame yourself, do you?"

"Of course I do. It's what big brothers do." She understood all too well. But his wry effort at humor triggered a hot sheen of tears that stung her eyes. "May I?"

She followed his gaze down to the bench where her hand rested beside his. Little more than imagination separated their fingers, but he still waited for permission to take her hand.

She didn't give it. Instead she laced her fingers through his and squeezed his hand in a firm grip of her own. "You don't have to announce every time you want to touch me."

"Yeah, I do." He angled himself toward her, hooking one leg up on the bench and switching hands before reaching out and pressing his callused fingertips against her cheek. Jessica held her breath. But the touch was so gentle, so tender, that she turned her cheek into the cup of his palm and remembered what it felt like to crave a man's touch. "Until that 'what if' question disappears from the corner of your eyes and you believe I'm not going to hurt you, I'll ask before I touch."

It was a sad testament to her attack, and a remarkable bit of patience and understanding from a man who seemed so hard.

"I want to kiss you, too." He slid his fingers into the hair at her temple, massaging her there, never breaking contact with her skin. "But I have a feeling that's a little ways down the road. Especially…" He trailed the tip of his finger across her bottom lip, and Jessica felt the tug of that portentous caress all the way down to her toes. The promise of his desire warmed parts of her she hadn't wanted to even think about for too many months. But before she admitted, even to herself, how much she wanted that kiss, too, Sam pulled away. "If possible, you're going to trust me even less when you find out what it is I need from you."

He stared at her so intently that she hugged her arms around herself and leaned away. His eyes must have ached with their unblinking beseechment, willing her to understand the unspoken message there. *Wait a minute*. An awful, sick thought soured her stomach, spoiling the illusion of intimacy they'd just shared.

"Let me guess." Her voice sounded cold, even to her own ears. "Your sister was raped before she was killed."

He looked and sounded like a special agent now. "I'm fairly certain the man who attacked you is a serial rapist who's left a trail of victims in his wake. You're the only one lucky enough to have survived."

"Lucky?" she scoffed. Jessica withdrew, both figuratively and literally. She rose and crossed to the nearest post. Hugging it, she pressed the same cheek that had savored Sam's touch against the rough-hewn pine. "You knew about my attack before you ever came here. And I went through that whole painful confession. You were using me."

She heard the creak of wood taking his weight as he stood behind her. "I'm an agent conducting an investigation. You're an eyewitness. I didn't like lying to you. But I needed your cooperation whether you were willing to give it or not. I still do.

"Don't tell me to go away, because I won't," he went on. She felt his heat as he stepped closer, moving toward her in that determined, relentless way of his. "I need facts, details, so I can track down this creep and put him away where he belongs. I may have failed to protect Kerry, but I won't fail to bring her killer to justice. Whatever it takes."

"Whatever it takes." If only it were that simple. But then another thought struck her. This whole nightmare got more complicated by the minute. She held on to the post, but angled around to face him. His expression was hidden in the shadows cast by her porch light. "The FBI wouldn't let you investigate your own sister's murder."

"I said I was on leave" was his version of an explanation. "Local police departments are just now starting to connect these crimes. But they've reached a dead end at every turn. I won't. He struck again this week in Las Vegas. I can't wait for the Bureau to form a task force. This guy is too good. He'll hurt someone else. I think—" she didn't want to hear this, but she knew it was true "—he's trying to hurt *you*. All over again."

"I think he is, too." She might not have time to wait for a task force, either, and the prospect terrified her. She hugged the pole tighter, feeling too confused to seek solace in Sam's arms right now, though she suspected he'd be willing to give it. She was tired of being the victim, tired of being afraid. She'd been raised to be stronger than that. She *was* stronger than that. Summoning that strength, she stood up straight and looked Sam in the eye. "What do you need me to do?"

"Your report to Chicago P.D. was sketchy at best. Anything you can tell me might help. An MO. Something he said. Any kind of physical description—hair color, build, scars or other distinguishing marks. A name or nickname if you have it."

"Is that all?" She nailed the sarcastic tone in her voice, but neither of them laughed.

"If you're strong enough to talk about it." Sam's voice had gone soft. The Irish lilt that danced along her nerve endings and worked its way into her heart had returned. "I promise to keep you safe. I won't let him hurt you, no matter what happens with my investigation. Jess?"

"So you want me to tell you all about the night I was raped."

"I know I'm asking a lot. I know it won't be easy."

The black void inside her head mocked her. She wished she could turn on a light and pull out the details he wanted, the ones she needed to remember. She wished she could deal with the details and move past them and not have to carry around the constant reminder of all that had been taken away from her that night.

But she couldn't. Forget not being easy.

"It'll be impossible." All she had to do was hold up one hand to silence his apologies about lying and his insistence that she was the only one who could help him. "Because I don't remember a thing about that night."

From across the parking lot, Sam watched Jess standing on the porch, waving to a retirement-age couple who was driving away with a child-size sleigh and Santa Claus doll they'd bought from her shop. She looked for all the world like the classic beauty, friendly nature girl and successful businesswoman she was.

Amnesia?

Sounded like a damn convenient excuse to avoid dealing with reality. Her gaze connected all too briefly with his before whistling for the dog and disappearing inside the cabin. She'd explained what little she did remember—up to the moment she'd left the museum fund-raiser in angry tears, and then after the moment she recalled running from an alleyway with only a ratty blanket to cover herself as she hailed a cab and went to the hospital.

Everything else in between? A blank.

Sam knew his resentment and disappointment weren't fair. Jessica Taylor had dealt with a reality as harsh as any he'd faced. Harsher, according to the explanation her therapist had given her. Whatever she'd seen and experienced the night of her attack had been too horrible to bear for some reason, so her mind was protecting her from the pain by blocking it out.

Most of it, anyway. He'd witnessed two flashbacks himself, once with the sheriff's first visit, and then at the auction. She might not be ready for it, but her brain was trying to force her to recall something. He intended to stick around long enough to find out what that was. He just prayed she figured it out before the bastard leaving those hideous messages robbed her of the chance.

"This is the last one, Sam." Work and heat and tireless energy—unfortunately, not his own—brought him back to the job at hand.

Derek Phillips was a strapping eighteen year-old, well suited to the defensive tackle position he played on his high-school football team. They had a chance to win their district and play for the state title in their class for the second year in a row, Derek had told him. Several times. Sam grinned. Jess's teenage neighbor was the kind of person who never met a stranger. The kid had worked hard all afternoon and struck up one friendly conversation after another, despite Sam's distracted mood.

"It's about time," Sam answered, grabbing his end of the railroad tie Derek had pulled off the back of Jess's pickup and carrying it over to the edge of the parking lot. "I never thought we'd finish this job. Looks nice, though. I appreciate the help."

"No problem."

Sam set his end of the railroad tie and stood up straight, stripping off his work gloves and pulling the navy bandanna from his jeans to mop the sweat from his forehead. Damn. This air was too still, too hot for September. He hadn't seen today's weather report, but there must be a storm brewing. A doozy of one if the dark green-gray line of clouds gathering in the west was any indication.

He smoothed the hair back from his forehead and tied

the bandanna around the top. But he saw that even better relief from the heat was on its way. With the latest rush of customers gone, Jess was striding across the yard with a tray of that delicious, thirst-quenching lemonade. Hell. He couldn't help but smile in anticipation. The whole vision was delicious. Long legs. Swaying hips. Silky chestnut hair catching in the breeze created by her graceful stride.

A fanciful thought sneaked into his imagination. Her lips would taste just like that lemonade—smooth and sweet, with just enough tart to make it interesting. They were lips that could quench a man's thirst. And, man, he was dying of thirst.

But Jess's startled misstep brought an abrupt end to his sentimental journey. A trio of barn cats scattered in front of her as Harry bounded over to join them, turning this break into a little party. But was it the uneven ground, the cats or Derek that had caught her off guard? The teen had removed his shirt earlier, and made no move to put it on now. Did the kid's naked chest bother her the way his seemed to?

"Hallelujah!" Derek yelled as Jess handed him a drink. His brown eyes lit up as he looked down at her. "This is way cool. Thanks."

"You're welcome, Derek. You've earned it." Apparently, nothing more than the terrain had tripped her up a moment ago. Now she was playing the perfect hostess.

Derek beamed at the power of Jess's friendly smile. The young man seemed to stand up straighter, his chest seemed to expand to an even more impressive girth. Then he started talking football again. Something about making an all-star team and playing exhibition games around the Midwest. And winning them.

Sam thanked Jess and hid his amusement behind a long swallow of the cold, lemony, sweet drink, trying not to make the inevitable comparison to kissing her. The kid was

preening for the pretty lady. Showing off. Doing his
damnedest to make an impression.

Had he ever been that young and studly and full of himself? Sam mused. No doubt.

But then he found himself looking just as hard at her as
the two conversed. A genuine smile from Jessica Taylor
was a thing of beauty. No wonder the kid had a crush on
her.

He did.

As if feeling the intense heat that suffused his body from
the inside out, Jess turned to face him. There was no smile
for him, only the awkward stammer of an excuse as she
began her retreat. "Bring the glasses up to the house when
you're finished. I'm going to go in and start adding up
receipts. When you two get cleaned up, come on in for
dinner." She turned to Derek and winked. "Unless you've
got a hot date tonight."

"Uh, no, ma'am." Derek's cheeks blushed a bright pink,
and he'd worked on a farm too many years for it to be
sunburn. "Just meetin' some friends later. If you're
cookin', though, I'd be glad to stay."

"It's just Reuben sandwiches." She gave him an option
out.

Derek didn't want it. Sam supposed if the kid tried his
charm act on a high-school girl, he'd have her eating out
of his hand. But Jess was eleven years his senior. Couldn't
he see that her interest in him was only neighborly? Sisterly
at best. "They're my favorite. Sounds great."

With dinner set, Jess went back to the cabin. The view
from the rear was just as mesmerizing as the view from the
front had been. Sam felt his jeans grow tight. This was
some kind of cosmic retribution, he reasoned, downing the
rest of his lemonade and starting the cleanup part of the
job.

He'd been dead for months. Dead to his feelings, dead

to his hormones, dead to his heart. Thoughts of vengeance had been the only thing keeping him alive. But he hadn't really been living.

Jess Taylor was reviving him, making him care, making him want. Making him wish like hell that he was a better man and she hadn't been hurt so badly.

Because he wanted her. He was falling for her. He hadn't even kissed her yet, but every touch, every look, every word, awakened something in him. Something only she could satisfy.

But she'd been touched by violence, altered by it. She needed a gentle man who'd never carried a gun, who'd never wanted to kill a man. She needed—she deserved—a healing kind of love.

And unless he could find a way to heal himself first, Sam O'Rourke wasn't that kind of man.

Six o'clock came and went with only a few more patrons stopping by. Sheriff Hancock had stopped by with his wife to pick up two tabby cats. He reported that his department had found numerous trucks matching the description Sam had given him, and his deputies were "following up." To Sam's way of thinking, it was a politely vague way of saying they wouldn't have any helpful information for Jess anytime soon.

And then another of Jess's brothers stopped by. Gideon Taylor. His four boys had shown up with a slice of birthday cake for their favorite aunt, then gone off to explore the nooks and crannies full of treasures for sale in her cabin, with the delightful mission of each choosing something for themselves.

This brother didn't say much, but he didn't have to. There was something almost telepathic in his dark eyes as he shook Sam's hand and introduced his wife. Sam knew he was being sized up, but couldn't tell if he passed muster.

He'd warned Jess not to reveal his true occupation to

anyone. But the Taylors weren't fools. They must suspect that he was here for some reason beyond manual labor. But whether Gideon thought he was there to protect his sister— or if he was the danger she needed protection from—the man never let on. After the break-in, Sam wondered how many other family members would "happen by" to check on her, and her new hired hand.

Now that the shop was officially closed, and a chilly wind had picked up, Sam had hurriedly tied tarps down over the more fragile items on her porch, and locked down the barn and outbuildings. He parked her truck in the garage, removing the gun and holster from the glove compartment where he'd kept it locked up and close at hand all day long. Now that Jess knew the truth, there was no need to hide it or his ability to use it. And he wouldn't be caught again without that sure line of defense the way he had been last night.

Derek had been fed and, at Jess's urging, sent on home before the rain hit to get ready for his night out. Sam and Jess were alone again. Alone with the dog and the looming storm whipping in tumbleweeds and cornstalks and other debris from the west. As he climbed the stairs to his apartment, electricity crackled in the air, making the hair on his arms stand on end.

But the ten-degree drop in temperature wasn't the only thing riding in before the storm hit.

A bright red Porsche convertible, expertly tuned and fully loaded, judging by the smooth hum of the engine, sped down the hill from the north and careened through the brick gates marking Log Cabin Acres. Spitting new gravel from beneath its low-slung frame, the car flew like a jet leaving a contrail in its wake. Sam paused on the landing. The dark-haired driver spun a ninety-degree turn and skidded the car to a halt at the center of Jess's parking lot. He killed the engine, peeled off his mirrored sunglasses and climbed out before the wake of dust caught up and clouded around the car.

Man, what a waste of fine machinery. And what a seriously wrong picture this was. The driver, dressed in dark jeans and a polo shirt, and wearing a pair of tan leather shoes without any socks strode on up to the cabin as if he owned the place.

Was this another brother?

Sam quickly ran through his impressions of Sid, Mac and Gideon Taylor. They were forces to be reckoned with when it came to Jess's welfare. But none of them had struck him as irresponsible thrill seekers.

To hell with keeping a low profile. The back of his neck prickled with more than electricity. Obeying that warning instinct, Sam tossed his holster into his room and tucked his Sig Sauer into the back waistband of his jeans. He pulled his tattered white Fenway Park T-shirt down over the gun and vaulted down the stairs to meet this cocky son of a bitch head-on.

But Jess had heard the commotion, too. She dashed out onto the porch with Harry. The wind caught the screen door and banged it against the house. But even that racket wasn't enough to mask her heavy sigh. She planted her hands on her hips and marched down the steps to meet their visitor.

"What the hell are you doing here?" Not the friendliest of greetings, but clearly, she knew this man.

Interesting.

Sam held back half a step, ducking behind the corner of the porch to watch this meeting play out. Jess hadn't sicced the dog on the guy as he approached, but the ramrod-straight line of her posture didn't exactly say she was happy to see him.

"Jessica? Honey?" He flashed straight white teeth as if his presence here was obvious. "I drove all the way to see you as soon as I heard about the break-in. My insurance man called me this morning. *You* should have. Are you all right?''

His insurance man called on a Sunday morning?

"You drove all the way from Chicago?" She sounded skeptical.

Chicago?

"Of course." The man tossed aside his sunglasses in a dramatic gesture. "No matter what's happened between us, I am always going to care about you."

Alex Templeton. Marketing wizard. The man Jess said she'd broken up with that fateful night in Chicago. Sam made the connection to the newspaper photo an instant too late.

Alex Templeton scooped a startled Jess up into his arms and planted a solid kiss on her.

Sam didn't know which hit him harder—the notion that this man moved too fast, stood too close and took too much advantage of Jess's vulnerability—or the stab of jealousy in knowing that that egomaniac had kissed her first.

Chapter Eight

Jessica's panic was instant and intense.

She was trapped.

She wedged her arms between them and twisted her mouth away from those cool, confident lips. "Alex, stop!"

Harry barked. Alex shifted his body around hers, blocking out the intrusion.

That kiss she'd once thought was so spontaneous and seductive crept to the dent behind her ear. "C'mon, honey. You've got to forgive me sometime."

With only the toes of her tennis shoes touching ground, she stumbled as she rammed her palm up under his chin and pushed away. Jessica swatted his hand when he reached out to steady her. She steadied herself. Rock steady, on her own two feet. "Is that why you're here? To beg my forgiveness?"

The dog scooted between them and sat at her command.

Alex propped his hands on his hips and shook his head as that wily-Wall-Street-predator look entered his piercing blue eyes. "I don't beg for anything. For months you asked me to come here and see my investment firsthand. You know I have obligations. But I dropped everything because I was worried about you. Now I'm finally here and you push me away? What the hell is wrong with you, honey?"

"You have no right to call me 'honey.'" Jessica shoved

aside the hair that blew across her face and held it behind her ear. She should have let Harry have at him, but she'd been so shocked to see him. Alex. Here. As impetuous and uptown as ever. After all this time, he'd finally come to Missouri.

The charm was back in his handsome features as quickly as it had gone. He took a step forward. "I know we had a fight the last time we were together. But you and I have fought before. We always make up." She cringed. Oh, God, he was going to say it. "I always loved making up with you."

Jessica took a step back. She'd been a naive, starstruck young woman then. Alex had educated her in sex and exposed her to culture and sharpened her business acumen. But she was years more savvy to the ways of the world now. What had seemed like a wonderful adventure then looked like a foolish mistake now.

"There is no making up this time. I left. Six months ago. We broke up. We're finished." She made sure he knew things had changed. "How's Catherine, by the way? Your wife?" she reminded him, in case he'd forgotten the other woman he'd pledged his love and loyalty to.

"I'm working out an arrangement with Cat."

"Fine. Go work it out with her. I'm not interested." Harry darted up onto the porch as she turned to go back into the cabin. But she was suddenly struck by the uncomfortable notion of having her back to Alex. She'd let him leave first. "I'll send you a copy of the insurance report when I receive it. We can talk then. I'm sorry you wasted the trip." She looked up at the yellow cast to the sky and the roiling clouds above them. "You'd better get the top up on your car and find a place to stay."

"Seeing you is never a waste of my time. We're good together. I can give you—"

How dare he? "You're a married man. You can give me nothing."

"Don't be so cold. Don't you have any feelings left for me?"

Annoyance? Loathing? Humiliation?

"No."

"Honey—"

"She said no." That Irish voice, in a deep don't-mess-with-me tone, cut through the air behind her. Her knees wobbled like putty at the wave of relief that cascaded through her. "I'm right behind you, babe," Sam warned as he walked up and wrapped his arms around her waist, pulling her back against his chest.

Jessica fought her way through a momentary hesitation, then folded her arms over his and leaned into his strength. It wasn't rescue she'd needed so much as reassurance, and Sam's stalwart presence offered just that. He hadn't jumped in and shoved Alex aside, he'd simply let her know that she had an ally if she needed one. Jessica stood straighter, nestled closer, liking the embrace as much as she liked the expression of affronted shock on Alex's face. "Sam, this is Alex Templeton. He's my business partner."

She didn't label Sam. Their relationship was growing too complicated to say he was just her hired man anymore.

There was no shaking of hands. Alex's gaze traced the circle of their linked arms, darted up to Sam's face, then down to hers. "What is this? Are you trying to get back at me?"

"This isn't about you," she said gently yet firmly. "I've moved on. You should, too."

Alex shook his head, looking perplexed by her lack of welcome. "I suppose that offer you made this summer to buy out my share of the investment in your little company and get me out of your life entirely still stands?"

"Yes." Simple and direct seemed to be the best way to communicate with him.

He took half a step forward as if he wanted to argue his point or tear her from Sam's arms or claim some kind of reward for the sacrifice he'd apparently made in coming here. But Sam wasn't budging and neither was she. The first bolt of lightning streaked across the sky and thunder rolled like drums right over their heads. Nice touch.

Alex looked over his shoulder at his Porsche. Did he see it as an escape? A trapping of wealth and virility that had failed to impress her? Or was he simply worried his precious baby would get wet? When he turned to face her, his frustration and anger were evident. "I'll be staying in town. I'll talk to you later," he slid a pointed look toward Sam, "when you're alone."

"I won't be alone." She hoped. Sam's fingers squeezed in a secret promise around hers where they clung beneath the cover of their arms. The air was chilly and popping with electricity, but Jessica felt warm and snug and confident in a way she hadn't felt in months.

Maybe her healing had finally begun.

Alex snatched his sunglasses off the grass. His words were catty, though his tone was pure power broker. "This whole thing's a tax writeoff, anyway. I'll have my lawyers contact you. I won't make it easy for you to get away."

"I didn't think you would."

Jessica didn't move, and Sam didn't release her until Alex had closed the top on his convertible and gunned the car through its gears. Sam strode down to the edge of the parking lot and watched the Porsche speeding away, gaining momentum as it crested the hill and vanished from sight.

From this angle she could see the bulge at the back of Sam's jeans. He was carrying his gun. He'd been prepared to defend her in more ways than one. The knowledge was at once thrilling and alarming. When he turned, she nodded toward the weapon. "Were you expecting trouble?"

He reached behind him as if the gun was some sort of touchstone that ensured their safety. "I'm not taking any chances."

The wind caught the fringes of his midnight hair and whipped it around his face as he hiked back toward her, giving him a wild, untamed look. But she knew better. Beneath that rough exterior, Sam O'Rourke was all about calculating patience and precise control. He spoke to the mature woman inside her in a way Alex's blend of boyish exuberance and sophistication never had.

Jessica hugged her arms around her middle, protecting herself from her own chaotic urges as much as from the brunt of the chilly wind. "You noticed the Illinois plates?"

"I noticed." She didn't for one moment think Sam wasn't sizing up Alex as a suspect for the rape and murder of his sister and her own attack. He was. "I suppose his job takes him around the country?"

Jessica nodded. "He's a marketing consultant. In high demand, especially in the large metro areas."

"I'll have Virgil run his travel records, see if any of his trips match up with the attack sites. The guy's definitely got a temper on him, and we know he was in Chicago when you were…" His voice trailed away on an apologetic sigh. "I don't mean to sound so impersonal about it. I'm just trying to piece this together."

"I know. You're in agent mode right now. But I think you're chasing down the wrong path. Alex just drove in from Chicago. He couldn't have been here last night for the break-in."

"Technically, all we know is that he drove in from Highway 50. Maybe he's been in Kansas City for days." That was an unsettling thought. But not unexpected. It wouldn't be the first time Alex had lied to her. Sam shrugged as he sorted through all the possibilities. "Your old boyfriend doesn't strike me as a beat-up-truck kind of guy, anyway. He could easily have hired those men to throw a scare into you."

Waves of chill bumps rippled across her skin, but it wasn't from the drop in temperature. "For whatever reason, it worked. I'm scared."

"Was there anything about Templeton just now that seemed familiar? Something he said or a way he moved that you remember?" Lightning flickered like the Fourth of July in the cloud bank overhead, matching the colors and turbulence she saw in Sam's eyes. "I'm sorry, but I have to ask."

And she had to answer. "When Alex grabbed me, I did panic. I had this awful sense of déjà vu. I remember being overpowered, struggling." Without conscious thought, she reached up and touched her neck. She'd ripped the skin from her fingers freeing herself that night. The bindings on the bed had been so tight. If she hadn't reacted so quickly or been so determined…

"Jess?" Sam's gentle voice drew her back to the present. She splayed open her left hand and stared at it. Her fingers were covered with scars now, not blood. "What are you remembering? Is it Templeton?"

She looked up into his eyes, centering herself in the countryside of southeast Kansas City, near the heart of a brewing storm. The images that had tried to form faded away. She breathed in deeply, but the picture wouldn't return. "He couldn't strangle me because my fingers were caught in the ligature. That's why I didn't die. But I still passed out. He thought I was dead." She shrugged. "But I don't have a face for you yet. That part's still a blank." Frustration closed her hand into a fist. "Surely I'd remember the attack if it was someone I knew."

Sam propped his hands on his hips and stood, unswaying

against the buffeting force of the rising wind. He stood close enough to keep the worst of it from hitting her. It was a small gesture of comfort that threatened none of her usual hangups, and she was grateful for his consideration. "Maybe that's why you blocked it out. Someone you trusted betrayed you."

"But Alex? I do remember a few things. Like the morning after? I wasn't exactly in a part of the city that Alex would frequent. He'd be mugged or murdered there himself. He might be a jerk, but—" she had to learn to say the word "—he wouldn't rape me. He loved me. He liked being with me, anyway."

"He likes controlling you. A minute ago he insulted you because he didn't get his way."

A bolt of lightning split the sky, and a clap of thunder exploded right on its heels. Jessica shivered as the impact charged the air with energy. "He was tossing off words. His ego's hurt."

"That's been motive enough for some men to do the unthinkable. Rape is all about control and power." He dropped his voice to little more than a whisper. He leaned in to be heard over the tom-tom beat of thunder in the distance. "You asked him not to touch you, and he didn't stop."

Jessica wound her arms more tightly around her waist, reliving the crawling sense of dread that had swept over her when Alex had kissed her. She'd give anything to erase the sensation that clung to her skin like a sticky residue of evil intent. "That's just his way. He lives life in the fast lane. I used to like it when he swept me off my feet like that."

"Don't make excuses for him. It doesn't matter how many times you like it. The one time you don't and you tell him so, he needs to respect that."

His words, spoken in such hushed vehemence, almost

made her smile. "You've been studying up. You sound a lot like my trauma therapist."

"I learned that from my father. It's called being a man. A strong woman with talents and opinions of her own isn't a threat. She's a prize. An equal. It's a pity not every male grasps the concept. Including Templeton."

His sister, Kerry, must have been a prize like that. He stood up straight and turned his face into the wind. Anger, regret and sorrow passed across his features before he tucked it all away behind those icy-gray eyes and looked down at her. The interview was over. "The rain's about to hit. Anything else we need to batten down?"

He crossed over to the porch, securing the knots on the tarps he'd tied at the base of each post. Jessica stumbled back a step as the wind hit her full force. The symbolism of how sheltered she'd been when Sam was close by wasn't lost on her.

As he moved on to the next post, Jessica hurried after him. When he reached for the final knot, she grabbed his hand and stopped him. His fingers were long and calloused within her grasp. As strong and capable—and infinitely gentle—as the man himself.

She'd been strong once. She intended to be strong again. And she definitely had formed an opinion about Sam O'Rourke. Jessica met the questioning look in his eyes when he turned to face her. She didn't blink; she didn't hesitate. "I'm glad you're here with me. I'm glad we're in this together."

The tense line of his mouth eased. He turned his hand so that their fingers laced together, linking them in the way he had so many times before. "Me, too."

Sam's gaze had locked on hers and he seemed to drift imperceptibly closer, though she didn't think either of them had moved. Harry yelped at the next clap of thunder and circled around their feet, but Jessica ignored him. She was caught up in an awareness of something completely alien from the impending storm.

Sam's thumb moved gently back and forth, teasing her sensitive palm with the whisper of a caress. Her skin wasn't crawling now. Not with this touch.

Healing wasn't all about finding answers.

"You said you wanted to kiss me." It was a half-formed thought she gave voice to before she could second-guess herself. "If I said *yes*, would you?"

Something dark and sensual melted the ice in those beautiful gray eyes. Sam laid a finger against her cheek and stroked a delicate circle down to the point of her chin. "Say it."

Softly, surely, Jessica answered. "Yes."

Her breath rushed out a heartbeat ahead of the thrilling expectation that consumed her. Sam tipped her chin and leaned in, bringing his mouth inch by tantalizing inch closer to hers. She'd never wanted anything so much. She'd never been so afraid to want something this much.

Parched with anticipation, Jessica moistened her lips with the tip of her tongue. Sam's gaze dropped to her mouth at the tiny dart of movement. She caught her breath, feeling the portent of that look as profoundly as a caress. It was like that first big drop on a roller coaster ride. The tension that built as she climbed to the top was nearly unbearable. But the rush of excitement as she plunged over the edge would be…must be…

His lips touched hers, warm and firm, and Jessica knew the risk had been worth it.

It started out as just a gentle testing of pressure. Not much. A little more. Harder. Easing up now. Sampling this corner. That curve.

She knew he was taking things slow for her sake, and the consideration that Alex had lacked tugged at her heart. Jessica slipped her hand up to rest against Sam's chest. She felt a tremor of movement beneath her palm, and then every muscle bunched as he held himself in rigid check. But she had asked for this kiss. She pushed onto her toes and silently asked for all of it.

With a deep-pitched groan that was half gratitude, half desire, Sam sifted his fingers into the hair at her temple and opened his mouth over hers. Jessica parted her lips and welcomed the rasp of his tongue. She inhaled deeply and drank in the scent of the ozone-soaked air and the earthier fragrance that was Sam himself. He released her hand to frame her face between both of his, angling her mouth first this way, then that, daring her to sample him in the same way.

Accepting the challenge, reveling in it, she braced both hands against the muscled wall of his chest and plunged over that steep hill into passion. The soft, worn cotton of his shirt left nothing to the imagination. Crisp hair sprang up and teased her palms through the thin material. She kneaded the tips of her fingers into his solid strength and dug in as shock wave after shock wave of sensation skittered along her skin and sank deeper inside, gathering in sparks of electricity at the tips of her breasts and juncture of her thighs.

Jessica nipped the arc of his bottom lip, suckled at the indentation of his top lip and aligned her mouth to his to savor what it felt like to be a woman cherished, desired by a man who was all man. A man whose lips were blessed by a touch of Irish magic.

Though only their hands and mouths touched, the kiss was so achingly tender that Jessica felt herself falling into a place where no man had taken her before. Warmth, heat—fire—seeped from the pores of his skin into hers. His chest expanded in quick, deep breaths that matched her own. The whimpering sounds of need from her own throat mingled with the deeper sighs from his.

The ride was spinning out of control. She held on as tightly as she dared, tempting herself with the gentle abrasion of his beard-roughened skin and soothing herself on the smoother texture of his supple lips. Heat leaped between them. Their tongues twisted and twined. He lifted her higher, she pulled herself closer. They were hurtling toward something she'd forgotten long ago. She grew dizzy. She reached. She wanted.

An ice-cold raindrop splashed against her cheek, shocking her as if she'd been startled awake in the midst of a beautiful dream.

The thrill ride crashed to a disorienting halt as she rocked back onto her heels and they both came up for air.

"Oh, babe." The breath from Sam's ragged voice fluttered across her cheek. His fingers were still tangled in her hair as he rested his forehead against hers. She curled her fingers into the front of his shirt and a bit of Sam himself, trying to regain her equilibrium. They were both panting heavily for air and clear thinking. "I never…"

"Never what?" she breathed when he fell silent. More rain spattered her skin, cooling the fire that had nearly consumed her.

The sky rumbled overhead, and Sam smiled, right there, close to her face, his eyes warm and full of laughter. "You've been saving up for that kiss."

She'd been waiting all her life for *that* kiss. With a knowing smile of womanly delight, she tipped her head back into the basket of his fingers. "Yeah. I guess I have. It was worth it."

Another dollop of rain hit her face and splashed up onto his. An innocent giggle tumbled from her throat as she reached up to wipe the droplets off his nose and chin.

"You're getting wet," he teased, using the pad of his thumb to erase the moisture puddling at the corner of her mouth.

And then the heavens spoke. Sam and Jessica gave up the cause as the skies opened up and the rain blew in like a wall of water. In a matter of seconds they were drenched to the skin and barely able to see.

"Come on," he urged, tucking her hand into his and pulling her up onto the porch behind him.

Pressing their backs against the cabin's log frame, they tried to avoid the deluge. But the wind was blowing the rain in horizontal sheets now. Lightning lit up the dark, greenish sky, sending wicked forks of raw electricity down to earth. Harry howled at the ear-splitting crack of almost simultaneous thunder.

Jessica opened the screen door and he dashed inside, probably heading straight for the insulated quiet of the basement. She pushed the door shut and turned to take a closer look at the sky itself. The fireworks of their kiss were momentarily forgotten as Mother Nature's fireworks took on an ominous importance. "I'd better get inside and turn on the TV. See what kind of weather warnings we're under."

"You don't have tornadoes in September, do you?" Sam asked, turning his back to the rain and shielding her from the worst of the stinging drops with his body.

"Unfortunately, yes." Jessica raised her voice to be heard above what sounded like millions of footsteps running toward them. "But the sirens would have gone off. I'm more worried about flash flooding or—" The rain suddenly changed color and form and became tiny pea- and marble-size pellets of ice that bounced and pinged and piled on the ground. "Hail."

Sam turned and took a step toward the stairs. "This will blow over fast, won't it?"

Jessica thought of the farmers whose crops had yet to be harvested. She pictured a brief image of Alex's Porsche and the number of dings the hail would leave in its bright red finish. "Not before it causes a lot of damage. But, yeah, the temperatures will even out in a few minutes. I think the rain will stay with us for a while, though."

Sam's shoulders rose and fell in a heavy sigh. He faced her with a rueful smile. "I'd better get upstairs, then, so I have time to dry off by morning. I expect we'll have some cleaning up to do."

He'd taken two strides toward the end of the porch before common sense and personal desire had Jessica reaching out to stop him. "You'd better ride out the storm in here with me. I have a basement in case it gets really ugly."

Sam glanced down at her hand where it rested on his forearm, then up at her mouth, silently reminding her of the kiss they'd just shared. "It might rain through the night." His eyes were intent when his gaze met hers. "Are you sure?"

She understood what he was saying—how comfortable would she be, alone with a man in her cabin, possibly overnight?

Well, she had a bed and a sofa and a full-size basement. She had Harry and she had her shotgun. But most of all, she had her blossoming trust in Agent Sam O'Rourke.

"Jess?"

"Come in out of the rain, Sam." She reached up and brushed aside a lock of thick black hair that water had plastered to his forehead. She understood what he needed to hear. "I'm sure."

THE RHYTHMIC DISSONANCE of steel scraping against stone was the only sound in the room.

He'd had enough. It had built up inside him like this before, and he knew if he didn't act quickly, he'd lose control of the situation. And losing control was out of the question.

It had always been about taking control.

He sat on the edge of the bed, sharpening the blade of his pocketknife. His chest was bare above the waistband of his dark jeans. It was a man's chest, a strong chest, a symbol of his power and virility. But the bitch didn't understand that. She cast him aside as if he was weak or unimportant.

It was *her* face he saw in the whetstone beneath every sweep of the knife as he honed it to a razor-sharp edge.

''She can't have everything her way.'' No one but the shadows in his bedroom could hear him.

He sat in the small circle of light created by the lamp on the bedside table. Everything was laid out in order, ready to go. His bag was packed, his phone and laptop were ready.

Beside the black stocking cap, his collection of pocketknives was arranged on top of the bedspread, and from that selection he'd chosen this particular knife because of its fine teakwood handle. It had silver trim with two engraved initials that had been worn nearly smooth from years of use. The thing was an antique. It had cost him a pretty penny to obtain it. But there were few like it in the world, and *she* had such an appreciation for fine old things.

It seemed appropriate.

She really shouldn't have told him what to do. She should have appreciated the effort and sacrifices he had made to be there for her. But there'd been no thank-yous, no grateful kiss.

The muscles in his arms and chest contracted and strained to the point of shaking as the resentment and anger coursed through him. She had no right. ''The damn bitch has no right.''

She was still out there, walking around, commanding her little empire. She'd made him look foolish, as if *she* had power over him. He'd looked her in the eye and seen that she didn't recognize him. But she could hurt him if she ever did remember. She could destroy everything he wanted.

But he could destroy her first.

He would take away her power.

He might have failed once, but he would not fail again.

The tension passed as he remembered that he would be in control tonight. That was all he really needed to be happy—control. Love and affection weren't all that important anymore. Just seeing her grovel, apologize, beg. Respect his power. Believe in him. He'd tell *her* what to do tonight. He'd show *her* just how strong and powerful he really was.

He picked up the cell phone and made a call. He preferred the distractions of the city when he did his work. It was so much easier to get lost in the chaos there. It was a very clever cover for him. But since he couldn't get *her* to the heart of the city, he'd create his own distractions. His request was very simple to the man who answered at the other end of the line.

"Do you have it yet?" The responding curses and complaints about the weather and weird things were irrelevant. "Get it. Tonight." He disconnected and returned to his work.

The wildness of the storm outside was a distraction in itself. It would suit his purpose as well as any dirty, shadowed, overpopulated city street.

Her time was coming. He'd make her suffer. He'd make her pay. She would never tell him what to do again.

The knife moved in methodical circles.

Chapter Nine

The telephone rang at half past eleven, startling Jessica as she set the last letter of her word on the game board in front of her.

"I'll get it." She turned in her chair to reach for the phone beside the computer on her desk.

"Let me." Sam O'Rourke moved entirely too fast for a man who was so tall and big and packed with muscle.

She barely managed to get to her feet and block the phone with her hips against the front of the desk. "Don't be silly. My house, my phone."

"Jess." Overpowering her and wresting the phone from her grasp would have been easy enough, but Sam was hindered by his self-imposed don't-touch, don't-intimidate-the-hostess mode. Setting her aside or reaching around her would have brought them into contact with each other, something he'd been studiously avoiding ever since that kiss. "You really need a caller ID."

"Fine. Get me one tomorrow. I'm answering the phone."

"Dammit, Jess." The dire tone in his voice left no doubt about his thoughts. Whoever had sent that e-mail or trashed her shed or attacked her might be trying to terrorize her again.

"He wouldn't call me." There was no need to explain

who the *he* was. "He works by stealth and deception. He's not going to risk giving me a chance to talk back to him or recognize his voice."

The phone continued to ring, beefing up the tempo of urgency in the room.

"What if it's Templeton, inviting himself over? Trying to lay a guilt trip on you for not welcoming him with open arms?"

She'd never allow that. "More than likely this is my parents calling to check on me because of the storm. Now, if a man's voice answers my phone in the middle of the night, you're either, A, going to freak out my dad and put undue stress on his heart, or B, going to have to start answering a lot of questions, because my mom can't resist matchmaking for her kids. And right now you're on her short list for me."

"There's a list?"

"Missing the point." But his quizzical expression was all the distraction she needed. She reached behind her and picked up the receiver, twisting around to put it to her ear before Sam could wrangle it from her grasp. "Hello?"

"Hey, did I wake you?"

"Cole?" Jessica's first reaction when she identified the voice was one of absolute delight. "Hey. Why are you calling so late? Where have you been? I miss you. You're not caught in this storm, are you? Are you okay?"

"Whoa, slow down, kiddo." The deep-pitched laugh on the other end of the line flowed through her like a familiar hug and she took a deep, steadying breath. "It's the only time I've had free. Can't say where I've been. I miss you, too. No, and I'm fine. Did I cover everything?"

Her second reaction was one of self-conscious awareness. Sam stood right behind her, close enough for her to feel the heat from his body, waiting for silent confirmation that the phone ringing after eleven o'clock at night was neither an emergency nor a crank call.

She slipped her hand over the receiver and looked over her shoulder, up into those gray eyes that were braced to expect any danger. "It's my brother," she whispered. "It's okay."

She held his gaze, waiting for him to stand down. With the slightest of nods he finally returned to his seat and began rearranging the letter tiles on the rack in front of him.

Though she doubted his fascination with the task of forming a word to beat her last score was genuine, she appreciated his attempt to at least look as if he wasn't eavesdropping. Still, she moved into the kitchen as she talked. The cabinets weren't soundproof but they afforded her some privacy. She leaned her hip against the counter and pulled her attention back to Cole.

"I think you covered everything except that cryptic message you left on my machine last night," she accused with a rueful smile. "I'm sorry I missed dinner with you. But it's been raining here for four hours. We've had tornadic winds and flash flooding, so I'm not going anywhere tonight. If you need to talk, I'm here to listen."

But Cole's intuition about her had always been right on the money. "Are you alone?"

Though nothing as personal or profound as that kiss had passed between them since coming inside, it was impossible to ignore Sam's presence. He just didn't seem to fit her cozy, secluded home. His shoulders were too big, his eyes too sharp, his scent too enticing for her to completely relax in such close quarters.

She kept coming back to the way that kiss had made her feel, and wondered if she was ready to handle what those kinds of feelings might mean. Certainly a healthy man like Sam would want more than a kiss. Part of her wanted more, as well. But a bigger part of her—in that empty space where her confidence had disappeared along with her memory—wasn't sure she could ever give a man the emotional and physical satisfaction he needed, and deserved, from a woman.

She was learning to trust him as a friend. But could she ever trust him with her body? With her heart?

Could she be trusted with his?

"Jessie?" Cole prompted.

"No, I'm not alone," she hurried to answer, knowing her hesitation had already put him on alert. "The man I hired recently is here, too. I thought it was safer for him to stay in the main cabin during the storm."

"How well do you know this guy? Is Harry there with you?"

"Cole—"

"I have my reasons for asking." He took a deep breath as if catching himself before letting something slip. "Just be careful who you trust right now. Okay?"

"Now *that's* cryptic. What is going on with you?"

"Nothing."

"Liar." Her intuition had always been right on the money with him, too. "Something's happened, hasn't it? If there's anything I can do—"

"You can't."

Her own fears receded behind concern for her brother.

"Can Mitch or anyone else help?" Mitch Taylor was captain of the Fourth Precinct, a well-respected, well-connected cop. "You know we all love you."

"Hell. I love you guys, too. I wish…"

"You wish what?" But there was no answer. She hugged her arm around her waist, wishing she could hug him instead. He was really struggling with something. "Cole?"

"I want to come home. But I can't."

"Of course you can."

"I can't, Jessie. I want to see my nieces and nephews and eat Ma's cooking and find out why the hell you were in love with a guy last year and now you're holed up like some kind of damn recluse. But I can't. It's better that you stay safe."

"My God, Cole. Now I'm really worried. What have you gotten yourself into?"

The already-tight dimensions of her kitchen shrank as Sam appeared at the opening to the dining room. She must have been broadcasting her fears like a beacon. Instead of feeling trapped and retreating a step, she moved toward him, taking his hand before even realizing she'd made the connection.

"It's nothing I can't handle," Cole answered. "I just needed to hear your voice. My gut's been telling me you're in trouble. I'm not there to help and it's killing me."

"Don't worry about me." Sam's grip tightened around hers, absorbing some of her concern.

She could imagine Cole's blue eyes sparkling as he guessed her secret. "He's more than a hired hand, isn't he?"

"Cole—"

"He's there with you right now, isn't he?"

She lifted her gaze to Sam's, wondering if he could read her thoughts as easily as her brother. "Yes."

"Give me his name."

"Sam O'Rourke." Sam's eyes narrowed, questioning her.

"Sam O'Rourke," Cole repeated, as if he was writing down the name. "You tell Sam O'Rourke that if he so much as makes you cry, I will personally track him down and make him pay for hurting you. Understood?"

Track him down. Make him pay. Two very dangerous threats. One very powerful reason for not telling her brothers about the man in Chicago who had truly hurt her.

Though she'd changed into dry clothes hours ago, she suddenly felt chilled to the bone. She pulled her hand free and tucked it beneath her arm, feeling as vulnerable and overwhelmed and certain of her decision to face this alone as she'd been in that emergency room in Chicago.

"That goes both ways, you know." She, too, tried teasing to cover up her real pain. "If some woman is causing you trouble, point her out to me and I'll set her straight."

"Not to worry, kiddo. You and Ma are the only women I'll let into this heart."

"Oh, boo-hoo."

She wasn't the only one making a show of crying. At that very moment Harry ran up the basement steps and howled at the door. The long, mournful whine meant only one thing. "Sounds like supermutt needs you."

At last Jessica could muster a genuine smile. "You know how he hates the thunder. But I imagine he's finally realized he can't wait until morning to go. I'd better let him out."

"Okay. Say hi to Ma and Dad. And give everyone my love. That means you, too, kiddo."

"Are you sure there's nothing I can do?"

"Not this time. Just be safe."

Be safe. Ironic that he should somehow sense that she wasn't.

"I love you, Cole." But he'd already hung up.

"Problem?" Sam asked. He'd taken a step back as soon as she'd released his hand, giving her plenty of room to move past without touching him if she wanted.

He probably thought he'd frightened her again. Oh, yeah, she had a lot to offer a man like Sam. Secrets. Paranoia. Mood swings. The hypnotic drone of the dial tone played on like an ominous portent of her future.

"Yes." Harry howled again, breaking the spell of doom that had fallen over her. He trotted over to her, gave her a *let's go* look and then went back to the door. She fixed a smile on her face and hung up the phone. "But there's nothing I can do." She nodded her head toward Harry. "*This* problem I can help."

With Sam following at a respectful distance, she circled around the armoire and unlocked the back door. As soon as she opened it, the moldy smell of the rain-soaked earth hit her sinuses through the screen. Jessica crinkled up her nose and followed Harry out onto the porch, breathing in the dampness, desperately needing some fresh air to clear her head from the turmoil of her emotions.

Though the worst of the storm had passed, rain still fell in a straight, steady curtain beyond the edge of the porch. Harry hesitated at the top of the steps, sniffed the air, then slunk out across the yard and disappeared behind the barn.

Jessica shivered, huddling inside her blouse as the temperature finally felt like autumn.

"I'd offer you my jacket, but it's up in the apartment." Sam closed the screen door quietly behind him and walked past her to lean his shoulder against a post, again carefully keeping his distance. Like the dog, he, too, seemed to be evaluating the weather and their surroundings. "I'd offer you me, but—"

"I accept." Sam glanced over his shoulder, obviously surprised by her response. She was tired of tiptoeing around her feelings for Sam, tired of still being the victim of something that had happened months ago. She liked sparring with him, knowing she was safe and equally matched in any trade-off of words and ideas. She needed his strength and protection. And right now she very desperately wanted his comfort. "Unless you have somewhere to go?"

A pleased smile tugged at the corners of his mouth. "I'm in no hurry to leave you."

He held out his hand, and Jessica took it as easily as she had in the kitchen. Maybe she was finally getting used to touching a man again, or maybe it was just that this one provided such a tempting reason to move past her inhibitions.

But she was still taking it one cautious step at a time. She moved to his side instead of accepting his hug. Bless his patience, he didn't complain. Keeping their fingers entwined, she wrapped her arms around his and rested her cheek against his shoulder. The goose bumps that had pricked her skin dissipated quickly as she cuddled closer. "How come men generate so much body heat?"

She'd meant it as a rhetorical question, a compliment. But he'd inherited enough of the blarney to have an answer for her. He laid his free hand over hers where it curled around his bicep and winked. "So women need us for something. We had the whole jar lid thing covered, too, but then somebody invented those rubber grips."

Jessica laughed, allowing this man to warm her, inside and out. "Careful, Agent O'Rourke. Your tough-guy image is in jeopardy. I'm going to start to think you have a sense of humor."

"I like making you laugh." Jessica rode the expansion of his torso and arms as he breathed in a heavy sigh. The moment of shared humor quickly dissipated and was lost in the dark, wet silence. "It seems like a hundred years ago, sometimes, when laughter was easy. Kerry was the real comic of the family. Man, she had a wicked tongue. Dad said she was just like my mom—sharp and sassy. I used to laugh all the time." His fingers kneaded her hand in his grip. "God, that was a long time ago."

Jessica understood all too well how tragedy skewed the passage of time. She pressed her lips to the jut of his shoulder. "I'm sorry."

He shook his head. "Sometimes I'm so damn angry about all that's been taken from me, I…" For a split second his hand tightened painfully around hers. "I swear to God,

I'm gonna get this guy." He held up the first two fingers of his right hand and sighted along them into the darkness. "I will put a bullet right between his eyes."

An instant fear buzzed through her at the violence she felt simmering through every part of Sam's body she touched. She wasn't afraid for herself. This is what she'd feared her brothers would do. She'd never be able to stop all of them. She might not even be able to stop this one. She slid her hand from his arm to his chest, pressing her palm against the pounding of his heart. "Sam," she whispered, trying to soothe his grief and anger. "You carry a badge. You have responsibilities. You want justice for Kerry, not vengeance. Please say you understand the difference."

They stood like that for a few tense seconds that seemed like eternity. But gradually she felt his heart slow to a steadier beat. He covered her hand with his. "I will give him every chance to surrender himself. But if there's no other way to stop him…I won't let him hurt anyone else." He turned and pressed a kiss to the crown of her hair. "Especially you."

Jessica tipped her head back and ensnared herself in the vow that shone from his eyes. She wanted him to kiss her again. To seal that promise. She wanted to return his kiss. To ease the terrible burdens of duty and honor a man like Sam faced. His mouth moved closer, and she stretched up on her toes.

But just as they were close enough for the coffee on their breaths to mingle, a movement in the darkness caught her eye. A light flickered on and off through the trees. "Sam?"

He twisted around, pushing her behind him, his hand already reaching for his gun. He saw it, too. Mutual healing would have to wait. Someone was moving around in the trees near the storage shed again.

"Pretty bold sons of bitches to try it two nights in a

row.'' Sam cocked his gun to load that first bullet and leaped off the porch into the rain.

''What are you doing?''

''Checking it out.'' He spared her a glance over his shoulder. ''Get inside and lock the door. Call the sheriff. Tell him you have trespassers and that shots have been fired.''

''I didn't hear—''

''You will.''

''Sam!'' Oh, God, what was he going to do? ''Be care—'' But the rain and the darkness had already swallowed him up.

He'd left her. Alone. For a few precious seconds, Jessica's lungs refused to work. She'd been alone that night, too. Her vision blurred and swam before her eyes as her mind tried to take her back. ''No.'' She squeezed her eyes shut and shook her head, refusing to be sucked in by the debilitating fear. ''No. Call the sheriff. I can do that.''

A sound in the distance kept her from going in. Something low-pitched and unintelligible, muffled by the rain. She went to the edge of the porch and peered into the darkness.

Energy crackled through the air, as dangerous and unpredictable as the lightning storm had been. There was something evil in those woods. Something watching. Something waiting. ''Sam?'' she breathed into the night.

She wiped away the splashes of rain that chilled her face and tried to make him out as he darted around the barn toward the shed. In the distant shadows, one light became two, weaving in and out through the trees. He'd be outnumbered. She swallowed hard to keep her apprehension locked down inside. She should go help him. Warn him of her suspicions. But he'd told her to stay put, to stay safe. Experience with her brothers had taught her that a cop could focus more intently on his job and his own safety if he knew his loved ones were safe.

Not that she thought Sam classified her as a loved one. But she was a responsibility.

Then another sound, more distinct this time, reached her ears.

Frantic barking.

"Harry!" Galvanized by the same vicious warning that had alerted them to the vandals last night, Jessica flew down the steps. "Damn that dog."

Eternally grateful. Always protective. Ever vigilant. An innocent creature bound by instinct and loyalty to guard his territory and protect his mistress. The creep last night had said they'd be ready for him next time. What if they'd returned to shoot or poison him? "Harry?"

She slid to a stop in the wet grass at the corner of the barn, catching her breath and orienting herself before she ran into the trees. The rain quickly soaked her hair and dribbled blinding rivulets of moisture into her eyes.

The illumination from the yard light didn't reach this far, and the two roving lights had disappeared. She couldn't see to find her dearest friend.

But Harry didn't need to see to find her. Jessica pressed her tongue behind her teeth the way Cole had taught her and whistled. The loud, shrill sound pierced the darkness. Harry woofed in response.

"Yes!" She pumped a victorious fist in the air. "Come on, boy!" She whistled again. She'd head back to the cabin. He'd find her there. He'd be safe. She'd be safe. Sam would be safe. She whistled a third time. "Har—"

Her shout gurgled into silence as black-gloved hands clamped around her mouth and waist and lifted her off the ground. Her scream burned inside her throat and sinuses, fighting for escape. But the hands were rough, her abductor strong and fast. She banged her heel against his shin and tripped him up. He stumbled, hissed a wicked breath, but didn't fall. He dodged her swinging fists and squeezed his arm around her gut, jerking her flush against his sinewed body in a brutal mockery of an embrace. He carried her into the brush, into the shadows, into the trees.

Sam! She screamed his name behind the hand that pinched off her voice. Jabbing, biting, twisting, she fought for her freedom. She was wild and fierce, but the man who'd captured her was made of steel and stone.

With a heave of strength he threw her to the ground. She hit hard, landing flat on her back, knocking the air from her lungs. Even before the jarring pain and stabbing bits of twig and rock registered, even before she thought to inhale or scream, he was on top of her, pinning her down. His knee in her gut, his hand on her mouth, stretching her head back at an excrutiating angle.

Something sharp and cold pricked her throat. Circled around it. Cinched it tight.

Like that night.

Jessica's mind screamed as she flashed back in time.

The sounds of revving motors and gunshots in the distance became the sounds of city traffic and classical music inside her head.

The black figure above her smelled of wet, pungent wool that had been stored in mothballs. Just like that snowy night in Chicago. In the cab in front of the museum. The driver's clothes had reeked of the same musty scent.

No! He was taking her the wrong way.

She pounded her fist against his shoulder. *Stop the cab!*

They sped into the darkness. She threatened to open the door and jump out. The doors latched with an ominous click, and he swung his arm over the front seat, drawing the blade of a long, deadly knife across her throat and warning her to be still.

Air and consciousness faded. Memory and reality blurred.

Stop! Help!

"Die…" The voice was real. Here. Now. "Bit—"

The hounds of hell clamored in her ears. A charging beast hurtled out of the darkness and collided with the man on top of her, knocking him to the ground.

The noose around her neck went slack, and Jessica's chest swelled with a reviving breath. The duel beside her was harsh and unmerciful. Punctuated with curses and growls, it ended with an inhuman shriek.

"No." She mouthed the word. Her throat was too raw to work, her lungs too sore to breathe. She pushed herself up onto her hands and knees, tugging loose the band from around her neck and tossing it aside. "Stop."

Two red lights flashed in the distance. A concussion of sound exploded in the air and one of the lights went out. But this wasn't any flashback to a back alley in Chicago. This was real. It was definitely real. Oh, God. "Harry?"

She spun around on her scraped knees, knowing her enemy was behind her now.

"Get away from him." Her voice was little more than a rasp of sound. The coughing that seized her immediately inflamed every bruise and wound on her body.

Maybe her attacker heard something in the woods. Maybe he simply sensed the approaching danger. His hand stilled in midair, interrupting his gruesome work.

"Get away," she warned him, forcing herself to crawl forward, finding strength in the knowledge that she wasn't alone. Not this time. Because she could hear the sounds now, too. The thump of booted feet on the wet ground. Coming closer, ever closer.

Like a ghost leaving its abandoned body, the figure in black rose, hovered an instant over the still form at its feet, then scurried away into the night.

Chapter Ten

Sam cradled his Sig Sauer in a firm grip between his palms and pressed his back into the thick trunk of the ancient elm. His deep, silent breaths kept him alert and virtually invisible to the comedy duo of thieves who were trying to load Jess's green buggy onto the back of their pickup.

The buggy was heavy, and the rain made it almost impossible to get a good grip or secure footing. They were easy prey, rolling a wheel over a toe, landing ankle-deep in a muddy puddle. Dropping a flashlight into the same puddle.

Despite their slips and stumbles and curses, Sam hung back until he'd determined that neither man was armed. Neither of them was over the age of twenty-five. And while they were clearly thieves, neither one of these bumbling, wanna-be intimidators fit the profile of a calculating killer.

An uncomfortable sense of warning teased the fringes of Sam's subconscious mind. *Sam.* He felt the word inside his head as if he'd heard the call with his ears. He turned his gaze back toward the cabin, seeing little more than gnarled branches and the bulk of the barn silhouetted against the yard light. An edgy need to take action danced through his feet. *Figure it out, O'Rourke,* he commanded of himself.

He turned his attention back to Mutt and Jeff, creeping to the next bit of cover and crouching behind a fallen pine bough. Under pristine conditions, he could easily take down both men without firing a shot. But the mud and reduced visibility would work against him, too. One slip and he'd be vulnerable to a lucky punch.

But he'd love to ask those bozos a couple of questions. Namely, Why? Why frighten an innocent woman? Why steal and destroy her things? Why *her?*

What was their connection to Jess's rape? Or, more likely, what was their connection to Jess's rapist? The sick message they'd left in the shed last night was no coincidence.

Was the threat here real? Or an overreaction from the hyperawareness that had stayed with him ever since Jess's voluntary cuddle on the porch. He'd damn near poured his guts out to her, all because she'd pressed a hip, a breast, her hands and lips against his hungry body. She'd held *him.* He'd talked about things he'd never shared with anyone. Because she understood. She knew about vengeful thoughts and soul-eating anger and bottomless grief.

She knew. And yet she went on with her life. She moved forward. As tough as it was for her to trust a man, she could share a normal moment and care about his pain.

"What are you doing to me, lady?" Sweat popped out on his forehead as the force of his emotions tried to overtake him. He didn't deserve that kindess. He hadn't earned that trust. But he wanted it. He wanted her. Everything. If Jessica Taylor was willing to give any part of herself, he realized he was selfish enough to take it.

It was an unsettling admission for a man who'd counted on the ice in his heart to sustain him to the end of this mission.

A shrill tomboy whistle cut through the soupy air, jerking him out of his dour mood and planting him firmly back in the danger of the moment. "Jess?"

Stay put. Lock yourself in. Had he expected that of a

woman who boldly marched forth and greeted strangers with a shotgun?

She whistled again.

"Ah, hell."

The goons heard it, too, and jumped from the back of the pick-up. "Tie it down. I'll start the truck."

"Tie it with what?"

"Did you bring the rope?"

"I thought you were bringing the rope."

"I brought the hamburger for the dog."

These two thugs weren't the real danger. They were barely competent clues that could lead him to the man he was after.

They were a damn diversion.

"Son of a bitch." Sam bolted from his cover and charged the road. The men scrambled for the cab of the truck. "FBI! Stay where you are!"

The engine roared to life and screeched through its gears.

"FBI? Nobody said—"

"Go! Go! Go!"

The driver floored the truck, slinging up mud and rock until it found traction and lurched full speed down the road. They hadn't even taken time to latch the tailgate, and at the first jolt, the buggy bounced out the back. Sam dodged the rolling wheels as the carriage clattered past him and crashed into the ditch.

He fired two warning shots, but the driver wasn't slowing and he couldn't fly. Screw that. Sam didn't waste another step in pursuit. He'd ask his questions later.

Swiping the rain-soaked hair off his forehead, he blinked the moisture from his eyes. He squared himself off in the middle of the road, braced his right hand in his left palm and took a bead on the only clear target he had.

Breathe out. Think ice. Squeeze the trigger. Boom.

The right taillight was history. Before the satisfying jolt of the shot had dissipated through his arms, he was running.

The busted light would give the sheriff and his deputies something more concrete to search for in the light of day. The search tonight was his alone. "Jess!"

There was no whistle to guide him now, but he could follow the sound of the barking. More like a rabid, snarling version of his own thoughts. If Jess was hurt...

He didn't waste his breath with cursing; he didn't give voice to his fears. He raced through the trees toward the house, veered right, toward the sound, shoving aside branches and snapping twigs beneath his boots. Until a sudden and consuming silence more frightening than the sounds of battle stopped him in his tracks.

"Jess?" His call was a husky cry into the night.

With no answer.

Oh, God. He'd been too late to help Kerry. Was he too late to help Jess?

Sam's chest heaved with the exertion of his run, but he breathed noiselessly in and out through his mouth. Where was she? Where was the damn dog? Why the hell was it so quiet?

"Sam?" The froggy croak of a whisper came from behind him.

He jogged toward the pained sound into a clearing beneath a canopy of pine and oak. The branches overlapped here, reducing the rain to a drippy mist. Jess was in the center of the cavelike darkness, kneeling over a black, bulky object on the ground. The stark white outline of her bra glowed against her skin in the darkness.

"Where's your shirt?"

She angled her head and looked deep into the heart of the woods, opposite the direction from which he'd come. "He went that way. Toward the creek." *He?* Bloody hell.

The instinct to pursue his quarry jolted through his legs and he ran to the far side of the clearing. "If you hurry—"

But her voice cracked on a ragged sob, and Sam stopped in his tracks. Oh, God, she was hurt. He couldn't leave Jess if she needed him. Sam peered into the pitch-dark mix of rain and trees and night, knowing that son of a bitch was out there somewhere, just beyond his reach, eluding him. His chest heaved in and out, taking calming breaths as he warred between the urge to finish this job or to help Jess.

Hearing her fight back tears made the decision for him. She was poking at the object on the ground. "I can't move him."

He approached as quickly as he dared, making a wide circle around the perimeter of the clearing to ensure that they were alone, that her attacker hadn't doubled back to finish the job. His boot crunched against something shiny and silvery in a clump of pine needles. It looked like a broken link of a miniature chain. He picked it up and slipped it in his pocket.

"Sam?"

He'd figure out if the silver gadget was anything important later. Jess needed him. He wedged his gun in the waistband of his jeans and hurried over.

"Ah, hell." The black object was Harry. He sank to his knees beside her, piecing together the awful scene. "Are you hurt? What happened?"

Up close he could see the scratches on her back and forearms. And the mean red welt at the base of her throat. He reached out to inspect the severity of the wound but curled his outstretched fingers into his palm when she turned her pleading eyes to him. "I have to help him. I have to save him."

She demanded action, not comfort.

He intended to get something right tonight.

"Tell me what happened," he demanded.

The dog was bleeding from his neck, and Jess was using her shirt and belt to put together a pressure bandage. Harry's flank stuttered in uneven breaths. Sam knew he was in serious trouble when the mutt barely whimpered at the touch of his hand against his soft, woolly chest, feeling for a heartbeat. It raced beneath his fingertips. Not good.

"He stabbed Harry."

That damn *he* again. "Was it the same man? Did you recognize him?"

She didn't even hear the questions or comprehend her own injuries. "He had me by the throat and Harry saved me." Tears glistened in her eyes and spilled over. "He was doing his job. Protecting me."

The devoted pet had done a hell of a lot better job at it than Sam had. "We'll take good care of him," he vowed, burying his questions about the attack.

Unhooking his own belt, Sam looped a makeshift muzzle around the dog's snout. Once those teeth were secure, he stooped down beside the dog, wrapping one arm around Harry's chest and slipping the other beneath his hind legs. The dog snapped his head and protested the movement.

"What are you doing?" she tugged against his arm as he lifted the heavyweight beast in his arms and staggered to his feet. Harry whimpered. Jess's eyes welled with tears and she tried to pull the dog from his arms. "Stop it. You're hurting him!"

"It has to be done! He needs more help than we can give him here." Sam's voice was sharper than he meant it to be. He deserved a good smack when he saw the look on Jess's stricken face. "I'm sorry, babe. We have to keep our heads here, all right? Come here."

She moved a step closer, and Sam bent his head and pressed a quick, chaste kiss to her trembling lips. He couldn't tell if he'd startled her out of her panic or if that simple touch was the comfort and apology she'd needed.

She pulled back and stared deeply into his eyes, as if trying to read his intent. Then she took a deep breath, and an expression of relative calm eased the fear, if not the tension, from her face.

"That's it, sweetheart." He wished he had a hand free to hold on to hers. "Don't scare me like that. I won't let the big guy die. I promise."

"I know." She squeezed his shoulder, offering a bit of reassurance herself. "I'm the one who's sorry. I'm okay."

He'd reserve judgment of that until he had a doctor check her out and could get a few answers about what had happened in that clearing. But he could feel a sticky, warm fluid he knew was Harry's blood soaking into the sleeve of his shirt and knew time was running out. Adjusting the dog's weight against his chest, he headed for the garage, using the longest, quickest strides he could manage without tripping. "Let's go, then."

Jess's only answer was to hurry her pace to keep up.

Once the garage door was open, Sam laid Harry in the bed of Jess's pickup. "Stay with him," he ordered. "I'll be right back."

But she'd already climbed into the truck beside her pet. She cradled his head in his lap and stroked his fur, murmuring encouraging little phrases that soothed even Sam's troubled soul.

Knowing his talents were better suited to practicality rather than tenderness, Sam dashed up the stairs to his room and grabbed his phone, punching in 911. While he identified himself and gave a brief report of the night's events to the dispatcher, he methodically slipped on his holster and badge, gathered the blanket off his bed and the white button-down shirt he'd worn yesterday.

"Does this town have an emergency vet?" He descended the stairs two at a time. "Call him. I'm bringing in a dog who's been stabbed in the neck." He handed the blanket to Jess and helped her tuck it around Harry to keep him warm and shield him from the weather. "He's in shock and losing blood, but he's breathing on his own." He memorized the vet's address. "Got it." He hung up and reached for Jess. "Let's go."

"I'm going to ride back here with Harry." She couldn't hold a baby any more tenderly than she held that dog.

Man, he hated this. "I'm sorry, babe. I need you up front to tell me how to get there as fast as we can."

She reluctantly conceded the wisdom in his request. After situating the dog as comfortably as possible, she took his hand and stood. Sam didn't bother asking for permission. He circled his hands around her trim waist and lifted her down from the truck. He wanted to hug her tight in his arms, wipe away the tears that had dried upon her cheeks. But her hands rested all too briefly against his shoulders as she beseeched him with those clear-blue eyes. "Hurry."

Charged with a mission he would not fail, Sam climbed in beside her. He handed her the white shirt and drove as swiftly and safely as he could along the muddy back roads, heading for the highway.

Under any other circumstances he would enjoy watching her dress, taking note of how his oversize shirt draped and clung to her lean figure. But all he could see was the welt on her neck finally disappearing beneath the buttoned-up collar. All he could do was claim her hand once she got the sleeves rolled up past her wrists.

All he could think was that she'd cheated death twice. Once in Chicago. And tonight in the backyard of her own home. That crazy, faceless bastard had put his hands on her. Hurt her. He'd gotten by Sam for the last time.

The emotions roiling inside him weren't pretty or politically correct. They were self-damning and territorial and humbling in their depth.

He pressed his foot harder against the accelerator.

He didn't intend to let anyone or anything hurt her again—not in any way, shape or form.

She sat sideways in her seat, clinging to his hand with both of hers. But her gaze was fixed out the back window the entire trip into town.

Jessica Taylor could survive a lot of things. But he didn't think losing Harry was one of them

"THAT'S OLD NEWS, Virgil. Whoever sent that e-mail was at Jess's place last night. He put a stranglehold on her. He's definitely trying to cover up his tracks. I already figured it had to come from somewhere in Kansas City for him to get here so fast."

Sam had slipped outside to the parking lot of the veterinarian's office to take this call privately. It was good to see the sun again after the natural and man-made hell of last night. Besides, the waiting room was filling up with the vet's regular morning appointments and way too many Taylors for Sam to feel needed or welcome.

They were loud, they were loving—and there wasn't a puny one in the bunch. He wasn't intimidated by her family, but they presented a huge wall of resistance he'd have to fight his way through if he wanted to get close to her again. And as much as he did want to be the one providing that comfort, he didn't think a confrontation would help her right now.

He didn't begrudge Jess any support from her family while she was scared and hurting over Harry's prognosis. Emergency surgery had successfully mended the stab wound. But the cut had severed some of the nerves near the dog's trachea, and he was being monitored to ensure he'd be able to breathe properly on his own.

Sam's own lonely status as the last surviving member of his family had been brought home when Jess released his hand to hug her parents who arrived just after dawn. Her brothers and a cousin had arrived one by one after that, except for Cole. They'd traded hugs and circled around her and shielded her from the pain of facing this crisis.

Sam was already on his own by the time Virgil called.

"Please tell me you've got something else," he told his partner, strolling toward the picnic tables and exercise area at the side of the building.

"I can give you the twenty-four-hour copy shop where the e-mail orignated from." Virgil was ever the voice of reason. "But without a picture or description to give the staff, they probably won't be able to verify which customer sent that message."

Sam huffed out a breath in frustration. "Hell, it could be somebody on the staff."

"Any chance your girl could identify him if she saw him at the shop?"

He hadn't gotten around to asking any more questions about the investigation or seeing if any of last night's events had rebooted some of her memory. Jess had been too wrapped up in her concern for the dog. "I'm not sure yet. I've got another name I need you to run in the meantime. Alex Templeton. Chicago investment consultant. Likes antiques, apparently."

Virgil spoke in spurts as he jotted down the information. "Templeton...Chicago... What am I looking for?"

Sam brushed off the leaves and debris that had been blown down by the storm from the top of one of the picnic tables and rested his hip there. "Travel history. He's an old boyfriend of Jess's. Find out whatever you can on his wife, too. Catherine. There's something funny going on there."

"Checking out an old boyfriend?" Virgil teased. "You sure this isn't personal, Irish?"

He remembered all too clearly the way Templeton had ignored Jess's protests, and then had the gall to blame her for not welcoming him with open arms. "It's very personal."

Virgil blew out a long, low whistle over the phone. "You be careful, buddy. I know it all but killed you when Kerry died. I'd hate to see you get hurt like that again."

"This one's not gonna die."

"I don't mean just that. I know you better than you know yourself. You're falling for this Taylor woman. I can hear it in your voice. Are you going to be able to walk away when this is done?"

Walk away? Hell. Sam hadn't thought beyond the prospect of catching Kerry's killer. It had been his whole purpose for so long. But leaving Jess didn't sound like an option he wanted to consider right now. Maybe ever.

He laughed to cover his raw emotions. "You sure know how to spoil a mood, don't ya, Virg."

But his laughter didn't fool his partner. "I can take some time off if you need me there to help you. With whatever."

"You're helping me right where you are." That much was true. "Thanks for looking out for me. But I'll just take this one day at a time, okay?"

"Say the word and I'm there."

"You get me the word on Templeton and we'll call it good."

After they'd signed off and Sam tucked the phone back into his pocket, he became aware of another presence. A man—a big man—standing at the corner of the building, watching him.

Sam moved nothing but his eyes to acknowledge the man whose dark hair and clear-blue gaze labeled him a Taylor. "You're Jess's brother?"

"The oldest. Brett Taylor. Here." He tossed him a bundle of material that Sam caught in one hand. He inclined his head toward Sam's shoulder and chest. "You're a mess."

"Sam O'Rourke. It's nice to meet you, too."

Brett grinned at the sarcasm and strolled a few steps closer. Though this wasn't an enemy—yet—Sam automatically straightened to a more defensive posture as he approached. He'd tossed him a T-shirt with the Taylor Construction Company logo on the pocket. Sam's Fenway Park shirt was stained with Harry's blood and caked with spatters of dried mud.

"I keep a spare in my truck," Brett explained. "We're about the same size."

That was true. There weren't too many men that Sam could look in the eye. But Brett Taylor might even have a bit of an edge on his own six feet, four inches of height.

Sam peeled off his dirty shirt and changed into the new one, not so much because he cared about his appearance but because the blood would be an upsetting reminder to Jess. "Thanks."

"So you're the man living with Jessie."

Blunt and to the point, though a little misleading in its implication.

He'd wondered when the inquisition would begin. "I work for her."

"What kind of handyman work requires a gun?" Sam let the unspoken accusation that he had somehow been responsible for last night seep in and join the rest of his guilt. "The vet tech said you were wearing one when you carried the dog in last night."

"I've got a license for it." He'd locked up the Sig Sauer in the glove compartment at Jess's request. Against his better judgment, she wanted her family to think that nothing more dangerous than vandals had been on her property, and that Harry had been wounded chasing them away. She wanted no mention of gunshots and strangulation. But he refused to lie about everything. "I'm with the FBI. I work out of Boston. I'm on a leave of absence right now."

Brett processed the information without losing his smile. "So, basically you're an off-duty cop?"

"Basically."

Brett extended his hand. "Well, I'm glad you were around. Jessie said you saved Harry's life. Hell, you might as well have saved her, the way she feels about that dog. Thanks."

A peace offering? Sam cautiously reached out to shake his hand. "I'm glad I was there, too."

But big brother had a warning for him, after all. "Are you anything more than a hired hand or off-duty cop to her?"

Sam pulled back and splayed his fingers at his hips, meeting Brett's challenge. "You'd have to ask her what she feels."

"I'm asking you." Brett wasn't smiling now. "My sister's been pretty vulnerable lately. I'd hate to see anyone take advantage of that."

"She's stronger than any of you give her credit for." He wanted to add more in her defense, tell her family just how far she'd come mentally and emotionally, not to mention the physical healing from injuries too personal to describe. But he'd promised to keep her secret. "I don't intend to hurt her."

"Good." Brett flashed a smile again, apparently satisfied with that answer. "Let's keep it that way."

JESSICA WALKED her mother out to her parents' van, double-checking the parking lot to see that her own red truck was still parked where it had been last night. She was tired, she was sore—but she and Harry were in one piece. She wasn't so sure they would be if Sam hadn't been there for them yesterday.

But where was he now?

Sam had disappeared from the waiting room nearly an hour ago. So had Brett. She hoped that didn't mean trouble.

"Is everything all right, hon?" Martha asked, laying a comforting hand on Jessica's arm. Concern that her grand-doggie's condition might have worsened was evident in her tone. "Dr. Girard said she was keeping Harry here a few days just for observation, right?"

Jessica quickly summoned a smile, unaware that her worries had been etched so clearly on her face. "She said he'll be fine." Though Harry's long runs in the country and intensive training days were over because of the limited oxygen flow to his lungs, he was still going to lead a long, spoiled-rotten life as her favorite pet. "I can visit him every day and probably take him home Thursday or Friday."

Martha patted her heart and breathed out a sigh of relief. "Oh, good. You must be worried about Sam, then."

"Ma." Though her instinct was to deny any preoccupation with the tall, dark and distracting agent, her mother was right on the money. Scary. Maybe by the time *she* reached sixty-three, she'd have developed as good an intuition about people.

Having lost a lot of faith in her own ability to judge men, Jessica reluctantly sought out her mother's sage opinion. She glanced at the other side of the van, where her father and brothers were making plans that included hoagies and football, then spoke in a raspy whisper. "Sam doesn't scare easily. But—"

"We can be pretty intimidating en masse like this." Martha admitted, understanding Jessica's concern. "But I think your Irishman can hold his own with us."

"He's not *my* Irishman."

"Wouldn't you like him to be?" Martha leaned in, dropping her volume to a matching hush. "That fabulous voice and yummy body aside, I think he's a solid, dependable kind of guy. There isn't much that's going to ruffle his feathers.''

Though she had to work through the idea of her mother using a phrase like "yummy body," Jessica agreed. "But he's just doing his job, isn't he?" Whether as law enforcement or the hired hand, he'd be a formidable protector. "Do you think there's any kind of like, you know—a relationship?"

Martha pulled back, her eyes wide with a mixture of sorrow and surprise. "You don't see it?"

"See what?"

"The way he stands apart but never takes his eyes off you. Sam has been here all through the night. He's politely staying out of your family's way now because he wants us to focus on you and Harry, not you and him." Martha's smile of approval was usually saved for daughters-in-law and grandchildren. She smiled that way now. "He's still here. There's nothing quite like a man who stands by you when you need him most. It's one of the things I love best about your father."

Though she'd never doubted her parents commitment to each other, it was heartening to still hear the word *love* thrown out after forty years of marriage. This brief discussion was turning out to be as profound as any lengthy heart-to-heart she'd shared with her mother growing up.

Jessica had been crazy with fear and guilt last night, her mind torn by nightmarish glimpses of the past and present. Images almost remembered, fears she'd never forget. But a word, a kiss, a nearly constant touch from Sam had kept her sane and functional and gotten her through it all.

"Ma, this past March…in Chicago…something happened. I…" She felt a desperate urge to tell her mother the whole truth, but she took a moment too long to work up the courage, to rethink the risk she'd be exposing her family to. She could already see the worry in Martha's eyes. She was about to tear up herself. "Sam…he's helping me get through it."

Martha lifted her hands and gently framed her daughter's face. The fun matchmaking had all been cast aside. "Then he's a keeper in my book."

Definitely a keeper. If he wanted to stay on after her attacker was captured. If he wanted to stay with a crazy lady like her. A relationship with her wouldn't be easy. But she wanted to try…she was ready to try.

Jessica covered her mother's hands and smiled. "Ma, you know how much my family means to me. But—"

"You just say the word, and I will clear your father and brothers out of here." Her gaze slid over to the men who had turned to greet Sam, strolling around the side of the building with Brett. "See? All in one piece."

One strong, sexy, rough-around-the-edges piece. Jessica noted the clean shirt tucked into the jeans that were still wrinkled and dirty from last night. She also took note of the sly way his gaze kept darting over to her, even though her cousin Mitch had waylaid him to introduce himself and shake his hand.

While she met, returned and was warmed by the gray-eyed attention, Martha kept talking. "With two break-ins in two nights, I'm not sure I can keep them from making daily checks on you at home. But I can give you some time right now. I'll offer them a big, home-cooked breakfast. Go. Talk to Sam. Say whatever you have to say. *Ask* for whatever it is you want. I think he'll listen. You owe it to yourself if you love him."

Love?

The word felt strange inside her head. It turned over in her heart with a reaction different from anything she'd ever experienced with Alex. The idea of loving Sam frightened her, yet thrilled her at the same time. She hadn't thought she ever would, *could,* fall in love again.

She turned to her mother, knowing her frown expressed all her doubts and confusion. Maybe Martha knew her feelings better than Jessica knew herself. But love? "Ma, I don't think I can—"

"Go." She squeezed her hand and held on when Jessica would have pulled away. "If you ever need to talk about anything, I'm here to listen. *Anything,*" she reiterated with such a knowing look that Jessica wondered if her mother somehow knew the awful way she'd been violated.

"Thanks, Ma. And I will. Soon. I promise."

"Right behind you." Sam's voice alerted her of his presence an instant before she felt his fingers lightly brush against her arm. She didn't flinch. "With Harry in the clear for now, we'd better get back to the cabin and see how much damage the storm did. At the very least, you need a nap. You haven't slept all night." Like he had? "You are closed on Mondays, right?"

"Right." She'd scheduled an appointment with her therapist and had several errands to run. But right now *home* and *nap* and a chance to talk to Sam sounded like the best plan of action.

Jessica hugged her mother, taking her up on her offer to keep her overprotective brothers at bay. "Can you buy me a couple of hours before reinforcements arrive?"

Martha's girlish grin beamed at the challenge. "At least that much."

A woman with a mission now, Martha turned and grasped Sam's hand. "Thank you for all your help with Jessie. I know she's being well taken care of." She stretched up on tiptoe and kissed the dimple beside his mouth. Twin dots of color pinkened the apples of Sam's cheeks above the scruff of his overnight beard. Martha pulled away and winked at Jess. "Call me tonight."

She went on her merry way, an irresistible force that hooked her arm through Sid's and said something that gathered all her boys around her on the sidewalk in front of the truck.

Sam helped Jessica into the truck cab, then circled around to climb in behind the wheel. Once the doors were shut and the engine was running, a heavy sigh buzzed across his lips. "What was that all about? It's been years since I've earned a motherly peck on the cheek."

"She likes you."

"I'm glad somebody does."

So he had been grilled, tested, warned off by her brothers.

Impulsively Jessica slid across the bench seat. She laid her fingers against his stubbly jaw, turned his mouth to hers and kissed him. It was nothing lingering, nothing seductive. But it was confident, caring and completely spontaneous.

"And that was for…?" The question in his narrowed eyes made her smile.

What were her mother's words? "For standing by me when I needed you." Her sensitized palm scraped along his beard as she pulled away. She curled her fingers into her fist to savor the chain reaction of heat that simmered in her bloodstream and curled deep inside her. "I know you could have gone after those men, or looked for clues. But you came to me instead."

"I wanted to be with you."

As an agent protecting his witness? Or a man protecting his woman? Her mother seemed to think it was the latter.

Jessica didn't move back to her side of the truck. Instead, she buckled into the middle seat belt and rested her head on Sam's shoulder.

"Need some body heat?" he teased.

She nodded. But it wasn't just his heat she craved.

Sam reached out but paused, his hand hovering just above her knee. "May I?"

She pushed his hand down, relishing the possessive

brand of his fingers and palm encircling her leg. He dragged her right up against him, holding the length of her jeans-clad thigh against his harder, more muscular one. He dipped his lips against her temple and whispered some ragged words that filled her heart and touched the wounded, feminine part of her soul. "I've wanted to hold you all night."

Jessica wrapped her fingers around his wrist and granted him permission. "I need to be held."

Seven pairs of eyes stared at them through the windshield of the truck. She didn't care.

"Let's go home."

Chapter Eleven

The truck lurched as it hit a rut, jarring Jessica from her dozing state. She lifted her cheek from the pillow of Sam's shoulder and pushed herself upright, combing her hair off her face with her fingers. A passing glance in the rearview mirror revealed a long, deep groove in her face from where she'd lain against the strap of Sam's shoulder holster.

Holster?

Forget dozing. She'd been out. Completely unaware of where she was or what she'd been doing. Just like a mini-bout of amnesia. The comparison wasn't very comforting.

When had Sam strapped on his gun?

They were nearly home. What had she missed?

"Sorry," she apologized. She unbuckled her seat belt and moved to the passenger side where she could hold on to an armrest to balance herself as they pitched and rocked southward along the uneven terrain of Lover's Lane Road. The space between them gave her a chance to think, away from the subtle pull of Sam's protective strength. She'd made herself right at home, snuggling against him. "I didn't mean to take advantage."

The sun played up the shadows beneath his eyes from a night without sleep, but he still managed a smile. "I wasn't complaining."

She gently massaged the mark on her face and looked at the black leather strap of his holster. "Is anything wrong?"

It only required a quick glimpse for him to ascertain what she was really asking. "I intend to have this with me from here on out. I won't take any more chances with this guy. I have mighty big paws to fill when it comes to watching over you." He slowed the truck to steer through a low-lying section of road that had flooded out. "I'm your new official guard dog until Harry comes home."

His words were a mixture of awe and regret at the sacrifice Harry had made, but his tone was all matter-of-fact. Jessica hugged her arms around her waist and slumped against the seat. Her neck was bruised from where her attacker had wrapped something around it. Her body felt like one big ache after her life-or-death struggle.

"You think he'll be back, then?" They both knew she wasn't talking about the dog.

"I know he will." She felt, rather than saw, Sam glance her way to apologize for the cold, hard facts she needed to hear. "He'll be a whole lot trickier next time. He's used the cover of the city to carry out an anonymous attack. Last night he used the storm and a couple of would-be thieves to distract our attention. We won't see him coming. But I'm making damn sure this guy won't be leaving." The truck splashed up out of the water and gathered speed. "I'll be ready for him."

Jessica considered the absolute certainty in Sam's voice. If determination alone could make it happen, then her rapist—his sister's killer—was about to see his anonymous reign of terror come to an end.

And Sam wasn't the only one determined to have this all done and over with. She sat up straight, then reached across the seat to brush a raven curl away from Sam's temple and tuck it behind his ear. Her fingertips strayed into the kinks of midnight silk, bravely linking them in that subtlest of ways. "*We'll* be ready."

Sam tore his gaze from the road and probed her so deeply with those icy eyes that she pulled her hand back into her lap as a subconscious means of defense. "That means I'll be with you 24/7. Are you ready for that? I know you like your space, and whatever's happening between us is probably scaring you as much as it's scaring me. But I won't go away until this is done."

Then he *would* go away? The idea that he'd have no reason to stay after her attacker had been caught played right into all the self-doubts about her womanhood that were still negotiating some shaky ground.

But the logical part of her brain reminded her of that once-in-a-lifetime kiss. The gentle touches and the heated looks. And the idea that—as annoying as they might be—her mother's talents were historically right on the money when it came to predicting future mates for her children. And she thought Sam O'Rourke really cared for her in some way.

It was a frightening prospect.

They crested the hill in front of the Phillipses' farm and were both momentarily distracted by the devastation of last night's storm, leaving a field of ripe corn shredded and pummeled into the ground. "I don't know much about farming—" Sam was shaking his head "—but that can't be good."

The Kent farm on the opposite side of the road was equally hard hit. But with Trudy's inherited wealth and Charles's real estate investments, the damage would be a minor inconvenience. For the Phillipses, on the other hand, it could mean disaster. She'd be sure to offer Derek as many paid hours or as much time off as he needed to help his family.

And though it was easier to focus on someone else's problems for a change, Jessica had never been one to ignore a challenge simply because it was difficult. She'd fought her rapist and last night's attacker. She'd sought out professional counseling to help her deal with her trauma and amnesia. She protected her family from their own good intentions.

And though it *was* scary, she couldn't ignore her feelings for Sam O'Rourke.

"What *is* happening between us?" she asked.

"Not as much as I'd like." His sexy mouth twisted with a wry grimace. "Sorry. True as that is, it's too cutesy an answer." He tapped his fingers, one by one, against the steering wheel, pressing them precisely, purposefully into the gray vinyl, channeling his tension there. "I came here to do a job. To catch a killer. To use you if I had to."

Regret was stamped in every line of his face. He didn't have to apologize for his initial subterfuge, she felt his self-reproach seep into the air surrounding her as he exhaled.

"You expected me to be a star witness and make your case. Instead you met a recluse with no memory of what you need to know."

"I met a beautiful woman who was rightfully scared yet willing to do whatever she had to, to protect herself and the people she loves." His description of her eccentricities sounded like praise. "And you are remembering things. Bit by bit. It'll come."

The brick gates of her property came into view at the bottom of the hill. They drove through the gates before she responded. It was her turn to fill the truck with regret. "It'd be nice if I'd remember it all before he showed up again. That's the scariest part." Her breath shuddered out on a sigh. "I can't see the enemy coming. He could be looking me right in the face, and I wouldn't know it was him."

Sam's fingers stopped their drumming. He reached clear across the seat and squeezed her hand where it rested in her lap. "We'll know."

We. There was such power, such comfort in that teeny, tiny word.

Jessica turned in her seat, easing the stretch of his arm,

massaging his hand between both of hers. For a few moments she studied the light tan of his skin, the sprinkle of black hair along his forearm. She ran her thumb across the rise of each solid knuckle and skimmed the sinewed strength of his long fingers. This was the hand of a craftsman—undeniably strong, softly callused, beautifully shaped—an elegant sculpture of muscle and bone and purpose.

It was a hand that could love a woman—or kill a man—with equal skill.

"Sam?" She stilled her explorations as he pulled the truck up to one of the railroad ties that lined the lot. She clutched his hand tightly and lifted her gaze to his rugged profile. "Last night I know you made a choice to stay with me. And I'm grateful. But, if it comes down to it again, if you have to choose between protecting me or capturing…him—"

"I'll keep you safe. I promise."

"—I want you to get him."

His hand chilled within her grasp. "Jess—"

"Promise me that." She unknowingly started the massage again. Taking strength, giving it. "He's killed five women. He wants to kill me. And a man like that, with all that rage yet clever enough to hide himself behind a mask and bring a condom when he attacks—he'll kill again. My life would be hell, knowing that. Knowing he got away because you stopped to save me."

Sam pulled away long enough to set the gears into park and unbuckle himself. He killed the engine, then turned in his seat. His shoulders swelled beyond the depth of the seat as he leaned closer. Reversing his grip, he consumed both her hands within his grasp. The conflict in his eyes was unmistakable. "I don't want you to get hurt."

"I've *been* hurt." They both knew she was talking about more than the scratches and bruises she'd received last night. His gaze darted back and forth, desperately searching her face for some weakness in her defensive armor so that he could argue his point. He wouldn't find any. "I don't want him to hurt anyone else." Of that she was certain. "Promise me that, Sam. Say it."

The long silence that followed resonated throughout the truck cab and pounded in her ears. Sam pulled away, resting one hand against his thigh and scraping the other across his beard-roughened chin and jaw. He looked at her again. He struggled. She waited. And then a reluctant vow filled his eyes. His words were firm, though some husky emotion tinged the Irish in his voice. "I'll get him. No matter what. I promise."

Relief mixed with a bit of dread as the danger of the request she had made poured through her. Giving her trust to a human ally, seeing an end to this nightmare for the first time shook her with feelings that were as frightening as they were freeing. She blinked back tears as fatigue and emotion threatened to overtake her. Instead of weeping, she acted on an impulse she hadn't felt for far too long.

In a flurry of movement, Jessica unhooked her seat belt and crawled right across the seat. She looped her arms around Sam's neck and hugged him tight. "Thank you." His unshaven cheek brushing against her softer one was an unexpected seduction. His strong arms folding around her and pulling her snug into his lap was pure heaven. "Thank you."

His arms shuddered around her and she felt his lips nuzzle her ear. "I'm not sure you understand what you're asking of me. When I first started this thing—months ago, the night I saw Kerry in the morgue…" Jessica held on tight and rode the ragged rise and fall of his chest. "I wanted him dead. Dammit, babe, I'm a sharpshooter. I could do it. If I knew who he was I could do it. I could say he put up some kind of fight and I could take him out. I wanted him to put up a fight." Now one hand was stroking methodically up and down her leg, from hip to knee and back again, creating a delicious friction between the denim and her skin. "But now…" His hand clutched around her thigh, dragging her impossibly closer. "I hadn't counted on getting…involved."

Jessica leaned back against his arms so she could read the truth in his eyes. "Is that what we are? Involved?"

Sam swept his hands all the way up her back and caught her beneath the fringe of her hair, cupping her jaw between the gentle assurance of his skilled hands. His eyes darkened with flecks of charcoal and slate as he studied her upturned face. "Yeah. I think I am."

His accent wrapped around the hushed words, warming them like a caress that thrilled her heart and nurtured her battered confidence.

"I think I am, too." Sam's gaze lingered on her mouth, triggering a wistful, needy feeling inside Jessica. When he abandoned her mouth to study her eyes, she was left wanting. But his eyes—and something deeper inside—demanded her attention. "What's wrong?"

"That bastard took what was left of my family. I don't want to lose you, too."

Shaking her head, Jessica offered him a serene smile. She understood his anger, his sorrow. "I don't want to be lost," she reassured him. She brushed her fingertips across the point of his chin, setting every sensitive nerve ending abuzz with the masculine rasp of his skin. Then she pressed the pad of her index finger against the fullest arc of his lower lip and gave a gentle tug. "All I'm asking is if it comes down to it—don't let him go."

His lip trembled beneath the stroke of her finger. A shiver of sensation? Or a hint at emotions spinning beyond his control? "He won't get away."

Ask for whatever it is you want. I think he'll listen. Her mother's words replayed themselves inside her head.

Then and there Jessica decided to risk her heart. "Sam. Will you kiss me?"

His eyes grew brighter, the shades of color there sparkled in richer hues. "I'm dying to." His face relaxed with a smile. And then he was moving closer. Ever closer. "If I go too far, too fast—" He finished the sentence by closing his mouth over hers.

It was a gentle mating at first, as sweet and tender and full of restraint as that first kiss had been. There was a poignancy in all his strength and passion being contained in such a soft, reverent kiss. Jessica melted into the connection—feeling safe, growing bold—sliding her fingers around his neck and up into his hair. She clutched up handfuls of the silky stuff and marveled at the wonderful textures and heady scents that made Sam O'Rourke the man he was. The man she wanted.

The man she wanted more of than ever before.

She was consumed with a single thought. *More.* She moaned low in her throat, sighed deeply. She even breathed the word against his lips. "More."

"Yeah, babe." He shifted her in his lap, sliding one hand beneath her bottom, the other behind her back—lifting her up, drawing her hip into his groin. He traced the seam of her lips with his tongue, then pushed his way inside. Jessica tilted her head back and welcomed him.

And suddenly, what was once full of restraint was full of wild, seeking passion.

Jessica's breasts flattened against the wall of Sam's chest. His heat seared the tips and hardened them, igniting a slow, simmering trail of desire that wound its way through her, gathering in a syrupy warmth in parts of her body that hadn't felt—that hadn't wanted to feel—alive and alert and filled with need since that awful night.

Her breath caught and mixed with his, eliciting something like a husky growl in his throat. Her own vocal cords hummed in a feral response.

She touched her tongue to his as he slipped inside her mouth. A tentative stroke here, a bolder taste there. Every venture of her lips or tongue was rewarded with a pluck, a press, a claim. His mouth was warm and supple as he explored her inside, his hands hard and sure as he explored her everywhere else.

"I want to feel your skin." His words were an urgent request along her jaw before his tongue did something wicked to the dent beneath her ear. He followed the cord of sinew down the side of her neck, pushing aside the collar of the shirt she wore with his probing lips. His hands were already beneath the long tails of his oversize shirt, clinging almost painfully to the waistband of her jeans, refusing to go any higher.

"You don't have to always…" She gasped as he nibbled on a sensitive spot at the juncture of her neck and shoulder. For a split second she couldn't think as a shower of fireworks ignited at the spot and shot out through every nerve of her body. She clutched her fingers against the curve of his scalp and forced a rational thought into her head. "You don't have to ask."

"Yes," he took his sweet time at that bundle of nerves, stoking the fire inside her, "I do." He kept talking, his voice little more than a whisper of accent as he retraced his path, then finally dropped delicate, taunting kisses against her lips. "I'm not…like…him. I won't just…take."

"You're not."

She could have argued the differences between an act of sex and an act of violence. She could have pointed out the number of times he'd held himself back, or announced himself before touching her so she wouldn't be startled, much less frightened. She could have reminded him that she was the one who'd asked for this kiss in the first place.

But Jessica recognized a stubborn will, an innate sense of justice, a kind heart that had been pummeled by life. Talking wasn't enough.

She untangled her fingers from the silk of his hair and dodged his distracting mouth while she reached down to the top button of her shirt. The instant she started unhooking buttons, his hands were there to help her. "I want this." She angled her head to look him straight in the eye. "I want you."

An instant later he pushed the shirt off her shoulders, peeled it off her arms and tossed it aside. The mild chill of true autumn air danced across her bare skin, leaving a trail of goose bumps in its wake. But before the cold could take hold of her, Sam's hands were there, with hard palms and callused fingers spanning her back, dragging her up to his chest. A sizzle of raw heat leaped between them before their mouths ever reconnected.

"You're so beautiful," he murmured, praising her with his words and his lips and his hands. "So soft, so perfect. So damn beautiful."

It was a quick, greedy embrace now. Jessica slipped her hands beneath the hem of his shirt and demanded the same liberties for herself. His flanks were hot and smooth as she seared her palms against his skin.

With a core-deep sigh of satisfaction, Sam scooted them both to the center of the truck's bench seat, giving them room to move. Anything they could touch—the ridge of a spine, the nip of a waist, a proud, pert nipple—was fair game to their exploring hands. His fingers slipped beneath the elastic of her bra, tunneled into the fringe of her hair, dipped into her jeans to squeeze her bottom. Her fingers slid across the quaking response of his flat stomach, abraded themselves in the tickle of curly chest hair, dug into the muscle that defined his shoulders.

And all the while their mouths were joined.

Kissing Sam—being kissed by him—was the truest form of seduction Jessica had ever known. Every touch had a purpose, every stroke conveyed a feeling, every gasp whispered her name.

The scents and sounds of their passion filled the cab and reverberated in her senses. Heat and musk and giggles and sighs. Her blood seemed to thicken, slowed by the volcanic heat that consumed her. But her breathing went shallow, thrusting her chest against his and drawing away in a quickening rhythm that mimicked the more intimate urges that had her squirming in his lap.

He slipped his hand between her legs and worked his way along the inside of her thigh, kneading her through her jeans, sending shimmering trails of warmth straight up to the junction at the very heart of her where every ribbon of heat seemed to be flowing.

It was nearly overwhelming and just a tad frightening how easily, how quickly, Sam brought her to this point. But it was all so delicious. So right. It was so damn liberating to feel like a woman again. It was as if she'd been in hibernation, lying dormant for months and months on end. And Sam was the sunshine that awakened her, the hunger that coaxed her out of her cave and back into life again.

"Mmm...Sam. I want— Oh!"

Her breath rushed out in a strangled sigh as he found the crisscrossed seams of denim at the base of her zipper and rubbed the stiff folds of material against her swollen center. She squeezed her legs together around his hand to intensify the pressure as molten desire demanded its release.

"I know, babe." He spread his legs apart and Jessica's rump slid down to the seat between them. Her hip butted against the unmistakable proof of his need for her. "I want it, too."

Her fingers fumbled with the snap of his jeans, but got no further. She clung to his shoulders and hung on as he leaned her back across his arm and opened her body to his questing mouth.

With one hand behind her head, the other at her waist— working open a snap, lowering a zipper—he closed his lips around one distended nipple, moistening the cotton of her bra with his tongue. Then, pushing the cloth aside, he rubbed her with an exquisite torment. The damp tip hardened and beckoned the instant the cool air hit bare skin.

He murmured something low and hot against her before reclaiming the breast. He pulled deeply on her, plunging her closer and closer to the brink of the eruption of heat that was bubbling to the surface inside her. Jessica threw her head back as he kissed the swell of each breast, branding her as his own. He peppered a path of maddening kisses into her cleavage and up along her sternum until he dipped his tongue into the hollow at the base of her throat and kissed her there.

The first kiss at her throat blended into the haze of passion that consumed her. But when she felt the pressure there a second time, her mind exploded with a deceptive clarity that eclipsed all conscious thought.

Can't breathe. Too tight.

"No!"

Suddenly *he* was there. A silver necklace tight around her throat. That horrible pain stretching every joint and tendon beyond its limits. The stale, mothball-scented wool cap pressed close to her nose as vile, filthy things were shouted into her ear.

"Stop it!"

She clawed at the face that was too close. She beat at the arms that were too strong.

"Get off me!"

That damn cat leaped in front of her face and she twisted away from its stifling presence.

"Stop it!"

"Jess!" Viselike hands cinched around her wrists, pinning her flailing arms. "Jess, it's me!" A voice called to her across the distance of nightmare and time. "Dammit, Jess! Open your eyes. It's Sam." *Jess.* Not *bitch.* "I won't hurt you. It's Sam."

Oxygen and sanity returned in one huge gasp for air. "Sam?"

Her back was flat against the seat, her chest wedged beneath his. Her legs were hooked in a scissorslike vise between his, while her jeans had ridden down around her hips in their struggle. Her arms were crossed and pinned above her head.

And those eyes—icy gray impenetrable doors of steel—fixed on her with a force that showed no mercy for the demons that tortured her so. Jessica shrank from the intensity of that gaze, fighting to see the real man instead of the monster.

But those eyes were surrounded by lines of strain and concern. And that deep, Irish voice kept whispering her name, over and over, until she knew who she was. And where she was.

And what she had done.

"Oh…oh, Sam." The instant Sam knew she was back with him, he released her and sat up.

Feeling as frozen and lost and humiliated as she had ever felt in her life, Jessica scrambled backward on her hands and bottom and squished herself into the corner of the truck. The cold metal frame bit into her back, but the softer velour of the door liner didn't offer her any better comfort.

She yanked her jeans up to her waist and snatched up her discarded shirt, clutching it in front of her exposed torso as if it was a shield of armor. The blood pounded in her ears, but she could feel very little of it flowing through her veins.

"I'm sorry." She shoved her hair out of her eyes and hugged herself into a tight little ball. "I'm so sorry."

"Are you all right?" he asked, slowly backing toward his side of the truck. His chest heaved in and out, his nostrils flared as he fought to regain control of his breathing. The scratches along his jaw—four well-defined marks that she had put there—shone like crimson brands across his skin.

Was *she* all right?

"I hurt you. I'm sorry." Instinctively she reached out. But long before she made contact, she retreated into her corner and swiped at the tears that burned her eyes. She felt heat staining her cheeks—mortification blending with rapidly dissipating arousal. "Oh, God, Sam. I was afraid I'd do this. What I want and what I can deliver aren't…" Her gaze fell to the jutting evidence of his erection inside his jeans. "I left you…" She collapsed into a sniffle of tears she angrily wiped away. "I'm so sorry."

"If you apologize one more time—"

"Dammit, Sam. You must think I'm some kind of freak. A tease—"

"I would love to shake some sense into you right now, if I didn't think it'd scare you even more." His voice was harsh, ragged, clipped. But she could see it was frustration, not anger—concern, not disappointment—that fueled his words. He grabbed the steering wheel in his fists and vented his emotions there. "I said if I went too far or too fast that I would stop. I just didn't realize…" His white-knuckled grip relaxed. His eyes narrowed as he scrutinized her shaking reaction. "It wasn't me at all, was it? I did something that reminded you of him."

If nothing else, she needed Sam to believe that *he* hadn't done anything to repulse her—that it was her past, creeping in and snatching her away at the worst possible moment. "My throat. When you put pressure there. You didn't hurt me. But, suddenly I couldn't breathe. I was back…there. Then. I wasn't here with you."

Sam—the man, the protector, her would-be lover— turned his gaze out the far window and swore. When he faced her again, the special agent was reluctantly back in place. "Did you remember anything? Any details that could help us?"

Her yes got swallowed up by a sob and she pressed her fist over her mouth to stem the raw tide of emotions.

"We need to talk about this."

"I know, but I—"

"No buts. We'll talk about this later. When you're ready." He shifted in his seat. "After I've showered."

Her sob turned into a humorless laugh. "A long, cold one? I wasn't being fair to you. I'm sor—"

"Jess!" He reached out and palmed the back of her head. "I'm going to kiss you now."

He leaned toward her as he pulled her from the corner. Her mouth opened on a startled gasp. But Sam bottled it up with a firm, no apologies kiss that reminded her of the passion that was possible between them. Just as quickly as it had happened, he released her and pulled away.

"That's to prove a point. This is not your fault. I'm not angry at you. But I am pissed off at what's been done to you. You're a passionate woman. And a brave one. A few minutes ago you rediscovered that. And I… Hell. I forgot. I went after what I wanted without considering what could happen." He sucked in a huge, steadying breath that absorbed whatever rational energy was left inside the cab of the truck. "I never meant to scare you."

"*You* didn't," she insisted. "*He* did."

But he wasn't ready to accept her forgiveness any more than she was his. And apparently the subject was closed. Just like last night's storm, the tempest passed, leaving a cooler, gentler atmosphere in its wake. "We need to check for storm damage and get some rest. Then we'll talk." Sam stopped her protest before she even got started. "It's your turn to promise me."

She couldn't look into that fierce, wounded gaze and say no. "Later," she answered meekly. Then she put some backbone into it. "I promise."

He seemed satisfied with her answer. "I'll shower up in the apartment. I want you to lock yourself inside the cabin until I'm done. Then we can inspect the grounds together. Understand?"

She nodded. She dabbed her tears with the sleeve of her wadded-up shirt, then shook it out and slipped it back on.

Waiting for her to exit first, Sam climbed out of the truck and followed her up to the cabin. It was the first time she'd ever seen him move without that innate grace he possessed.

But the control was there. As much discomfort as he must be in, he was still cognizant enough to be thinking about her safety. He walked through the cabin first, making sure it was empty. Then he waited on the porch until she'd locked the dead bolt on the interior door behind him.

Once he'd gone, she ran a shower for herself and stepped in, leaning in to let the warm water pelt the crown of her head. Soon, tears were streaming unheeded down her face to be lost in the curtain of water sluicing over her body.

She cried for Harry. She cried for Sam. She cried for his sister, Kerry, and the other women whose deaths he wanted to avenge. She cried for the woman she used to be. The one a man like Sam could have loved.

She cried until the only warmth was the tears themselves.

When the water ran cold, she turned it off, grabbed a towel and headed up to her bedroom to dress. She hated herself for being so weak. During those all-too-brief minutes in Sam's arms, she'd been in heaven. She was normal. Alive. She was in love.

Now she was a quivering mass of indecision, consumed by regret and glimpses of the hell that was finally resurrecting itself in her mind.

Chapter Twelve

Sam kept a watchful eye on Jess as she carried a fresh pitcher of lemonade out to the porch and refilled his glass and that of their guests—a big blond bruiser who knew how to tell a joke, and a compactly-built Hispanic man whose golden eyes seemed to question the strain of Jess's smile as much as Sam did.

Jess's youngest brother, Josh, a Kansas City Police Department detective, and his partner, A. J. Rodriguez, had stopped by with the excuse that they were "in the neighborhood." Jess greeted each man with a hug, laughingly accused them of being liars and promptly put them to work.

Sam had already replaced a few shingles that the storm had torn from the cabin roof. Jess had determined that the green buggy that had bounced off the would-be thieves' truck was totaled. She could salvage some of the parts for resale, but most of it was headed for the junk pile.

But Sam had noted that her smile disappeared the instant Josh and A.J. turned their backs and headed down the gravel drive to pitch in with the cleanup around the storage shed. Sam had an idea they were doing some coplike snooping, as well. And though they treated him friendly enough, he could tell that thieves and vandals weren't the only thing Josh Taylor was here to check.

A while later Jess's smile was firmly back in place as

she served them all lunch, though she barely touched her own. Josh was as verbal as A.J. was quiet, but the two carried on a lively conversation that only occasionally demanded a response from either Jess or Sam.

Yes, they'd reported the truck with the bullet hole to Sheriff Hancock. A.J. promised to run the description on the K.C. Metro wire as well, in case their vandals were city boys. No, she didn't need any brothers setting up a twenty-four-hour surveillance of her property, though Sam admitted he'd appreciate an extra pair of eyes to watch things that night so he could get some much-needed rest.

And as hard as he stared at Jess, as strongly as he telepathically urged her to share the truth with her family and friends, she made absolutely no mention about her own attack. As far as the Taylors knew, they were on guard against a band of thieves and vandals.

And a handyman from the FBI with designs on their sister.

Sam no longer hid the fact he worked for the Bureau, though he respected Jess's wishes and made no mention of his real reason for being there. He wore his gun and carried his badge despite the chafing of his holster across his shoulders from chopping up fallen limbs and carting the pieces to the stack of firewood. If the Taylors wanted to relegate him to an off-duty agent earning some extra money as a security guard, let them. He fully intended to uphold his promise to *get* the man who'd attacked Jess. With or without their cooperation.

Whatever happened after that would be up to her.

"We'd better be reporting in, amigo." A.J. held up his watch as a signal to Josh.

Josh downed the last of his lemonade and stood. "You'd think having Cousin Mitch for a precinct captain would make it easier to get away with taking a long lunch, not the other way around."

Jess rose from her chair and helped him slide his leather jacket on over his shoulders. She was smiling again. But the effort it required looked almost painful. "You know how Mitch is. He runs a tight ship. We count on him to be tough. That's why we love him so much."

"You sure he's not pickin' on me?" Josh turned and twisted up his face in a mock show of intimidation.

Though he stood a head taller than she, Jess playfully punched him in the shoulder. "No, but I will if you get in trouble for being late." She glanced around his shoulder to include A.J. in her teasing. "You know, detective, you've got to keep this boy in line."

"I don't do miracles." A.J.'s laconic humor earned a laugh. He tipped the bill of the ball cap he wore with a flourish of Old World panache. "Good to see you again, Jessie. C'mon, hotshot." A.J. pointed a commanding finger at his partner, then headed for the low-slung black car they'd arrived in.

Josh swung his arms wide and shrugged as if he didn't have a clue. "See? Everybody at the Fourth gives me grief." When his arms came down, he wrapped them around Jess and hugged her tight. "One of us will be out here tonight," he promised, his outrageous charm temporarily on hold. "You won't even know we're here. So you get some sleep."

Jess kissed his cheek before he pulled away. "I'll try."

"Love ya." He winked.

"You, too. Give my best to Rachel and Anne-Marie." Josh's wife and baby girl, he'd learned from earlier in the conversation. Just mentioning them brought on a beaming smile.

"Always. Sam?" He turned to shake Sam's hand. His smile belied his firm grip. "There's something going on with you I just can't figure out. I mean, what's a Boston boy doing all the way out here?"

''Josh.'' Jess's reprimand fell on deaf ears.

He released Sam's hand but leaned in half a step. His blue eyes narrowed; he was still trying to solve the puzzle. ''Unless you're trying to woo this lady. Maybe you met her on one of her trips, and now you're making a dramatic, romantic trip to—''

''Joshua Taylor.''

This time, big sister's reprimand shut him up. He thumbed over his shoulder at Jess. ''I warn you, she's stubborn.''

Sam couldn't resist the obvious. ''You think?''

When Josh laughed at the shared joke, Sam had the fleeting notion that he could like this man. He considered how, under other, less threatening cirumstances, his respect for the Taylor men might have evolved into bonds of friendship.

But these weren't other circumstances. As far as they knew, he could be as big a danger to Jess as the unknown enemy he was trying to protect her from. The situation wasn't exactly conducive to long-term family harmony.

''Take care of her,'' Josh reminded him needlessly.

''I will.''

Sam trailed Josh down the steps and stood watch over the two departing detectives while Jess began to clear the table. But as soon as the black Trans Am had driven out of sight, she sank into the nearest chair and dropped her face into her hands. Exhaustion, that had to be emotional as much as physical, radiated from every curve of her posture.

''Jess?'' Torn by her pain, Sam jumped the steps onto the porch, kneeling beside her and reaching out to scoop her into his arms before reason could kick in. ''I'm going to…''

But reason did hit. Hard. He curled his hands into fists and let them fall to his sides. Any effort to comfort her might do more harm than good at this point. The last time he'd touched her, he'd lost control of his desires and triggered a flashback.

Some comfort.

He blew out a steadying breath, refusing to let either his emotions or his hormones make another mistake. "Are you okay?"

He tried to mimic one of Josh's nonchalant laughs but failed. This was too much, too serious to be healed by laughter. Instead, he forced himself to think like a special agent charged with protecting a witness. He braced one hand on the back of her chair and the other on his knee, hovering close, but not touching her.

Her blue eyes were dull with fatigue when she met his seeking gaze. "Sometimes I think I'll never be okay."

"You should tell your family what you're going through, let them share your burden. It's too much to handle on your own."

But she was already shaking her head. "I tried this morning with Ma. But I can't. I'm so afraid one of them or all of them would make this their personal quest. They'd set their careers aside, their family and friends, just to help their sister."

"Like I did?"

He could read the shock, the comprehension, the apology on her stricken features. But he wouldn't let her say the words, he wouldn't let her absorb any more misplaced guilt. "I didn't—"

"Josh was right." Sam gentled his voice to a soothing pitch. "You need to sleep. Why don't you go in and lie down for a nap. Sleep through the night if you can. I'll finish cleaning up out here."

She shoved a shock of her chestnut hair behind her ear, refusing to be helped. "I promised to tell you what I remember."

"It can wait." He stood, allowing himself to take her hand and pull her to her feet. But he held on only long enough to steady her, then he quickly moved to the door and held it open for her. "I want you rested. You'll be able to think clearly. You'll want to feel strong to handle the questions I have to ask."

Jess nodded, wrapping her arms about her waist in that habitual, heartbreaking hug that made it appear as if she could find no other solace. She paused in the doorway beside him. "You've been up as long as I have. You need to sleep, too."

Sam waved aside her concern. "As soon as I know one of your brothers is out here on patrol, I'll come in and sack out on the couch. We'll talk in the morning."

Her gaze fell to his mouth and lingered as if she saw something there that caught her eye. She studied his mouth long enough that Sam could feel the answering heat rushing to that spot—preparing, reaching out, wanting to taste the same heat from her lips. But then she blinked and turned to the open door, dousing the sudden fire. "Until morning, then."

Sam rooted his feet to the planked porch and watched her walk away. Kissing her was out of the question. Holding her was taboo. Falling in love with her wasn't an option, either.

Jess needed a genteel, patient man to love her, to be a passionless companion who could help her heal. She didn't need a greedy son of a bitch like him who saw her as a smart, sexy, desirable woman. A man whose body and soul still ached for her in ways a long, cold shower could never fix.

When the door closed softly in his face, he took that as a sign. The irony of his punishment was complete. He'd come here a few long days ago with the devious intention of using her to get what he wanted.

He finally understood that vengeance wasn't what he wanted, after all.

He wanted love. He wanted a family again.

He wanted Jessica Taylor.

JESSICA HAD FALLEN INTO BED wearing her T-shirt and panties. Despite the maelstrom of emotions inside her, exhaustion had claimed her for a couple of hours of deep, dreamless sleep.

So she was a little disoriented when the phone rang beside her bed, startling her awake. The clock read almost 5:00 p.m., but she hadn't turned on any lights upstairs and it seemed much later. Her face felt hot as she pressed her palms against her cheeks and pushed the tousled mop of her hair back off her face.

The phone was ringing a fourth time when the downstairs door flew open and Sam stomped inside in a hurry to answer it. Jessica leaped to her feet and dashed to the log railing of her loft. He'd been working outside and she hadn't even been able to do this to help him. She was embarrassed to be such a basket case and call herself a Taylor.

She shouted down into the cabin below. "I've got it up here, Sam."

"I didn't want to wake you. You were sleeping so soundly." He popped out of the dining room and stood below the railing, looking up at her like a modern-day Romeo with his shaggy black hair and that navy bandanna tied on top. His gaze raked over her body with such heat that she looked down to verify that everything was decently covered.

In this rumpled look, she was certainly no Juliet. But Sam's pinpoint attention didn't seem to care. The answering machine was picking up now. "I have a business to run. I'll get it."

She ran back to her cordless phone, pushed the button to turn off the answering machine's message and picked up the receiver. "Log Cabin Antiques. Jessica speaking." She cringed at the breathless quality of her voice, due as much to the man standing in her living room as to her dashing back and forth.

Fortunately, a friend answered. "Jessica? Charles Kent. I wasn't sure you were home."

"Uh, no. I was just busy. Sorry I didn't catch the phone sooner." She crossed to the railing and waved Sam toward the door, trying to tell him there was nothing to worry about. He didn't budge, making good on his promise to be her temporary replacement guard dog. Jessica turned her back and leaned her hip against the pine-log railing that lined the edge of the loft, giving herself the sham of privacy in the open cabin. "What can I do for you?"

"Two things." She could count on Charles to get down to business. "First, I'm appalled at this sudden influx of crime in our little hamlet. Sheriff Hancock was here this morning, asking about one of the locals I'd hired to do some work on my arboretum. He said your place had been broken into. Are you all right?"

"I'm fine. Vandals damaged some of my merchandise, but thanks to Sam nothing was stolen. Insurance will cover everything." She didn't want her troubles to become neighborhood gossip, but something Charles had said caught her attention. "You said the sheriff was there? Who was he asking about?"

"The younger Phillips boy."

"Derek?"

Charles ignored her surprise and continued. "Hancock said there was something suspicious about his truck. Asked him to account for his whereabouts the past few days. If he's going to be trouble, I'll have to fire him."

"Derek's a good kid." Or so she'd thought. Jessica

sprang to attention as disjointed facts tried to come together and make sense. She whirled around and found Sam looking straight at her, as if he sensed something important about to happen, too. "He's at football practice every evening until six, then he goes home and does chores on his parents' farm. He worked here Sunday afternoon. When does he have time to work for you?"

"Well, Saturday he was here at the house—transplanted some trees for me. I've had him and a few other young men here on and off through the past few weeks. I think his father has had a run of poor crop yields. Mr. Phillips even approached me about selling off a few acres. Could be they're hurting for money."

"I had no idea things had gotten that bad for them." Her concern for the Phillipses' plight quickly changed to suspicion. Derek would know where her storage shed was located. He'd know the most valuable items to destroy if he wanted to inflict some damage or make a point. But *Die Bitch?*

"Jessica?"

She pulled her attention back to the conversation. She needed to end it quickly and share the information with Sam. "I'm sorry. You said there were two things?"

Charles cleared his throat. His businesslike tone perked up with an uncharacteristic energy. "As you know, my arboretum has a seating area—for guests to relax or to study the flora."

"Yes?" She remembered the patiolike area, paved in a mosaic of terra-cotta tiles.

"I've gotten a lead on some wicker furniture from the 1940s. Postwar pizzazz style, if you will. It's at an estate sale tomorrow over in Mission Hills."

She shook her head, not understanding what he was asking of her. "Sounds perfect."

"The executor called to see if I could come over tonight to preview it, to make sure it's what I want."

"I'd go for it, then." Mission Hills was one of the wealthiest neighborhoods in the Kansas City area. "The stuff should be awfully nice. And if they're giving you a break before anyone else snatches it up—"

"Would you come with me?" he asked. "I could use your expertise to appraise and inspect the furniture. Advise me on its condition and whether or not they're asking a fair price. You know I want only the best. But I won't be robbed."

"Tonight?"

"I realize it's short notice. I just got the call myself. I'll pay you for your time as a consultant, of course. Maybe you'd allow me to take you to dinner afterward. Someplace on the Plaza."

Now his business proposition was starting to sound like a date. She'd gotten that same vibe from him before. But Charles was a friend. Charles was boring. Charles wasn't Sam. And if she couldn't make a relationship work with the man she wanted to be with, then... She shrugged. "I'm not sure—"

Sam was shaking his head and mouthing the word no. Then he pressed his hands together and rested his cheek against them. *Sleep,* he mouthed this time before pointing at her.

She supposed his adamant refusal was more about her health and safety than jealousy of any kind. Still, she was glad for the rescue. "I can't tonight, Charles. I'm exhausted from being up all night at the vet's."

"With your dog?" Charles sounded more perturbed than disppointed. He probably didn't appreciate a canine altering his plans. She suspected courtesy, more than real concern, made him ask, "Is something wrong with him?"

"He got hurt last night." She almost added that he'd

been hurt saving her life. Instead, she gave a more vague explanation. "He was guarding the place."

"I see." A renewed brisk tone changed the subject. "What about tomorrow, then? I could call and ask them to hold the pieces until you inspect them."

She was out of excuses. She'd be rested by then. Charles *was* a friend. And appraising antiques was part of her job. "Tomorrow sounds fine."

"Excellent. You could come to the house for lunch. And then we'll drive into the city together."

"I'll be there. Bye."

When she disconnected the call, Sam was still there, his icy eyes looking up and demanding answers. "Well?"

"Charles Kent has a consulting job for me. I'm going to his house tomorrow around noon. He was a little testy that I wouldn't go with him tonight."

"Is that right?" He seemed more interested in her suspicions about Derek Phillips. "What else?"

"Just a sec." There was no need to continue this *Romeo and Juliet* charade. She hung up the phone and pulled on her jeans. She eyed her bra folded up on top of her dresser, but opted for speed over modesty. Leaving the big shirt untucked, she hurried, barefoot, down the wooden stairs.

Sam was waiting for her at the bottom. The wary tension from his body radiated at full alert. "Something about Derek Phillips?"

Jessica nodded and moved past him into the wider space of the living room. "Charles said Sheriff Hancock asked him about Derek's whereabouts. I guess Derek's been moonlighting at the Kent place." She spun around to face Sam, leaving the width of the coffee table between them. "The taillight you shot out last night? It sounds like it's on Derek's truck. He and a friend might be our vandals."

She didn't know whether to be disppointed that her

young neighbor was a suspect, or excited that they were finally making progress on the investigation.

Sam, however, wasn't showing any emotion. "The kid has a crush on you, yet you treat him like a brother. Maybe Derek wanted to take what you wouldn't give him. Or punish you for not noticing him as a man." He hinted at a horrible possibility. "He said his football team travels to other states."

Jessica crossed her arms around her waist to ward off the instant chill. "To Chicago, maybe. But not to Boston or anywhere else those women were killed."

"He's a big kid. He could overpower you easily enough. But I'm open to possibilities if you have other ideas."

This was way too unsettling. She desperately wanted to seek out the comfort of Sam's arms, but she wasn't sure she'd be welcomed after this morning's fiascolike version of making love. Besides, he was all agent right now, and the caring man who'd reawakened her as a woman was buried somewhere deep inside.

"If Derek was involved with the vandalism, more than likely someone paid him to do it," she reasoned. "Charles said his family needs the money. But I don't think he'd rape me." The very possibility sickened her.

"You said you wanted me to get this guy. To do that I need facts, not your compassionate opinion. If Derek *is* one of our vandals who painted that message, then he has to know something about the man who told him to do it." There was something cold and absolutely lethal in Sam's eyes right now. Unwittingly, her gaze strayed to the black steel gun that hung below his left arm. The two shared uncomfortably similar characteristics. "I think I'll pay him a visit."

"Not tonight, Sam." Would he take that gun and use it on Derek if he thought the teenager was in any way responsible for hurting her or his sister? Would his legendary control extend so far as to give a young man the benefit of the doubt? She suspected Derek wasn't guilty of anything more than extremely poor judgment in how he raised extra funds. But the grim lines of fatigue around Sam's eyes had her worried. ''Tonight is all about recovering, you said. I need you to stay here with me. Please.''

His head jerked as if her request had taken him aback. His pale eyes flooded with color. But then he blinked, and just as quickly the show of emotion had passed. ''All right. Tomorrow, then. I'll drive you to the Kent place myself, and then track down Derek to ask some questions. .

''Tonight it's just you and me.''

She didn't know whether to be thrilled or frightened by the prospect.

SAM REPLAYED Jess's soft words over and over again in his head. *I need you to stay here with me. Please.*

His heart heard them as an invitation—words of forgiveness that welcomed him. But his mind had wised up quickly enough. He might not possess the gentle finesse Jess needed in order to love, but he did possess the experience and skills she needed to live.

Night had fallen hours ago, but the floor lamp at the end of the sofa was the only light he'd left on in the house— partly out of respect for Jess's attempt to sleep after a silent dinner of Martha Taylor's lasagne, and partly because the shadows seemed to fit his own dark mood.

He'd tossed off his shirt and his boots and socks after Jess said good-night and went upstairs. His gun was beneath the pillow, and his jeans were unsnapped. Josh Taylor sat in an unmarked police car at the end of Jess's driveway. Sam's bones were weary, his muscles sore. He should be sound asleep.

But something unsettled inside wouldn't let him.

He sat at the edge of the circle of lamplight, studying

the tiny piece of silver he'd picked up at the scene of Harry's stabbing. He fingered the tiny mechanism in the palm of his hand. It was the clasp of a necklace, similar to one he'd seen on his mother's jewelry long ago. The clasp of a silver necklace not unlike the one Jess had seen at that auction, which had triggered the first of the flashbacks he'd witnessed.

He considered the long, thin scar that cut across the fingers on Jess's left hand. He didn't need forensic proof to make an educated guess that she'd been strangled with a necklace, or that the scars were evidence of her struggle to save herself.

But how could he turn that knowledge and this clue into something useful?

Jess moaned in her sleep. Her mattress creaked as she tossed in her bed in the loft above him. Sam tilted his head and peered into the darkness. His body practically hummed with the need to go to her, to chase away her nightmares. But a man at her bedside in the dark of night?

He huffed a humorless laugh between his lips and stayed put. He'd already frightened her badly enough in the bright light of day.

The one thing he could give her without fail—the one thing she'd made him promise—was to get the man who'd hurt her. With a willpower that shriveled his soul into dust, he tuned out her whimpers and concentrated on what he knew thus far.

A call to the sheriff had verified that the truck Sam had shot belonged to Derek Phillips. With little encouragement from Sheriff Hancock, Derek had confessed that he and a teammate had broken into Jess's shed and tried to steal the buggy. Someone had left $200 and an anonymous note in the truck, daring them to steal the buggy. The note said that everything would be taken care of with Jess, that they were actually helping her reconnect with an old friend by taking it. Another $500 would be theirs when they delivered the buggy to an untilled field north of Derek's home. A phone call had prompted them to try a second time.

But paint that sick message for Jess? No way, the kid swore. The destruction inside the shed had already been done by the time he broke in.

Sam was inclined to believe that story. It made Derek the perfect fall guy for someone with bigger, more sinister plans for Jess. Who? Could Derek provide a name? A voice? A number? Sheriff Hancock didn't know to ask those questions. He was looking for a vandal, not a murderer.

"No! Stop it." Sam jerked his head up to the loft. Jess's cry, pure and anguished, cut straight through him.

This time he got up and crossed to the base of the stairs, following the needs of his heart and conscience. He wrapped his fingers around the pine log that served as a newel post and looked up toward the sound. "C'mon, babe," he whispered to the darkness. "It'll be all right. He isn't here. You're safe."

He squeezed his eyes shut. If a man could wish a thing and make it so, he wished her peaceful, dreamless slumber. He wished her strength and self-assurance. He wished her love.

Amazingly enough, her struggles quieted. It wasn't until he opened his eyes and turned away that he heard the soft rustle of sound above him.

"Sam?" Jess stood at the top of the stairs, her shape barely discernible with the drape of the quilt she hugged around her shoulders. As she descended toward him, the farthest reaches of the lamplight illuminated the russet streaks in her dark, sleep-tossed hair, which framed her face in a come-touch-me disarray. When she paused on the step above him, he could see the translucent pallor of her skin as well as the doubts and determination in her eyes. "Let's

talk now." Her voice was a soft caress befitting the quiet
shadows surrounding them. "It's all coming back to me
and I can't sleep. I don't want to face it alone."

He wanted to reach for her, but he didn't. He merely
linked their gazes and promised, "You're not alone."

Her game smile of gratitude flipped over the resolve that
had hardened inside him, leaving him feeling in vulnerable
danger himself. He stepped aside, then followed her to the
sofa.

She stopped at the edge of the coffee table and took note
of the badge and notepad lying on top. She glanced at the
unused pillow and neatly folded blanket on the rug. Her
gaze skittered across the dimensions of his naked chest with
something that might be hunger or fear. "Looks like you
haven't slept well, either."

"I'm all right. Do you want me to put on a shirt?"

"No. It's a beautiful..." She tore her gaze away. "Don't
change for me."

Sam tried not to read too much into the half-spoken compliment, still it felt as if she'd just made some sort of con-
cession. They both continued to whisper, as if a raised
voice might shatter the tenuous truce between them. "We'll
do this however you like."

She nodded. "I'll sit, then." In the dim light he could
see the determined set of her jaw, the tight clutch on the
quilt. She looked down at the sofa beside her. "You, too."

Sam lowered himself to the couch, keeping the width of
a seat cushion between them. He didn't realize he'd been
bracing himself for this conversation until he heard his own
breath seep out in a pent-up sigh. "Do you want me to ask
questions? Or let you talk first?"

When she didn't answer, he held out the silver clasp. "I
found this in the woods where you were attacked. Do you
recognize it?"

Jess recoiled as if she'd been struck, and Sam was ready

to end the conversation right now. But fear and shock weren't going to stop this brave lady. Unfolding one arm from the quilt, she picked up the silver in his palm. "It's from the necklace I was wearing that night in Chicago." She turned it to the light and studied it more closely. "A silver chain with an amethyst pendant. Alex bought it for me on a trip we took to Dallas last year." She pushed it back into his hand, eager to be rid of the macabre souvenir. "He…strangled me with it. I guess he kept it until he had an opportunity to finish the job."

She stared blankly at Sam's hand until he tucked the clasp away in a pocket. "If he's smart, he'd take anything that might leave fingerprints. And our guy's smart."

Jess shook her head. "He wore black leather gloves. Last night, too. Even when he was—" Sam caught his breath along with her. But she pushed through the unpleasant memory. "Even when he was naked, he wore gloves and that damn, stinky stocking mask that hid his face. He smelled of mothballs. All his clothes reeked of it."

"So it wasn't his regular outfit," Sam reasoned. "Our man dresses up, so to speak, for his outings. That shows premeditation."

Jess perked up at that. She turned in her seat to face him. "Yes. He was waiting for me at the museum—driving a cab. He pulled right up to the curb so I didn't have to flag one down. I thought he was just looking for an easy fare." Without thinking, she reached for his hand on the seat between them. The quilt fell from her shoulder as she linked her fingers to his. Sam held on tight, needing the contact as much as she seemed to. "When I complained about him going the wrong way, when I demanded that he stop and let me out, he pulled a knife on me."

Sam's fingers clutched convulsively around hers. "Can you describe the knife?"

"It folded up. But it was bigger than a pocketknife. It

had a hunting blade, you know, the kind that curves down to a point at the tip?'' She freed her other hand and gestured in the air. The quilt pooled around her hips.

Sam couldn't help but notice the strong curve of her shoulders beneath the man's T-shirt she wore. He couldn't help but wish the T-shirt she wore was his. *Irrelevant,* he warned himself. *Focus.* "I know the kind you mean."

"It had a fancy handle. Some kind of polished wood. And it had silver trim."

He dared to take her hand between both of his. She didn't flinch or pull away. "So that's how he got you to that dive neighborhood. All his victims have been successful professional women who wouldn't have any reason to be in a place like that. That and his *outfit* tell me he's planned his attacks almost obsessively. Probably to throw off authorities."

"Or to degrade us." Jess's visible shiver shook through him. "It's all about putting women down for this guy. The things he said. The things he wanted me to say." She curled her legs beneath her, folding her long body into a tight, protected ball. "*Master.* He wanted me to beg. To apologize." Sam swore at that one, an instinct he instantly regretted when wide, terrified eyes locked on his. "He said he wanted to prove that he was superior to any *blank*-ing woman. And that I was damn lucky he'd chosen me so—" her voice stopped on a stuttered breath and the first hint of a tear glistened in her eye "—so I could learn that lesson."

Rage more profound than he'd felt that night in the morgue with Kerry's body, battered Sam from the inside out. He exhaled deep, ragged breaths, trying to purge the anger. He'd known this would be hard to listen to, to hear the horrendous things that had been done to Jess. But he kept his head, knowing however difficult this might be for him, it was nothing compared to what Jess was going through.

Sam wanted to do more than hold her hand. He needed more comfort for his own raw soul than what that platonic touch could provide. But he couldn't ask and he wouldn't take. With the pad of his thumb he wiped away the tear that spilled onto her cheek. The tiny drop was hot to the touch, but her skin was cool. Chilled, even.

Damn, he wanted to hold her.

"I'm sorry, babe." It was killing him to see her hurting like this. "I'm so sorry."

It was the only tear to fall. She shook her head slowly, back and forth, stirring up the spice and ginger scent of her hair. "I need to finish this while I still can. I…" She pulled his hand from her cheek. "Could I sit closer?"

"I don't want to frighten you in any way. I don't want to trigger a flashback. Especially when you're talking about this."

She sat still for an interminable minute, considering his worry. When she finally spoke, she scooted across the sofa. "Just put your arm around me, and we'll see what happens from there. If I feel anything, I'll try to let you know. Before I hurt you or embarrass you."

Sam looped an arm around her shoulders and pulled her to his side. "Jeez, baby, no. Never that." She hugged the quilt and took his free hand into her lap, then leaned her head against his shoulder. His anger at the injustice done her eased, though his fears of hurting her kept him on edge. "Holding you is the best therapy I've ever tried. It's the only thing that's given me hope since Kerry died. Don't ever apologize for that."

The darkness of the night and the stillness of the cabin cocooned them in their own little haven. Sam dipped his nose into the spicy silk of her hair and absorbed the gentle warmth of her body snuggled against his. For several minutes they did nothing but sit together like that. It was a chance to find some peace before the rest of the nightmare arrived.

Jess started playing with his hand, absently rubbing her thumb back and forth across his knuckles. He knew she was sorting through her newfound memories. He held his tongue and listened as she began to recount the details of her attack.

"I was on the bed. It was a horrible place. Filthy. Scratchy." She shivered and he began drawing slow, smooth circles along her arm. "He…I was tied to the bedposts." Now Sam's skin crawled as he worked through the images she shared. "I'm sorry. I know this is hard to hear."

"Dammit, Jess, don't be sorry. Tell me anything—everything—you remember."

She squeezed her eyes shut and huddled closer. "He's a white man. Tall. He tied me…each ankle and wrist, but my left hand…" He watched her fingers mimic the actions she described. "He'd used his belt. I worked it free while he was yelling…calling me names…" She swallowed hard. "He got up to put on a condom—more planning, I suppose. He didn't notice my hand just lying there, unbound. Because then he was…on top of me…"

"Oh, babe." He kissed the crown of her hair. "You don't have to say it."

She turned and wrapped her arms around his waist, pressing her cheek against his heart. He curled both arms around her now, pulling her as close as he dared. "When he was done, he started to tighten my necklace around my throat." Her fingers automatically went to her neck, reliving the horror. "I caught my free hand there. He pulled so hard. He cut…"

Sam pulled her hand away and spread it flat beneath his against his chest. "That's how you got the scar on your fingers."

"I passed out. He must have thought I was dead. When

I came to he was gone. I was covered up and positioned as if I was in a coffin. He'd taken all my things—my clothes, my purse, my necklace—''

"A lock of your hair." He sifted his fingers through the short, wavy locks that had probably been layered like this to camouflage the shorn tendril.

"And I remember a cat. Right in my face."

"Are you sure it was a live cat? Maybe it's a dissociative memory. Someone's name or something he said? Was there fur on his coat? Maybe it describes his eyes."

"That's the only thing that isn't clear." Her body jerked in frustration. "Something about a damn cat."

"That's okay. Don't force it."

Jess trembled and sagged against him. "I don't want to do this anymore."

"It's okay." He had a general description to put on the wire now—tall, white male. He had a knife to look for. A souvenir necklace. He had the smell of mothballs, a black stocking cap, and a suspect with an insane need to prove his manhood by denigrating and murdering strong women. It was a lot of information compared to what he'd known back in Boston.

And he owed it all to the brave woman at his side.

For the first time that night, Sam yawned. With that much of a barrier broken, fatigue finally grabbed the foothold it needed to rush in.

Jess had been so quiet for so long that he thought she might have dozed off. He nudged her gently. "Do you want to go back to bed now?"

She blinked clear eyes at him. She hadn't been sleeping, after all. "Not really."

She hadn't moved away yet. "Do you want me to keep holding you?"

"God, yes." A frown creased her forehead. "Do you mind?"

He answered by falling back into the pillow he'd propped against the arm of the couch, pulling Jess with him so that she was draped on top of him. There was no startled reaction as he stretched himself out on the cushions beneath her, no hesitation as he covered her with the quilt and tucked her soft curves against the harder planes and angles of his body.

Within minutes she was sound asleep. Her breath teased his skin as she snored softly against his neck. Her heart beat a gentle tattoo against his. Sam watched over her, his blissful contentment at having Jess so close, so trusting, marred by vile images of what some beast had done to her, and the equally violent images of what he intended to do to the bastard once he got him in his sights.

Chapter Thirteen

Charles Kent's arboretum really was a beautiful place, Jessica thought. The clear roof with its individual panes of antiqued glass reminded her of crystal palaces of ages past. Exotic tropical scents, summerlike warmth, soothing greens and grays with surprises of bright red and yellow made this addition to the mansion a serene, rejuvenating escape.

Charles needed a quiet place to escape, judging by the raised voices out in the main hall.

"Mother! You have servants to answer your beck and call, not me." Jessica had politely stayed put when Trudy Kent had asked to borrow her son for a minute. The minute had stretched to five. "I'm meeting with Mayor Benjamin tomorrow. That will be soon enough. I won't change my plans to join his golf game this afternoon."

Trudy's voice was equally sharp. "Timing is everything in business. I thought I taught you that. If Fergus Industries makes their pitch tonight at dinner, then tomorrow will be too late for us."

There was a beat of silence. Jessica found herself turning her head, waiting in anticipation for the next exchange. "No." Charles's voice had returned to its softly articulate level. "I have plans with Jessica this afternoon. She's already here, and it would be rude to change them."

Oh, Lord. The last thing she needed today was to be

somebody's scapegoat. She'd awakened feeling hopeful for a change. She'd finally remembered her life, even the worst part of it. She'd expected to feel raw and dysfunctional this morning, but she'd slept amazingly well, cocooned in the haven of Sam's arms. She didn't want someone else's family tiff to spoil the illusory confidence she felt.

Maybe she'd exorcised the demons that haunted her dreams by sharing her ordeal with him. It hadn't been easy to finally relive that horrible night, but she'd gotten through it because Sam was there, offering whatever she'd asked for. God, he had a big heart. And patience she never would have expected from a driven man like him.

Sam seemed to think she'd actually been helpful, that their professional relationship was a success. He would report the details she'd given him to his partner, Virgil, to feed into the FBI's criminal database. After dropping her off here, he'd gone to talk to Sheriff Hancock about setting up an interview with Derek Phillips. They were going to piece this together, he'd promised. And she believed him. He'd get her attacker.

And then maybe she could persuade him to use that patience and heart to give her another chance to develop a more personal relationship with him.

"You'd think those damn trees were more important than the future of our community." Trudy's cultured voice had taken on an unladylike sneer. "Your father was the same way. Frittering away my money on things that were inconsequential. I thought you were stronger than that. I raised you to know your duty."

Jessica drifted toward the archway that led into the main hall. Maybe she should just bow out of this buying expedition gracefully, and let Charles and Trudy make peace with each other. Sam had given her his cell number and told her to call as soon as she was ready to be picked up.

She didn't doubt that even if she called early, he'd drop whatever he was doing and come for her.

Her cousin Mitch was taking a long lunch himself today to keep a protective eye on her, and was parked down the road out of sight. It'd be a long walk or a short phone call to catch a ride with him, too.

That was the ticket. She'd make a polite excuse, then head outside and call Mitch. She hurried her steps toward the front door.

"This conversation is over, Mother." Charles's voice was closer now. She heard clipped footsteps on the marbled foyer.

"Charles Kensington Kent." Three names. In any class, that was a mother's warning. Time to leave before the fireworks really started.

Jessica pasted a smile on her mouth and rounded the corner into the hall. And plowed into Charles. She tacked an apology onto her startled yelp. "Sorry."

But Charles's hands closed around her elbows to steady her. "My fault," he grinned. "I apologize."

Her hands had braced against the finely cut tweed of his suit coat, and for a fleeting instant the discovery blipped through her mind that her gentlemanly, pale-skinned neighbor had been working out. Unexpected. Odd.

Jessica quickly pulled away, straightening the sleeves of her brown leather blazer, breathing slowly in and out to get past the notion that boring Charles had pecs. Maybe that redhead he'd been so attentive to at the party wasn't interested in him only for his money. "Look, if this isn't a good time for you, I'd be happy to come back tomorrow."

He frowned as if she'd spoken gibberish. "But the sale is today."

"Yes, but," she looked beyond his shoulder to Trudy's stern, matriarchal countenance, "if you have other business? I could go to the sale by myself and report back to you.''

"You see, Charles?'' Trudy needlessly patted her silver hair into place. "Jessica understands the concepts of good business.''

Charles turned to his mother. "As do I.'' He gripped Jessica by the elbow and escorted her to the front door. "That's why I asked the expert to evaluate the goods before I purchase them. Goodbye, Mother.'' Despite their quarrel, he paused to lean down and kiss his mother's cheek. "I'll be home for dinner.''

Once Charles had seated Jessica in the passenger seat of his white Range Rover and pulled out onto the gravel road, he reached inside his suit coat and pulled out his wallet. Handing it to her, he said, "Check inside, if you would. There's a business card with directions to the estate sale on it. Would you get it out?''

"Sure.'' He pulled on his driving gloves while she thumbed through a sheaf of credit cards and photographs. She stopped at the picture of a beautiful young woman. Her Mona Lisa smile seemed familiar, but she didn't recognize the blue-black hair or considerable cleavage exposed by the low-cut gown. "Who's this?''

He glanced across the seat, then returned his gaze to the road. "That's Mother.''

Jessica nearly dropped the wallet in her lap. "You're kidding. I thought she was a girlfriend.''

Charles laughed. "It's a restored photo taken before her engagement to my father. She was a widow and prematurely gray before her twenty-third birthday.''

"Wow.'' Jessica flipped a few more pages and found the card. "She's some lady. I'll bet she has quite a story to tell.''

"Yes.'' He returned the wallet to his jacket. "You

should ask her to tell you about all her accomplishments sometime.''

''I'll do that.''

Jessica recited the directions from the card, then settled back into her seat. In the side-view mirror she spotted Mitch's car turning around to follow them and relaxed. Charles slowed the Range Rover as they neared the cross-roads. When they stopped, she automatically looked up the hill to her cabin.

''Oh, no.'' She nearly uttered something considerably less ladylike when she saw the red Porsche in her parking lot. Alex Templeton was pacing back and forth beside it, intent on winning the argument with whomever was on the other end of his cell phone.

Charles bent down to peer out her window. ''Customer?''

''Old friend.'' Alex stopped and waved as soon as he spotted her. She felt as if she'd just been sighted in the crosshairs of a target. Her panic was instant and intense. Why didn't he understand no? Why wouldn't he leave her alone? Jessica turned and shielded her face with her hand. ''Just drive. I don't want to deal with him right now.''

''Is there a problem?'' Charles's face was wreathed with concern. ''He's not one of your vandals, is he?''

In a Porsche? ''Could we just go?''

''Of course.'' Charles punched the accelerator. Playing the hero wasn't his forte. The car lurched forward, kicking up gravel and mud. She was thrown back into her seat as they raced up the hill. ''Hang on!''

''We were supposed to turn left back there,'' she yelled, clutching the armrest. She *was* hanging on.

''You said to drive,'' he argued.

Another engine revved into overdrive. The crunch of gravel spat in the distance. Jessica pushed herself up in her seat and turned around in time to witness a near collision as Mitch wheeled his Jeep into her driveway to block Alex's speeding Porsche. Alex's horn blared. Mitch climbed out and braced his arms between the door and windshield, a gun in his hand. He shouted something.

"Oh, my God." What was going on? What was Mitch doing? Had Sam found out something about Alex?

"Hold on!"

The whole scene disappeared as the Rover went airborne at the crest of the hill, then crashed back down onto the road. Jessica's cheek smacked against the side window. Pain radiated through her skull as the car fishtailed and spun toward the ditch. "Charles!"

"Shut up!"

Shut up? She clutched at her throbbing temple. She was hearing things. The car came out of its skid, then jerked back toward the opposite ditch. His foot still hadn't hit the brake when they crested the next hill. The car tilted onto two wheels and threatened to roll. Jessica's stomach churned with the motion. She grabbed the dashboard to catch herself from falling into the driver. "Charles," she warned. "You have to slow down. You're gonna wreck the—"

"Shut up, bitch!" He jerked the wheel to the right.

Driving gloves. Black leather driving gloves.

The car bounced down on all its tires again, throwing her into the door again. But she was already going into mental shock and didn't feel the pain.

"What did you call me?" She barely heard the words herself.

The car ran out of road and hydroplaned across a pool of standing rainwater. Then it hit mud, trapped the left front wheel and pitched into a roll. Air bags popped open and her world careened into black.

Seconds later, or maybe it was minutes, Jessica blinked her eyes open. Her chest burned with the bruising of the seat belt that had caught her and saved her life. Her head felt like gelatin and she wanted to throw up. She was surrounded by the fractured stalks of a cornfield, but she was alive.

She looked across the front seat at Charles. His head lolled against the deflated air bag and his arms hung limp at his sides.

Jessica squinted her world into focus and purpose. She unbuckled herself and crawled across the seat. But she wasn't checking to see whether Charles was unconscious or dead. She pushed him back against his seat and tugged at his tie. Her addled brain made her fingers fumble with the buttons of his shirt. Tears stung her eyes. Anger kept them from falling.

At last, she gave up on the buttons and ripped his shirt open. She was almost screaming now, frantic with the need to know the truth. She yanked at the neckline of the undershirt he wore until she reached bare skin.

She already knew what she would find.

She jerked away as if the man had singed her fingers.

It was the damn cat.

Charles Kent had the tattoo of a tiger on his chest.

"CAT BOYCE TEMPLETON. Her father made a fortune with one of the largest advertising firms in the country." Virgil's research had been thorough. "I can see where Alex might have a grudge against women. His wife made him sign a prenup, so he doesn't get a penny of what she brought into the marriage if they divorce."

"You think that's a motive?" Sam asked, switching the phone to the other ear to unlock Jess's truck and climb in.

He could sense Virgil shaking his head. "Cat and her daddy may have provided the start-up money, but Alex has earned a cool eight million in his own right. The guy's a player, rumored to have dated women all over the country, but he didn't rape your girl in Chicago. He has an airtight alibi.''

''What's that? Stooping some other mistress?''

''You really don't like this guy, do you?'' Sam didn't comment. Virgil knew him too well. ''Sorry, Irish. It's not that sordid. The fund-raiser he was at that night? Guess who was the main speaker?''

''Templeton?'' He started the truck and drove out of the county sheriff's office parking lot. His interview with Derek Phillips confirmed that he'd found his vandals, but he was still looking for a murderer.

Alex Templeton had been in Miami and Chicago at the time of those attacks. He was a tall, white male and he mistreated women. That and the fact he'd hurt Jess emotionally made him a decent suspect.

''He was at the podium at the time Miss Taylor was abducted.''

Sam swore. He wanted it to be Templeton. He wanted an excuse to hurt the fool for the way he'd used Jess.

Now he was back to square one.

That meant staying close to Jess until her attacker showed his hand again.

He'd be with her in five minutes.

JESSICA FOUND HER PURSE on the floor of the back seat and dug out her phone and sunglasses. She climbed out of the wrecked Range Rover and tried to orient herself. Even damaged by hail, the corn was too tall to see the road, but it was easy enough to follow the path made by the car. The goose egg on her cheek was nothing compared to the way her skull throbbed with every step. She slipped on the shades to keep the sun from piercing her brain and aggravating her headache, then punched in Sam's number.

When she got a busy signal, she ended the call and dialed 911. There was the road, twenty feet ahead. Her feet

weren't steady, but she kept moving. "Come on, people."
Maybe she should have called Mitch instead. "Pick up
the—"

A viselike arm covered in expensive brown tweed
grabbed her around the neck, pulling her back off her feet.
Her scream gurgled in her throat as a hand reached over
her shoulder and snatched the phone from her fingers and
hurled it into the corn. At her first twist to free herself, a
knife pricked the soft skin below her jaw. She felt the heat
of her own blood trickling down her neck.

"I had it all planned out," Charles complained. "I can't
do it here." He jerked Jessica by the neck. "Move it,
bitch."

"WHAT THE HELL is going on here?" Mitch Taylor had
earned every bit of his authoritative reputation. Sam had
been scanning the horizon beyond the hills that surrounded
the Lover's Lane crossroads, but he snapped to attention as
if he'd been addressed by a ranking agent. "I had the deputy pick up Templeton on suspicion of trespassing, but a
good lawyer will have him out in an hour and he'll be suing
my ass. This isn't about vandals, is it, O'Rourke?"

An edgy sense of his world about to go horribly wrong
was eating him from the inside out. "Where's Jess?"

"Answer the question."

"You answer mine."

Two leviathans going head-to-head. Two men who knew
their business better than just about anybody else. Two men
who loved the same woman in very different ways both
sensed the danger.

Captain Taylor pulled back the front of his jacket and
splayed his fingers at his hips. He carried his gun and his
badge and his attitude with intimidating force. "I was told
we were looking for a threat to Jessie's property. That's
not the whole story, is it?"

Sam debated for several agonizing seconds before he decided that losing Jess's trust was the painful price it would cost to save her life. "I'm breaking a promise, but you need to know."

He told Mitch everything as completely and concisely as he could in a few minutes' time. The stages of shock, grief and anger that crossed the police captain's face had stoically vanished by the time Sam had finished. "Her attacker's here in K.C. now. She's not safe on her own."

"She and Charles Kent are in a white Range Rover, heading east up that road," Mitch reported. "Toward the Stuyvesant place."

"I thought they were going to Mission Hills."

"Only if they're taking the scenic route. Mission Hills is across the state line." He thumbed over his shoulder to the west. "In Kansas."

Sam ran to the truck. Mitch pulled out his phone and shouted over the gunning of the truck engine. "I'll have the cavalry here in twenty minutes. We'll find her."

Sam floored it. Charles, the snob, hired Derek Phillips to plant trees at his house. Charles, the tall, white male, knew a lot about antiques and collectibles. He'd bet his shield the man collected knives and jewelry. Charles, the country gentleman who flaunted his money and status, had pressured Jess over the phone when he didn't get his way.

Sam prayed.

She might not have twenty minutes.

"THERE." The silk pinched her wrist as he gave it a final tug. "Now sit there and shut up."

"Charles, you won't get away with this."

Jessica pleaded her case even as he began pulling out all those sick, familiar items from the black duffel bag he carried. A stocking cap. A foil-wrapped condom. A plastic bag full of long shocks of dark hair.

A translucent white mothball rolled across the dusty floor.

She was too frightened to cry, too smart to scream. She concentrated on breathing evenly—inhale, exhale—so she wouldn't hyperventilate or pass out. She had blisters on her feet from the hike to the Stuyvesants' abandoned barn, blood on her white blouse from her cut and the gash on Charles's chin he'd received in the crash. He'd already removed his belt and tie and bound her wrists and ankles together so he could work without fear of her running away. He'd built a crude bed out of straw inside a horse stall.

Now he was changing his clothes. Stripping off the fine wool and imported leather that defined his landed-gentry persona, and putting on the musty stocking cap and grease-stained jeans that transformed him into a cab-driving bum.

Like some sort of macabre magician he turned to her and beat his chest. "Do you see this?" The mask muffled his articulate tone. "This is a man's chest. Can you feel my strength and power?" He rubbed his palm across the tiger tattoo. "I've killed other women. They understood that I was their master."

Jessica tried to think of a plan. Right now she was completely at his mercy. But she'd broken her bonds the last time. She'd survived.

Until she could get her hands on his knife or free herself, she prayed for deliverance. Someone would see the wrecked car and start a search. Sam would come looking when she didn't call.

Sam. Oh, God. If she could just see him one more time, feel his arms around her. If she could tell him how much she loved him and beg him to give her a chance—give them a chance. Would he go to counseling with her? Would he be patient as she learned about lovemaking all over again? Would he destroy this man the way he'd promised her?

"Answer me, bitch!" Suddenly, Charles was on top of

her, stretching her arms up over her head, running his knife along her throat. He ground his hips into hers and Jessica did scream, fighting down the gag reflex that tore through her. "Shut. Up."

Charles sheathed his knife somewhere behind him and pulled her silver necklace out of his pocket. With a deft sleight of hand, he circled it around her throat and twisted the ends together until it cut into her neck and silenced her.

She instinctively sucked in a breath of air, but it got blocked at the tourniquet around her trachea. Her lungs refused to expand. Her sinuses burned with the moldy scents of rotting boards and damp straw. She fought off the panic that tried to set in, but she was powerless against the dizzying spots swirling before her eyes.

"That's better." Charles sounded much calmer now, a sick parody of his former self. "No woman will ever tell me what to do or criticize me or say no to me. Right?"

Jessica's lungs ached to breathe. With the blow to her head, she wouldn't stay conscious for long. *Play along.* She could stall for time if she played along. She forced herself to nod. Once. Twice.

The gruesome black face laughed. "That's better."

He released the tension on the chain, and Jessica sucked in a deep breath of reviving air. But the reprieve was only temporary. He released her arms, but dragged the blade of his knife down the front of her blouse, snipping the buttons one by one.

She couldn't endure this again. He sliced through her belt and flicked open the snap of her jeans. *Keep talking.* "Your mother must have been a tyrant to grow up with. So demanding. So intolerant."

"We don't talk about Mother, is that clear?" He ripped open the fly of her jeans.

Jessica rammed her fists against his chest. "Stop it!"

He reached for the snap of his own jeans. "That's wrong,

wrong, wrong!'' he said. Jessica hit him again. ''Women have no power over me!''

The musty barn flooded with light as doors and windows swung open.

''Charles!'' An Irish accent tinged with lethal menace shouted from the main door. Jessica's heart screamed with joy. ''I'll put a bullet in your head if you don't let her go right now.''

In a matter of seconds her joy turned to absolute terror.

Charles rolled over, slicing through the belt that bound her ankles. Then he was on his feet, pulling her up in front of him as a human shield.

''Back off!'' he warned. ''Or I'll kill her.''

''YOU SON OF A BITCH.''

Jess had blood on her. Her wrists were bound. And that bastard had her lined up perfectly between himself and Sam's bullet. If Jess had been a petite little thing, he'd have aimed above her head. But she was tall and strong and a perfect shield for a man Kent's size.

The only shot was right beside her ear. An inch one way and Kent would be dead. An inch the wrong way and she'd be dead.

Sam had trained his entire career for a moment like this. He'd done it in training. He could make the damn shot.

But he'd never counted on the woman he loved being lined up in the crosshairs of his Sig Sauer as well.

Mitch Taylor shouted commands to the sheriff's deputies and KCPD officers who'd surrounded the building. He ordered Kent to surrender, to drop his weapon and release his hostage. He listened to Kent's demands and warned him of the charges being brought against him. He told Kent the difference between prison and death, depending on his cooperation now.

And all the while Sam never moved. His hands never wavered. His eyes never left Jess.

When the knife first nicked her breast he flinched inside. When it cut into her cheek, he seethed.

Jess struggled with the pain and fear, but her gaze stayed fixed on his. *Shoot him.* She mouthed the words. He'd promised, one way or the other, he'd get this bastard for her.

Charles Kent pressed the knife to her throat.

"Anybody have a clear shot?" Mitch demanded.

"Yes."

Sam squeezed the trigger.

Chapter Fourteen

The wheels of justice moved slowly but surely in every part of the country, it seemed.

In the three days since Charles Kent's death, Sam had spent some of his time at the hospital, checking on Jess. But there were always family and nurses and therapists of one kind or another around that prevented him from doing little more than ask how she was feeling and apologize for letting her get hurt. For being too tired or too obsessed or too damn distracted to see the real enemy right next door.

He'd spent more of his time writing reports and talking on the phone. Mitch Taylor had covered his butt with Chief Dixon in Boston, claiming he'd been working in cooperation with KCPD on the serial rapist case. A search of Charles Kent's rooms had revealed a collection of knives, including the one Jess ID'd as the weapon used on her in Chicago. And the souvenir hair samples from his duffel bag had been sent to the DNA lab to match to the deceased victims.

But Sam already recognized the curly, raven-dark lock of hair that had once been Kerry's crowning glory. It was just a matter of time now before the five murders and Jess's rape were officially marked as solved. His leave of absence was over in two days, and he'd been summoned back to Boston.

He didn't want to go.

He'd come out to Log Cabin Acres to clear his gear from Jess's garage apartment. But he'd walked around the place, too, and noticed the benches that needed painting and the shrubs that needed pruning. He'd even like to take a stab at rebuilding that buggy. He'd stood in the spot where he and Jess had shared their first kiss, and sat on the porch where she'd served him lemonade. He planted the memories deep inside his heart and knew he had to move on.

Sam tossed his backpack in the trunk of the car he'd rented, slammed it shut and flattened his palms on the cool steel to steady himself while the pain buffeted through him. He'd picked Jess up in his arms that afternoon in the Stuyvesants' barn and carried her outside. He'd sunk to the ground and cradled her in his lap, holding her for the last time.

The last time before brothers and paramedics and reality stepped in to tear them apart. He'd proved beyond any doubt that he was a man of violence and passion—when she needed healing and peace.

Sam inhaled deeply and raised his head to take one last look at the lush golds and reds and greens of the autumn trees. Missouri was a beautiful place. But it was time to leave it behind. He had to. Jess had her memory back. Her rapist was dead. And he would be an uncomfortable reminder of all she'd gone through.

After loosening the tie he'd worn to court that morning—to testify that Derek Phillips's crime deserved community service, not jail time—Sam shed his suit jacket and tossed it onto the passenger seat of the car. He heard the crunch of gravel and saw the long cloud of dust to the north long before the caravan of cars, trucks and a van crested the hill. "What the hell?"

When they pulled through the brick gates and drove up

Jess's driveway, he wasn't surprised. His day of reckoning had come.

Sam closed the car door and braced himself as one by one, the vehicles stopped and the Taylors climbed out. This was going to be the ''set him straight'' talk about shooting at, deceiving, using and taking liberties with their sister.

''O'Rourke.'' Mitch Taylor acknowledged him first. Then the others gathered round. It was a pretty damn intimidating lineup. But he balanced himself on the balls of his feet and dangled his fists loosely at his sides.

''I don't want to fight you,'' he said, swinging his gaze to include each man. Even one he hadn't met yet. A dead ringer for Jess in coloring, though this guy was built on the big and brawny side and sporting a long ponytail. It had to be Cole Taylor.

''Fight?'' countered Brett.

''I deserve it, I know.'' Sam understood about wanting the best for a sister. He respected their concern. ''I'll take any of you on, one-on-one. But the six of you together would beat the crap out of me.'' He included Sid Taylor, who stood at the end of the line. ''Seven, sir. Though I'd rather not—''

''Nobody wants to fight,'' Sid interrupted. He looked down the line at his sons. ''Right, boys?''

''Well, I don't know,'' Josh started to tease. ''If he hurt Jessie—'' But he was glared into silence by his father.

''We're just here to talk, son,'' Sid explained.

Son? A friendly conversation with all of them? Right.

''Let me save you the trouble.'' Sam rattled off a list of his transgressions against Jess, and ended with an honest apology. ''I never meant to hurt her. God knows I never wanted to. But I screwed up. So I'll leave. I don't want to hurt her any more. I don't want to remind her of all that's happened.''

Since no one seemed intent on throwing the first punch,

he pulled his keys out of his pocket and opened the car door. "Take care of her."

But before he climbed in, he wheeled around and demanded some terms of his own. "Don't let her settle for some ass like Templeton. She deserves better. She deserves someone who loves her. Who treats her as an equal. She deserves someone who wants only her. Who sees her for the brainy, sexy, softhearted knockout she is. You make damn sure it's someone who loves her." So much for ice in his veins. His outburst faded on one spent breath. "Don't let her settle for anything less."

"You know anyone like that?" That was Cole.

Sam glared at him. There. He'd confessed it. He wanted their sister. "Yeah."

"Then what can we do to convince you to stay?"

"What?" Cole might as well have thrown that punch. This wasn't a lynch mob?

"Enough!" A car door opened and closed. Harry bounded through the line of brothers and trotted right up to Sam. "Harry, sit."

At Jess's command, the giant mutt plopped his haunches on Sam's foot and nuzzled his head into his hand. *Interesting.* Not an ally he'd expected. Sam raked his fingers through his hair, confused. Somehow he'd been transported to an alternate universe where the Taylors wanted him to stay and Harry liked him.

But the only universe that made any sense was in Jess's blue eyes as she pushed her way between Mac and Gideon. "Did you mean what you said?"

She crossed straight to him, coming closer, ever closer. Close enough to smell the spicy ginger of her hair. Close enough for him to see the tiny stitches that mended her cheek. Close enough to reach out and...she turned away.

Jess looked to her family and said, "I love you lots, but...could you all go away?"

Martha Taylor came to her aid and shooed them all back to their respective vehicles. Sam almost laughed when he saw who really ran the Taylor show. It wasn't until they were all driving away that Sam realized Jess and Harry had positioned themselves in a protective front to shield him from her family's good intentions.

But once they were alone, she sent Harry out to check his territory and laced her fingers together with Sam's. He latched on tight, helpless to resist her gentle touch. "I was afraid I wouldn't get here in time," she said. "So I asked if someone would drive out here to delay you. I didn't think they would all volunteer."

Sam rubbed his thumb in circles against her palm. "What's going on, babe?"

Jessica looked up into the eyes of the man she loved. She saw the compassion written there. She saw the courage and nobility. She saw the love.

Now she just had to make him see it. Accept it. She had to make sure he gave them a chance.

"Sam? Would it be all right if I kissed you?"

"Ah, babe, you don't have to ask."

She grinned at the dawning on his face, and felt a uniquely feminine strength growing inside her. Three days in the hospital had given her plenty of time to think this through, to understand that he had always put her needs first. But a man, even one so strong and sure as Sam, needed to be asked, too.

"I don't want you to be afraid of me," she said, brushing her fingers across the bold jut of his chin, smooth shaven now. "I'm not perfect, but I'm stubborn. And I'm not going to give up on the possibility of *us* just because some days will be harder than others. Some days we'll have doubts. I might feel shame. You might feel guilt." She slid her fingertips across his taut lips and tugged gently at the lower curve. "But I am certain that we love each other and that we are stronger together. That, together, we can heal. That we'll have more good days than we'll have bad, and that one day—'' his hand came up to cup her cheek ''—the bad days will be over.''

His ice-colored eyes blazed with fire. ''I'm ready to kiss you now.''

And he did.

Their lips met in a crush of fierce possession that held nothing back. He lifted her off her feet and carried her into the cabin. She looped her arms around his neck and hugged him close, gave him the acceptance he needed, found the trust she required.

''Sam?'' Her fingers were tangled in the lush silk of his hair.

He was nibbling at that crazy spot at the top of her shoulder. ''Hmm?''

They'd made it to the sofa. Their shirts were open, their hearts were racing, and a feeling of utter rightness drowned out the remnants of fear inside her.

''I think I'm ready now,'' she said.

''For what, babe?'' She pulled back and looked at him in *that* way, and bravely reached for the buckle on his belt. ''Oh.'' The reverent stroke of his trembling fingers across her lips gave her more reassurance than any words. ''You don't have to do this for me.''

''I'm not. I'm doing it for me.''

Sam's loving was gentle and slow and achingly thorough. She asked to be on top and he asked her to just keep talking so he'd know she was with him all the way. They found their completion together, right there on the sofa.

And then again in her bed upstairs. It was better the second time around. And it would be even better the next.

And when they were done, he pulled her on top of him and wrapped them together in the quilt. Jessica rode the quieting rise and fall of his broad, warm chest.

"Kansas City has a Bureau department," he whispered in that beautiful Irish voice. He drew lazy circles across her back. "I wonder if they could use another agent. I'm a fair shot, a decent investigator, and I seem to have a pretty good working relationship with the sheriff's department and KCPD."

Jessica snuggled close and smiled. "If not, I know Boston has wonderful antiques."

They were both thinking out loud now, planning their future. "I'd like you to come to Boston with me some-time—to meet my family. I know that sounds corny, but I've met all of yours." His arms tightened with a sudden flinch. She let him stew a moment in silence. "I have, haven't I?"

"Every last one of them." She kissed the underside of his chin and felt him relax. "I'd love to go see where your family is. I'd like to say a prayer for them. And thank them. For you."

She tasted the salty tears that gathered at the corner of his mouth. Tears of happiness.

Sam was wonderful.

He'd saved her life. He'd taught her to trust again. He'd shown her that she could be loved. Was loved. Did love.

He was a gift she would never forget.

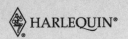

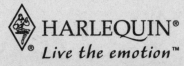

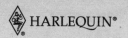

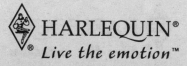

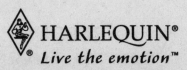

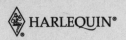

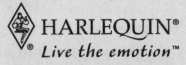